Dress Jeans, Disco, and Dating

*To Missy, Enjoy my look
back to the 70's. We grew
up in such a great neighborhood
filled with love & friendship.*

Enjoy b

A NOVEL BY

FRANK MARASCHIELLO

Frank

8/30/19

PAGE PUBLISHING, INC.
New York, NY

First originally published by Page Publishing, Inc. 2019

ISBN 978-1-64462-535-4 (Paperback)
ISBN 978-1-64462-538-5 (Digital)

Printed in the United States of America

For my parents, Frank and Jeanne, who always showed me the way.

ACKNOWLEDGEMENTS

Writing this book was one of the most exciting and difficult things I have ever attempted. Thanks to Jon, Lisa, Patti Jo, April and Melissa for the words of encouragement. Thanks to my wife Maureen and my family for listening to endless stories of growing up on the wonderful West Side of Buffalo. Thanks to Jeff for introducing me to your grandfather's writings and making me believe. And most of all, Mr. Coleman, my English teacher at Cardinal Dougherty High School, for exposing me to the power of a book.

INTRODUCTION

A Friend's Funeral

Life is very funny sometimes. It makes you laugh. It makes you cry. It gives you so much, and then sadly, as we approach middle age, it begins to take things away. Most of the "things" are the people most important to us.

It was during one of those sad occasions when someone was taken away that I was taken to another time and place that I hadn't thought of in so long. I also started to think about what made me who I am today. Why certain things are important to me, and why some things aren't, and most importantly, why friendships and family shape who we are.

The occasion was the funeral of a friend's mom.

It was in the spring of this year. I haven't spoken more than a few sentences to that friend in the last thirty years, but in spite of that, I still attended her mother's funeral. It was the right thing to do, to help her and her family say goodbye to their very special mom, a mom that always made me feel like I was part of their family.

I had spoken to her mom within the last few years under similar circumstances. I knocked on a familiar door with flowers in hand and a heart filled with sorrow. I sat with her at her kitchen table and talked about everything and nothing, the same way I had with her many times so long ago.

Nothing had changed, and at the same time everything had changed. I didn't know that that would be the last time I would ever speak to her, but regrettably, it was.

As my friend and her family entered the church, I realized how important she had been to me. I had only seen her once in the last few years. Then it hit me, your first love never really leaves you. It stays around in the back of your mind to remind you of a time before mortgages, children, and a real job.

Those memories can make you smile, make you laugh, or maybe even cry. It makes you notice young love as teenagers walk by holding hands on a warm summer night. It makes you think of your first car, your first kiss, and your first heartbreak.

All those memories came rushing back to me as she passed by on the way to the front of the church. I thought about my feelings for her, for her mom, and a bunch of long-forgotten thoughts and memories of a younger me.

How sad I began to feel sitting alone in that small chapel on the grounds of a nunnery waiting for the service to begin. To be truthful, death forces you to think about life, and I thought about how each member of her family was special to me, how each one of them was also part of me, and I hoped I was part of them.

I got the empty feeling that someone from my own family was now gone.

I started to remember dress jeans, disco, and dating. I thought about roller-skating parties, green station wagons with wood contact paper on the side, pet rocks, eight-track players, Donny and Marie, transistor radios, and *Saturday Night Fever*. I also thought about certain songs from the past that bring me back to my teenage years. When I hear them, I smile, and in fact, I am a teenager again as I sing along, hoping that no one hears me.

And most of all, I remember a friendship between a very shy boy and a special girl. And though we never officially dated, and we were never even officially boyfriend and girlfriend, we did spend many years together laughing, crying, experiencing teenage firsts, and learning about this crazy thing called life.

We talked about being married to each other and laughed about it. We wondered what our lives would be like when we were old like our parents were. We also wondered if disco would last, what happened to John Belushi, and what was a Three Dog Night?

We wondered if we would become like all the old people we knew as we aged. Would we ever graduate from college? What did our future really have in store for us?

All these questions were discussed with the youthful exuberance that only teenagers have. And now here we were, so many years later, now our parents' age, dealing with what our parents did. Births, deaths, sickness, weddings, good and bad news—we now *were* our parents.

But I realized one more thing as I sat quietly in the back of the church. We were still there for each other. Our bond of friendship had lasted for almost forty years. It is said that if friendship is true, those bonds will never break. It may take twists and turns, be dormant for years, but it will always return when that friend needs you the most.

When she noticed me in the church, her smile and tear-filled eyes told me our friendship had never ended. I also knew that I had to write my thoughts and feelings from so long ago before they went dormant again.

As I said before, this is a story of a very shy boy and a very special girl.

CHAPTER 1

It was 1976, our bicentennial year. Gerald Ford was president, and gas was fifty-nine cents a gallon. The whole world seemed to be red, white, and blue. Houses, jeans, and cars—all were our country's colors. I was fourteen and on my way to high school. So was she. So was my cousin Ronnie, and his graduation celebration was the next get-together in an endless parade of graduations, first communions, and confirmations that spring.

I approached Ronnie's party with a healthy combination of eye rolling and dread.

Not another graduation party, I thought. I knew there would be orange drink in solo cups, hot dogs, hamburgers, and potato salad on top of folding tables with flag-colored tablecloths.

And all the older friends and relatives at the party, they would try their best to act like they wanted to be there too. Most of them would be grabbing peeks at their watches to see when they could sneak out to be home in time to catch Johnny Carson's monologue on *The Tonight Show*.

And don't forget about the teenagers, they would be there too, out in the driveway, listening to throbbing disco beats coming from a portable record player in the garage. Kids would be mulling around outside in groups based on who went to what school, what neighborhood they were from, or who they were related to. They would be loud (that's why they were outside), and inevitably, there would be a girl crying over a boy sitting cross-legged on the front lawn.

As my family and I pulled up to the house in our station wagon, as predicted there were kids in the driveway, on the porch, and in the garage. We got out as a family, and my parents walked toward the front door of the house. Being a recent eighth-grade graduate myself, I wouldn't want to be seen walking in with my parents, so I walked slowly up the driveway. As an expert of these types of parties, I knew the kids' snacks would be somewhere outside. My parents, also being experts of such affairs, made a beeline for the house and High Ball/ Tom Collins section.

I walked toward a group of my cousins near the folding tables filled with food. Pretzels, cheese puffs, and chips have a way of making even the most boring parties better. At the table were a bunch of older kids that I didn't know chowing down on anything and everything in sight. They surrounded the table like a group of Vikings at a feast.

I edged my way in, trying to find a bowl that had anything left in it, and it was there that I saw her for the first time.

I saw a girl that I couldn't take my eyes off. She was walking toward the garage. Her confidence and poise was evident. She had a friend with her, but I couldn't tell you what she looked like. I barely noticed her. The girl smiled and spoke to all of Ronnie's classmates in the garage and driveway. She wore white painter's pants and a red blouse. Her hair was brown, so were her eyes, and she seemed to be walking in slow motion through the crowd.

But it was her smile that startled me the most. Even with her braces, it was warm, honest, and real.

I started to think that maybe this party wasn't going to be like the rest of them after all. I kept sneaking looks at her as I was turning my fingertips orange eating cheese puffs and my lips blue from the Kool-Aid I was drinking. I knew that she was very special, not like any other girl I had ever seen before. The closer she got to me, the more my heart pumped.

If there really is love at first sight, I had just experienced it. I never had a girlfriend and quite frankly never saw the reason for one. But now I did. Every reason to have one was now only a few feet away me.

My heart was beating in a way it never had before as she walked past me and stopped at the record player in the garage. As was the custom of the time, the record player played 45s, and when the song ended, the next person put on their favorite song. A lot of the time the same song was played over and over. Her choice was George McCrae's "Rock Your Baby." She turned to her friend and started to talk. I stood there watching her. They were just ten feet from me, but at that point, it felt like we were the only two people in my fourteen-year-old world.

As she talked, she swayed to the beat of the music, just a subtle swaying that caused all the people standing around her to disappear from my sight. Everyone around her was blurry, but she was perfectly clear to me.

I was motionless for a few moments when I heard a loud "bang", it was my cousin Ronnie busting out of the side door with more snacks for the table. The noise snapped me back into reality, and I turned toward him. He put a couple of bowls on the table, and the crowd quickly moved back toward me in search of more chips and pretzels.

I reached in my back pocket and gave Ronnie his graduation envelope with a crisp twenty-dollar bill in it.

"How much do you figure cash in tonight?" I asked as he ripped open the card.

"I'm hoping about $500, maybe I'll use it for my first car."

Ronnie and I were the same age and about to start at the same high school in September. He was the youngest in his family, and I was an only child. He had an older brother named Harrison, and two sisters, Louise and Jennifer. His mom was my dad's older sister, and as we grew up, we were more like brothers than cousins. I spent many Friday nights sleeping over at his house watching the "Vincent Price Friday Fright Night Late Show." We would get so scared that we would fall asleep with the lights on because we knew that some vampire was waiting for us under the bed. Ronnie was always more confident about worldly things than I was, especially with the girls. He also acted like he was my big brother and had no problem telling me what to do, what to wear, and what to say in order to impress the girls.

And one other thing, I knew he would make sure that no one would ever do anything to hurt me. That's how close we were.

"Who is that girl?" I asked as I fumbled for the last Dorito in one of Aunt Vera's bicentennial bowls.

"Nicky, there are about twenty girls over there" was all he said as he refilled a bowl with Bugles.

"The one in the red blouse and white pants by the record player."

"That one over there?" he said as he turned and pointed right at her, making it as obvious as possible that we were talking about her with a smirk on his face.

"Why do you have to make it so obvious?" I yelled at him.

"Her name is Stephanie Pacifico. We've been friends since sixth grade. Don't even think about it. She's cool, way too cool for you, and she's way out of your league."

Stephanie Pacifico, even her name is beautiful, I thought to myself.

He turned around and walked back into the house in search of more food without saying another word, leaving me standing alone. So there I was, shot down before I even had the chance to smile or even mutter a word to her.

I looked for a familiar face to talk to while staying close to the garage and record player. I found my cousin Patti Jo and started to talk about high school, all the time looking at the girl right behind her.

One thing was for sure. I knew Ronnie would be back with lots more grub because my aunt Vera always made enough to feed an army. I talked with Patti Jo and continued to watch the girl as she moved from group to group talking.

The more I watched her, the more interested I became. Then I made the mistake of starting to think about what Ronnie had told me. So I was out of my league?

What does that mean? So he thinks I will never make it to the big leagues? Or am I only now in the minor leagues, waiting for my chance at the big leagues? Being a teenager is so confusing.

And why should I give up that easily? I mean, I had just seen the girl of my dreams walk past me in the most unlikely place, an eighth-grade graduation party.

I had never dated a girl and was very awkwardly shy around them. I decided that I was now on a mission, and I had to get to know her.

As it became dark and the smell of mosquito candles filled the air, many of the kids started to leave. I knew my cousins would be the last ones to go home, so I stuck close to them.

Stephanie stayed and was still by the garage talking to a group of girls when my mother came out looking for me. Here I was for the first time in my life trying to look cool, and my mom appears out of nowhere telling me it's time to go home. (There is nothing more embarrassing when you've seen the girl of your dreams and one of your parents comes out of the side door yelling your name, telling you it's time to go home and past your bedtime!)

"Time to go home, your dad fell asleep on the couch again", Mom said as she walked out the door. "Say goodbye to your cousins, we are going to take "Sleeping Beauty" home now." She turned and walked down the driveway toward the street and our car.

I didn't care if I said goodbye to my cousins. I saw them all the time. I wanted to say goodbye to that girl standing by the record player, but I couldn't work up the nerve to talk to her.

I took one last look at her as I walked down the driveway. She was still smiling and certainly didn't give off an unapproachable vibe, and I wished again that I had the guts to walk over and say something, anything to her.

But I didn't.

As we piled back into our Saab for the ride home, my mom talked about the next graduation party we would be attending, and being the mom that she was, how excited she was, that the party was mine. I paid little attention to the front-seat conversation because I was thinking about the girl I had just seen.

I figured I would never see her again.

Boy was I wrong.

C H A P T E R   2

I almost forgot to mention that my name is Nick Carnavale. Our family had a long, long line of Nick Carnavales starting with my great-grandfather. We lived on the West Side of Buffalo in a typical Italian working-class neighborhood. Most of the fathers on my street fought in World War II and worked two jobs to make ends meet. Our moms stayed home and took care of the family.

Being an only child was difficult for me at times, but all the kids in the neighborhood and my large number of cousins more than made up for that. My mom told me I was an only child because I was the perfect baby and perfection would be difficult to duplicate again. I don't know if that was true, but it sounded good to me when I was a kid.

My father owned a landscaping business and moonlighted as a nightclub singer. His name, you guessed it, was Nick too. He was hardworking, and did he ever love to perform. In the late fifties, he had lived for a short time in New York City trying to make it as a singer. It definitely was his passion, and I grew up with music and musicians all around me.

My father was the youngest of twelve children born to Italian immigrants. He was short, strict, and played by the rules and was to the point. He was a natural athlete, good at any sport he tried, and his favorite was golf. He was also the type of person that you knew exactly where you stood with him at all times.

We had a huge family consisting of many cousins, aunts, and uncles. As was the custom in most Italian families, I also had a bunch of aunts and uncles that weren't really related to me. If they were good enough friends of my parents, they earned the name aunt and uncle. It's hard to understand if you're not Italian, but that's how I ended up with four Uncle Joes. One was really my father's brother, one was a cousin, and two were my father's good friends. If you add them in with my real cousins, it could get really confusing around the dining room table.

My mother, Elizabeth, was the complete opposite of my father and his family. She was of Irish and German descent and like me an only child, and she grew up in North Buffalo. My mom was taller than my father by a few inches, and was very pretty with brown hair and blue eyes. Mom stayed home and took care of my dad and me. She was the kind of overprotective mom that took you to the pediatrician every time she thought *anything* was wrong with you, including bringing me there because I ate the tails of shrimp at a barbeque, or the time Mitchell Pasquale hit me in the head with an ice ball.

Mom was also an expert in winter attire. I never left the house without mittens, scarves, hats, rubber golashes with the metal buckles, and Wonder Bread bags on my feet to keep them dry.

In her own way, my mother was very funny, often zinging my dad with remarks from her favorite spot in front of the kitchen sink. My mother also had more friends than anyone I ever met. Maybe it was because Mom was an only child too and had to learn to make friends quickly, or she would have spent a lot of time alone. She was friendly with the stock boys at the supermarket, the waitresses at Your Host, the owner of Liberty Shoes on Grant Street, and the kids that pumped her gas. She truly was a friend to everyone she met.

My father and I were mom's whole life. She had no hobbies and just took care of us. And one other important thing to her, she loved Tom Jones and went to see him with my aunts every time he came to Buffalo.

And rounding out the family, we had an Airedale Terrier named Humphrey that weighed 120 pounds and thought he was a lap dog. My Aunt Mary bought the dog for my father as a birthday present. She knew nothing about Airedales except that they were loyal dogs and good with kids. We were quite amazed that the little puff of black and orange fur grew into the huge dog he became. Besides my mom and me, that dog was my father's best friend.

Our neighborhood was loaded with large homes built in the early 1900s. The houses were filled with charm and lots of woodwork. We also had large front porches that were great to sit on, especially as a kid growing up. The whole world walked by while you sat up there. And it was also a great place to play on and, with a little imagination, when it was raining out often became a fort or even a spaceship.

Most of my neighbors were Italian too. On one side of our house was so close to our neighbor's that we could pass things to each other through our bedroom windows.

My bedroom was small. The walls were covered with posters of Gilbert Perrault, O. J. Simpson, and Bob McAdoo. All three of the Buffalo professional teams had the best player in their respective league. It was a great time to be a fan of the Sabres, Bills, and the Braves. (I still found room to have my Partridge Family posters on the wall too.)

I also filled my room with the models I bought every Friday at Woolworth's while my mother shopped next door at Loblaw's. I built cars, planes, and Aurora scary glow in the dark monsters. When the lights were turned out, I would watch them softly glow as I fell asleep.

One corner of my room had a record player with albums and 45s that I bought at The Record House in the West Side Plaza. I loved listening to music while I did my homework. I had an eight-track player, cassette player, and a stereo that let me listen to hockey games being broadcast from as far away as Chicago.

We had corner stores that gave credit, let you buy cigarettes with only a note from your mom, and had penny candy that actually cost a penny.

John's on Forest Avenue was my favorite store. The clerk was named Tony. He was always reading the horse racing forms when I walked in. I would get my football, baseball, and hockey cards, and he would never look up from the paper he was studying as he took my money.

And if I didn't have enough money left over for a Grape Crush and the ten-cent deposit on the glass bottle, he would let me drink it on the stairs leading up to the store and bring the bottle right back in.

In our neighborhood, everything was within walking distance. Elmwood Avenue was the place to be. That's why the butcher knew your mom's name, so did the dry cleaner and the girl in the Fotomat booth. There was only one drugstore, and the owner knew your name too.

Growing up, my immediate neighborhood stretched for two blocks in all directions. If you were a kid, you knew every other kid within that zone. We played football in the street (sometimes tackle), street hockey and ice hockey in the winter. We had to come home when the streetlights came on, and we never talked back to our parents.

It was *that* kind of neighborhood, and what a great neighborhood it was to grow up in.

The Marones lived next door to us. Donny and Alisa were both younger than me, and eventually became part of our family. However, it wasn't like that when we first moved in the block in 1970. Donny and his cousin Chuckie drew a line on the sidewalk and told me I couldn't cross it or they would "sock me in the face" if I did. After a few days, the chalk lines washed away, and so did the threats, and before we knew it, we were best friends.

On the other side of our house was the Pasquale family. Mitchell, Matt, and Paula also became like family to us. (They never put any lines on the sidewalk and welcomed us from the first time we met them.) As the six of us grew up together, we looked out for each other like we were brothers and sisters, fought with each other like we were brothers and sisters, and in fact, we became so close; we were brothers and sisters. We were always there for each other, and still are like one big family today.

My best friend from the neighborhood was Jim. He lived around the corner on Richmond Avenue. Our friendship began one day while I sat on my front porch in sixth grade watching him get bullied by a group of kids from Public School 52. He was very small for his age. Every day he would run home being chased by the same group of punks from his school. And every day they would catch him and throw him in Mrs. Simon's bushes. They would laugh at him while he tried to pick up his books and lunchbox and try to get away from them.

Since he was so small, he couldn't fight back against the group of them. I felt really sorry for him, and one day I decided to stick up for him even though I didn't even know his name.

No one should have to put up with that every day walking home from school, I told myself.

When he came running by me, I stepped in, and with the help of Matt next door, we confronted the group while they were trying to throw him into the bushes.

I guess a few punches, and more than a few threats from some Catholic school kids, were enough to have them move on to the next kid they were going to pick on, because after we were done with them they never bothered Jim again.

"What's your name?" I asked him as he was picking up his books from the ground.

"It's Jim, why did you help me?" he asked.

"Just because," I told him, and I walked away.

The next day he walked by my house without the gang chasing him. He thanked me again. We started to talk, and he told me he lived around the corner on Richmond Avenue. After that we became the best of friends.

Jimmy and I went to the Buffalo Braves NBA games, watched TV at each other's house, and even had a *Buffalo Evening News* paper route together.

Our favorite night of the week was Tuesday because we would watch "Happy Days" and "Laverne and Shirley." At nine when they were finished, Jim's mom would call my mother and say she was "sending" me home. She would watch me as I ran down Richmond, and when I got to the corner, my mother was on the porch waiting for me.

Those were such great times.

The other families in the block were the Moroscos, Barones, Palladinos, LaDucas, Genoveses, Guercios, Boncores, McMullins, LaRoccas, and the Gugliuzzas.

On our street, we didn't need a neighborhood watch. Everyone kept an eye on your actions. As you walked down our street, you were expected to say hello to everyone as they sat on their porches trying to escape the heat of an old house in the summer.

Our street also had the cleanest driveways in Buffalo because every dad made it an art form to hose them down on Saturday mornings after cutting their lawns.

With the houses so close together, there weren't many secrets. When the windows were open, you were likely to hear all the latest "discussions" taking place over the dinner table, and some of those discussions were sure not meant to be broadcast to all within earshot.

My graduation party in June was a big event for my mother. (The most important thing for me was the count and the amount at the night's end.) She, along with my aunts, would prepare all the food for the event. Aunt Pat's garlic bread and sauce, Aunt Vera's stuffed hot peppers, Aunt Lee's pastries, and Aunt Charlotte's cookies made the trip to my house for the party worth it.

With the help of Donnie and Alisa next door, we set up aluminum folding tables in the driveway and in front of the garage. All this was done with the intention of keeping the kids outside as far away from the adults as possible.

When the party began, a lot of the same people that were at Ronnie's house got in their car and paraded over to my house and tried to act like they were having fun at another graduation party. An endless line of Impala four-doors and Chevy station wagons would stop and drop of their passengers at the front of our house, and I greeted them at the bottom of the porch stairs. The envelopes were quickly stuffed into my back pockets as dreams of a new ten-speed bike and new watch rolled around my head.

In one sense, my party was kind of sad. My class was the last to graduate from Coronation of the BVM School. I was one of only eight to walk down the aisle. The nuns that taught us ruled with an iron fist and a wooden yardstick. I was good in school, not great, and served mass every Sunday. As was the custom for most Catholic grammar school students of the time, we were expected to attend a Catholic high school. My choice was Cardinal Brennan, an all-male school in North Buffalo.

At my party, I did the right thing, kissing my aunts, shaking my uncles' hands, and keeping the teenagers in the driveway. Paula and Alisa helped me string party lights across from the house to the garage and back. Each string had green-and-white plastic covers that looked like they were from a bad sixties beach party movie. The record player was in the garage with plenty of records around it and was manned by Matt and Donnie, my neighbors.

When my cousin Ronnie showed up, I had to ask the obvious question after his rather exciting graduation party the week before.

"Do you know what that Stephanie girl is doing this summer?" I asked.

"How am I supposed to know? I guess that maybe we will have to make an appearance at the Monday night He and She's dances this summer. Harrison and his band will be playing, and we'll get in for free. It will be cool. Most of the girls were talking about going there at my party."

Now the thought of going to a disco was, to say the least, a foreign concept to me. Ronnie didn't think anything of it because he had older sisters and an older brother that always sneaked him along with them, and I knew he had heard his brother's band many times at dances and bars.

I was a rookie at this disco stuff and was in no hurry to start, but Ronnie quickly convinced me I had to go.

"Look you're in high school now. It is your job to start sneaking into bars and making your parents wonder what you're up to. You know what Alice Cooper says, 'No More Mr. Nice Guy.' You've got to be a rebel, your parents are expecting that, and that's what the girls like too!"

As usual, Ronnie in his crazy way was right. Grade school was now behind me, and I had to start acting like a teenager, but a rebel I was not.

He and She's was an old warehouse that was converted into a disco. It was across the parking lot from the Fun and Games Amusement Park and the Blue Whale car wash. The amusement park had a few batting cages and rides, not much to write home about. On the other hand, it did have a car wash that was painted blue and made to look like the whale from Moby Dick. You drove in through his tail and came out through his mouth.

Only in the 1970s would anyone think it was cool to have a car wash shaped like a whale!

The bar was dark, and a mirrored disco ball hung from the ceiling. It served liquor every day except Monday nights in the summer, when it became "teen night" and specialized in 7 Up and Pepsi drinks.

"Come on, help me out, do you know where she lives? Or where she hangs out? Who are her friends? What high school is she going to?"

"I know she lives on Parkside Avenue and has a brother and sisters, that's all I know. I'm not a spy, and like I told you at my party, don't bother with her, she is way out of your league, and why would a girl that looks like that want to go anywhere near you?"

"What does that 'out of your league' stuff mean?" I asked, ignoring the "she's too pretty to go anywhere near you" remark.

"Too pretty, too cool, and too smart to want to be seen anywhere near you!"

Ronnie was starting to realize how interested I was in her, so I figured it was time to back off and stop asking all the questions.

My graduation party went great, and I made $385 for the nine-year effort to make it to high school. I gave the money to my mom except for $25. She put the balance in my "money market" account at the M and T Bank. I told her I would use it to buy my first car, which I did a few years later.

The $25 I kept was going to be used for a special purchase. I had seen in the window of Leeds Jewelers on Grant Street the newest style watch. The first LED watches were showing up in ads on television and in magazines. With a press of a button, the red crystal gave you the time in digital numbers. I had to have the one in the front window of the jewelry store, which was a silver Gruen LED watch. I walked over first thing in the morning and bought it from the jeweler, Mr. Leed. He looked old enough to have sold pocket watches to President Lincoln but was a neat old guy with a bald head and a big smile. He took a few links out of the watch, and I was on my way home, pressing the time button to see it light up at every corner.

I was now officially on my way to high school and really had no idea what was in store for me.

CHAPTER 3

After all the excitement of Ronnie's party and mine, summer went back to the usual routine. My summers growing up revolved around playing baseball and going to the beach with my mother, grandmother, and some of my aunts. We cooked on the hibachi in the backyard and went for ice cream at Frozen Whip on Grant Street. We also made one trip to Fantasy Island and one to Crystal Beach amusement parks. If we were lucky, we would go to the farm and see some animals and ride a horse.

Most days I got up and went to the park and played baseball. Four brothers that lived down the street from me usually organized the games. The Mullers—Niall, Greg, Jeremy, and Mike—were the wildest and funniest family in the neighborhood. They were all great baseball players and probably could have played a team all by themselves and won the game.

They lived at the corner of Bird and Baynes. The whole neighborhood at one time or another took their turn standing on that corner talking the night away. Their porch held high-stakes poker games with ten-cent antes and betting on every professional game. Their driveway held basketball tournaments, free-throw contests, strikeout games, and any other game that could be played by teenage boys. (At one of the free-throw competitions, I watched Beaver Brady make fifty-six free throws in a row!)

Mrs. Muller was a saint for putting up with the commotion that happened daily in that house, on the porch and in the driveway. She was like a mother to the entire neighborhood, and Mr. Muller had some of the best one-liners I have ever heard. They were wonderful people that the whole neighborhood loved.

On the way to the diamond, we would grab the neighborhood kids to play the games. I rode my Huffy banana bike with a peace sign sissy bar as fast as I could all the way there, yelling for everyone to come out and play. At the field, all the neighborhood boys were there, bikes lying on the ground, with mitts and bats ready to play the day away.

Many of the players from my little league team were there. A quick ride down Grant Street summoned the two Charlies, Mike and Bobby. We would practice all day and then practice again at night with our real team.

The games went until lunch. We went home and ate, and then went back and picked right up where we ended. We would continue to play until the first of our moms called us home for dinner.

The majority of the boys on my street played West Side Little League Baseball. The teams were named after Major League teams and sponsored by area businesses. We played at LaSalle Park on the edge of Lake Erie. It was a beautiful park that was infested with sand flies, but it had the most unbelievable view of the lake. On game nights, the park was loud and filled with kids and their parents either watching or on the way to the diamond. The Mister Softee ice cream truck was always there playing its irritating song, adding to the chaos.

And little brothers and sisters were usually covered in dirt from playing behind the backstop on the ever-present dirt pile.

My team was the Giants. I played catcher, and Mike and Charlie from my neighborhood usually pitched. Our coach was Joe Starr. He worked for the City of Buffalo and was tough on us, which was what a bunch of us needed in order to learn how to play baseball. He also sat on the bench during games with a cigarette in his mouth and Pepsi under the bench. He also had a brand-new powder blue Camaro that he picked up the whole team with. Any coach with a car like that had to be cool!

We won the championship the previous year with a 15–0 record. This season though, we lost a lot of players and had won only a handful of games.

My next game after the graduation party I will never forget. In the second inning, a pop fly was hit between home and first base. I took my catcher's mask off and ran down the first baseline looking up to catch the ball.

I screamed "I got it" as loud as I could.

The first basemen did not hear me and was running full speed down the line toward me. We collided, and since I was taller than him, my teeth hit his forehead. The collision knocked my front tooth out, broke my nose, and my bottom teeth cut through my lower lip.

I hit the ground like a sack of potatoes. I was a bloody mess.

I knew this night wasn't going to end with a twist ice cream cone from Frosty Treat on Grant Street. I remember looking up at the sky with cartoon birdies flying all around me. I then saw my dad staring down at me.

"What hurts?" he asked me.

"Everything!" I screamed as I was rolling in pain on the ground.

I spit my tooth out and put my tongue through my lower lip while my dad continued looking down at me. Blood was streaming out of my mouth and nose, and was choking me. He rolled me on my side so I could spit out all the blood. He also pushed my nose back into place. (He must have learned some first aid when he was in the National Guard in the 1950s.)

My coach and father picked me up and carried me to the car. Our dentist was one of my dad's customers, so he drove right to his house. I was bleeding all over the car as my mom cried in the back seat holding on to me.

"I told you he was too young to play sports, look at his beautiful teeth, they're gone, and his lips, his nose, he is scarred for life!" my mom screamed from the back seat in typical "hysterical mom" fashion.

"Stop crying, Liz, you're only making things worse. I saw a lot of guys get their teeth knocked out when I was boxing, he'll be okay," Dad responded in typical "he'll be all right" dad fashion.

On the way there, my dad did his best ambulance imitation running red lights and Stop signs all the way to Dr. Dante's house.

During all the commotion at the diamond, one of the mothers picked up my tooth and packed it in a paper Teem pop cup with ice and gave it to Charlie Cavaretta to hold on to. He got to ride in the front seat of Dad's ambulance and kept telling me how disgusting it was to have my tooth in a cup on his lap.

When Dr. Dante answered his front door, he found me and my uniform covered in blood.

"Get him into the kitchen" was all he said.

Dr. Dante entered the kitchen a few seconds later with a black medical bag that looked like it belonged to the doctor on "Gunsmoke."

"Hold him down. This is going to hurt" was all he told my father.

I don't know how he did it, but he managed to push my front tooth back in the hole it came from, and then he stitched my lower lip while I was bleeding all over his white-on-white *Better Homes and Gardens* kitchen.

"His tooth will probably live because you got him here so quickly. He is going to have black eyes, a crooked broken nose, and some scarring on his lips," Dr. Dante told my mom.

The word "probably" was definitely what my mother did not want to hear!

When we got back into the car, my parents started arguing about whether I would ever play any organized sports again.

I knew my father would win this one.

My head was pounding, my teeth were throbbing, and all I wanted to do was to go to bed. I kept the window rolled down so I could continue spitting the gobs of blood from my mouth.

"Dad, just get me home" was the last thing I remember saying.

The next morning, I got up and looked in the mirror. With the fat lip, stiches in my lip, black eyes, bent nose, pounding headache, and sore teeth, I figured all this was going to put a real damper on the rest of my summer of '76.

My Aunt Marie and Uncle Al hosted our family's Fourth of July party every year, but this year was going to be extra special.

Our country was two hundred years old, and they had planned an extra-special bicentennial cookout and party.

I loved taking the ride over the Skyway to Aunt Marie and Uncle Al's house in Hamburg. We would drive past the Bethlehem Steel plant with thousands of cars parked in the factory lots. And sometimes the huge overhead doors were open and I was able to see steel being poured out of buckets suspended high in the air. But that day the whole country was celebrating the bicentennial and the plant was deserted.

My Uncle Al was a World War II hero. He never once talked to me about it, but I knew he had been in a plane that was shot down over Germany. To me he was the bravest person I ever met, and my Aunt Marie always made me laugh with the loving insults she said to Uncle Al. When I would get to their house, I would head right for the kitchen. Aunt Marie, like all my aunts, had her special dessert that she was famous for. Her pizzelles were the best I have ever tasted. And when she saw me through the kitchen window on the way into the house, there was always one pizzelle waiting for me on a paper plate on the table.

Their family was large with four boys and one girl. Their sons were older than me, and I always looked up to them. They were great athletes and were more than willing to give me a hard time about my new scary look as soon as they saw me.

"What does the other guy look like?" or "Got beat up by a girl again?" was said to me over and over again.

"Ha, very funny" was about the only lame comeback I could come up with.

Thank God their younger sister Mary Jo was there with my other cousin Patti Jo to stick up for me. Without saying anything, I knew they felt sorry for me, so they asked if I wanted to go to the beach with them. I wasn't supposed to know that they were really going to meet some boys, but it was always fun to go for swim on a hot day.

But I wouldn't leave until after two o'clock because the entire country was going to ring bells at the top of the hour. I had sent away for a miniature Liberty Bell to ring on this special day, and I planned on using it. Right on cue, all the church bells rang. People were in their driveways ringing bells to celebrate the two hundredth birthday of our country.

I remember the sound of those bells and all the cheering that was produced vividly.

As we walked toward the beach with our towels and lotion, Mary Jo tried to tell me I would look normal again "pretty soon," but I knew she was only trying to be nice to me. And up until that point, I never really thought Patti Jo cared that much about me either, because when I went to her house, she always tried to scare me by making me watch the *Dark Shadows* TV show alone in her basement.

But the two of them cared enough to take me to the beach to try to make me feel better. And from that point on, they were always very special to me.

On the ride home, it was getting dark. On the top of the Skyway, we saw fireworks exploding in every direction all over the city.

When we got home, the neighborhood was alive with fireworks and loud booms. Even a walk down to the Mullins house and all the bedlam that was happening there didn't really make me feel any better. Although the sight of Jeremy chasing Beaver Brady down the street firing shots out of a Roman Candle at him did make me chuckle!

I tried to laugh it off, but I knew my much anticipated summer activities were now going to be very limited because of my appearance. Being fourteen years old was hard enough without worrying about people staring at you and asking "What happened to you?" ten times a day.

How could I go anywhere and try to meet any girl, especially the girl from Ronnie's party, looking like a jigsaw puzzle missing a few pieces?

I did make it back for a few games at the end of the baseball season, but it just wasn't the same. Quietly my little league baseball career was over. I also never made it over to Parkside Avenue or the dances at He and She's. I had made the decision that I had to limit my public appearances until my face didn't remind people of Frankenstein's.

The only thing that managed to make me forget my broken nose, black eyes, stitched-up lip, and most likely a concussion started the second week of summer. I was spending a lot of time on the couch watching the Summer Olympics being held in Montreal. They were amazing. I sat and watched another fourteen-year-old, as the cover of *Sports Illustrated* said, "She Stole the Show." Nadia Comaneci, a Romanian gymnast, was unbelievable. She scored seven perfect 10s. A feat that has never been matched in any other Olympics. In fact, the scoreboards could only put 1.0 for a score because 10s had never been scored before. Day after day, my whole family watched the gymnastics and rooted for her.

I, to this day, feel that she is the greatest athlete I have ever seen.

As the summer progressed, it started to sink in that high school was almost here. I had to make my plans, and for me, it was kind of scary thinking about a new school, new friends, and a bus ride back and forth to school for the first time. I hoped my face would be back to normal before school started. And I thought about what sports I wanted to play in school. I had played hockey for many years, and knew I would be able to make that team.

Baseball would be easy too. But what about football?

I asked my dad if he thought I could play football.

"Sure you could, you'll be a chip off the old block!"

I rolled my eyes and walked away quickly because I knew some "Mr. Cleaver" piece of advice was coming whether I wanted it or not.

"Football will make a man out of you" was all I let my dad say before I ran upstairs to my room and my eight-track player.

As I mentioned before, my father was an excellent athlete, the kind people hated to play against. He was the guy that was good at every sport he tried. And according to legend, one of the best football players that ever went to his high school. He played with a leather helmet, no face guard, and bragged he had broken his nose five times playing.

It was in honor of this legend that I decided to try out for the Brennan football team in August. I had never played organized football, and I knew I had to get into real shape. I started jogging and lifting plastic weights in my neighbor Mitchell Pasquale's basement.

I ran, lifted, and ran again every day to get ready for the tryouts. They started on August 19. Our coach, Mr. Nixon, was right out of a Vince Lombardi movie. He screamed at us, called us girls, and made us run until we puked. And even after all that abuse, I have to admit it, I liked him. He was funny and told us stories about his years playing basketball at Notre Dame University while spitting chewing tobacco all over the field.

After five days of practice, we were issued equipment. I put it on and felt like I was now playing for the Bills. I ran out onto the practice field as fast as I could. One of the coaches asked me what position I wanted to play. I hadn't really thought about what I wanted to play until he asked me the question; I just wanted to make the team.

Since my father was a running back in school, I said "Running back."

One of the coaches grabbed me by my jersey and asked me, "Freshman, have you ever played football before?"

"Just touch in my neighborhood with my friends."

I didn't know why he was laughing and shaking his head as he was mumbling something walking away. I soon found out.

"Freshman, get over here," the varsity quarterback said, calling me into the huddle.

All the varsity players were smirking at me and looking at each other as we huddled up.

I didn't know why, but I was about to get my first high school lesson without even making it into a classroom.

"Take the ball and run to the right, make sure you keep your head down when you hit the hole," the quarterback told me.

The ball was snapped. I ran through the hole and got hit the hardest I ever have in my life. Two seniors, Tony Hyland and Al Lincoln, hit me so hard that I regretted that I ever even thought of playing football. Both of them were over six feet tall and weighed about 225 pounds apiece. They stood over me laughing as I was flattened like a pancake.

I got up and walked back to the huddle and told the quarterback to give me the ball again. I must have been nuts because the same little birdies I saw a month before at my now-famous baseball game were back, and they were now flying all around my head as I staggered back to the huddle. He did, and I ran right at the two of them as hard as I could.

They creamed me, but this time they helped me up and told me I had guts to do what I just did. This time when I walked back to the huddle I had earned something that is hard to do as a freshman, a little respect from the upperclassman.

One of the senior players, Carlos Manuel, took me under his wing. He showed me how to run through a hole without getting killed and told me how to block without getting wiped out. He was the first upperclassman friend I made.

For the next three days, I gave all the effort my 135-pound body had to give. I told myself I was going to make the team no matter what. Every time I got knocked down, I got up and hit the next guy harder. I studied the playbook and started to understand how the game was played and made it through the second week without getting injured.

It worked. Mr. Nixon told me had I made the JV team. I thought it was a great accomplishment after all the bad things that had happened earlier in the summer.

The bus ride home that day seemed to be going in slow motion. I was so excited. I couldn't wait to tell my parents I had made the team. I got off the bus in front of Ray's Wicker Ware, ran past the comic book store, and the One Minute Stop all the way home.

I busted through my front screen door, and everyone was in their usual spots on the couch watching "Match Game '76."

"I made it!" I screamed.

"Made what?" my mother asked.

"The team."

"Water boy?" my father asked sarcastically as Nelson Reilly was giving an answer to Gene Rayburn on the RCA color console.

"I made the JV team, and I get to practice with the varsity till school starts."

My father smiled. "You have a lot to learn the next few weeks so you don't get killed in your first game."

"Dad, I got news for you, they have been killing me for the last few days. I gave it back as best as I could, and I think they like me."

I couldn't wait to get to practice the next morning. I had earned a spot on my high school team and a little respect too. Not bad for a fourteen-year-old freshman.

It was a great feeling, one that I will never forget.

One thing that I had never thought about as I walked into the locker room the next morning was that for every football team, there is a cheerleading team. Ours were from our sister school, Bishop O'Malley.

"Cheerleaders today!" one of the seniors in the locker room announced.

There was lots of hooting and hollering by all the players. It seemed like everyone got dressed for practice a little quicker that day. One of the guys said that the girls practiced on the field next to ours.

Wow, girls, I thought to myself, *this football thing just keeps getting better.*

I proudly put on my green practice jersey with "Brennan Cards" on the front and felt like a big shot for the first time in my life. I busted out of the locker room door into the sunlight without looking. When I did, I ran over Stephanie as she was walking on the sidewalk to cheerleading practice.

I was stopped dead in my tracks and stood over her as I tried to help her up. She just looked at me like I was the biggest klutz she had ever met. It was the closest I had ever been to her. She was even prettier with a tan and her hair up in a ponytail. She had on shorts and a "Brennan Cheerleading" T-shirt.

I just looked at her through my faceguard on the ground for what seemed like ten minutes. I am sure it was more like ten seconds before I finally did something.

Help her up, stupid! I said to myself.

I laughed and told her, "I'm sorry for running you over."

She just smiled, shook her head, and kept walking toward the other girls that were gathering to start their practice.

I walked to the practice field telling myself what an idiot I was. Of all the times, all the girls, I had to make my first tackle on her. How embarrassing!

Then I realized I actually talked to her, which made me a little distracted that morning at practice. I don't know for sure, but it might have been the worst practice in the history of organized football. It seemed like I spent most of it getting hit so hard I ended up on my back looking up at the sky.

But I knew on the next field there was someone very special, and I hoped that maybe I would have a chance with her after all.

"Haven't you ever seen a girl before?" one of the upperclassman running backs said as he ran over me like I was a stuffed animal because I was looking in the direction of the cheerleaders.

"Not ones like that!" I screamed back at him from the ground.

It was typical of my goofy cousin Ronnie to "forget" to tell me that Stephanie was a cheerleader and that she was going to O'Malley. And all this time, I thought I could count on him.

I thought this high school thing was going to be okay after all. I had made the team, and the prettiest girl I had ever seen was a cheerleader practicing on the next field.

I took my shower and got out of the locker room as fast as possible hoping to see her walking home or waiting for the bus. My plan was to apologize to her for clotheslining her earlier in the morning. But when I got outside, most of the girls were already gone from the practice field.

I did see a small group of cheerleaders at the street waiting for the bus.

I walked toward them down the sidewalk behind a bunch of the varsity players. I knew my place and kept my distance from the upperclassman, but I stayed close enough to them to hear their conversation. They were talking about the cheerleaders and especially the new recruits.

I couldn't help thinking that they might, because of their higher social status, be able to strike up a conversation with them much easier than I ever could.

35

I listened to everything they said. The usual high school boy boasting was taking place. I have to admit some of the things they said made me shake my head and blush. I definitely was not ready to start talking like that.

Then the worst thing that could have been mentioned was finally said. They started to talk about Stephanie, how pretty she was, and that she looked like Dorothy Hamill.

But most of all, she was off-limits because she had an older brother that would kill you if you went anywhere near her. He also went to Brennan and was a popular junior at the school.

I was quickly stopped dead in my tracks for the second time that day. But then I thought, if any girl was worth risking your life for, it was one like her.

CHAPTER 4

I was very nervous my first day of high school. My mother dropped me off, and I walked into school with the look every confused freshman has. There was a table marked "Freshman" on it. When I approached, I was given a schedule, homeroom assignment, and a pink Metro bus pass and sent in the direction of my homeroom.

I was hoping my cousin Ronnie would be in the homeroom. He wasn't. As I sat down, the boy behind me started talking to me immediately. He was from Riverside and was the first friend I ever made from that part of Buffalo. We talked about hockey and music until our homeroom teacher, Mr. Cavaretta, called us to order.

Once roll call was finished, we went to our first class, which was religion.

I had never switched classes before. My grammar school was so small; one teacher taught us everything. I was wide-eyed and no doubt looked like a dumb freshman as I tried to find that first class.

I cautiously walked in and sat in the back row. There was a boy sitting next to me that had no pen or paper to write on. I gave him both, and immediately, Dominic became my friend. (We have stayed friends until now.) I started to think that making friends in high school wasn't that hard and that all the worrying in the summer about fitting in was a waste of energy, because after all, we were all just trying to fit in. Everyone was eager to make friends, and no one wanted to be left out.

Our teacher was a young priest named Father Bentley. He wasn't much older than we were. He admitted to us he was only twenty-one years old. To be honest, I think he was more nervous than we were on his first day of teaching. Father Bentley became the advisor to the freshman class and a great friend to all of us. I went to three other classes before lunch. The teachers tried to come off as tough and expecting a lot from us. And for the first time, I was happy that the drill sergeant nuns from grammar school properly prepared me for anything that high school would throw at me.

At lunch, I sat with Ronnie and another cousin of mine, Joel, who was a junior. It was good to see some familiar faces in such an unfamiliar place. The cafeteria seemed to split up into classroom sections. The freshman looked scared and sat together in the back. The seniors were loud, in charge and in the front. The juniors and sophomores sat in the middle, waiting for their chance to move up to the senior section. The food was awful, but was better than the olive loaf sandwiches I had for lunch every day the last few years.

After my afternoon classes, I went to practice and took the bus home.

One other thing happened my first day of school as a freshman. It was the initiation ritual. It doesn't sound like such a bad thing, but it was. On the first day of school, the upper-class kids in the neighborhood would walk around looking for unsuspecting freshman, ready to hit them with rotten eggs, tomatoes, and any other spoiled thing they could find when you walked home from school.

All the while they are doing this, they scream "Freshman!" It didn't matter what school you went to. If they were older, they were out to get you.

I managed to get home without getting killed; this was accomplished by getting off the bus one stop too soon. My time came right after supper with the doorbell ringing. Dad answered the door. He started laughing when he saw the mob in front of our house.

He knew exactly what they were up to.

"Nicky, there are about twenty kids on the front lawn waiting to get you!" he yelled to me while I sat at the table finishing my chicken potpie.

I knew that I was next because they had gotten my friend Jimmy earlier in the day.

"Dad, what should I do?" I asked.

"Just go out there and get it over with. It will only hurt for a day or two," he said, laughing and walking back into the living room.

Imagine that, I thought, even my dad wasn't going to help me.

I put my sneakers on and walked out onto the porch. I surveyed the situation. Way too many kids for me to fight them. Some were on bikes, and the rest were on foot. I knew I was in the best shape of my life, so I figured I would run away and let them chase me until *they* got tired and gave up.

As I walked to the top of my stairs, the head initiator was a boy named Emil from down the street. He threw a tomato at me. I caught it and whipped it right back, hitting him in the forehead. While everyone was laughing, I took off running. I ran around the entire neighborhood. Not one of the projectiles launched at me actually hit me. I ran between parked cars, past the kids on bikes, up on porches, through backyards, and just outran all of them. I made it back home after about ten minutes in one piece. While they were chasing me, the number of people running into each other looked like a *Three Stooges* movie.

I kept running until I couldn't go anymore. I ran up on my front porch and shut the front door as fast as I could.

"You made it home alive?" my father asked, laughing.

No one ever made another attempt at initiating me.

My exciting first day of high school ended with me sitting in bed wondering what my high school life was going to be. Would I make a lot of friends? Was I going to be popular? Or just lost in the shuffle?

I surely didn't have the answer.

But just like she always did, my mother walked into my room and said "Bedtime, kiddo" and turned off my light.

"But, mom, I'm in high school now!"

"Well, you'll always be my baby, now go to sleep. You've had a long day."

And just like she always did, she shut my door. I put my head down and realized that everything was okay because of how lucky I was that both my parents were always going to be looking out for me.

CHAPTER 5

I quickly fell into the high school routine: get up, catch the bus, go to class, finish with football practice, and take the bus back home. I would arrive home from school at about five thirty, and my mother would greet me with the same questions as I walked through the door every night.

"How was school? What did you learn today? Did you bring home your sweaty clothes from practice?"

"Good, nothing, and no" was what I usually responded.

I saw Stephanie many times the first month of school at the football games. She was at pep rallies, a roller-skating party, and the Brennan dance.

Every time I saw her, she was prettier than the last time.

I don't know why it was so difficult for me to work up the nerve to talk to her. I had no problem talking to any other person I ever met. I just felt so awkward around her. I worried about the new pimple on my cheek, the clothes I was wearing, and all the other things fourteen-year-old self-conscious boys think about.

Our pep rallies were every Friday during football season. They were particularly hard too if you were a cheerleader. They took place in the school's gym. The cheerleaders would stand in the hallway while some crazy senior that wasn't on the football team riled up about five hundred high school–aged boys by saying that we were going to kill our opponent the next day.

Then girls would run in and get ready to cheer. The boys, acting like every high school–aged boy when a bunch of girls in short skirts get anywhere near them, whistled, screamed, and howled while they performed.

On one occasion, the nerdy senior named Edward J. Glasco went on about how Wedgewood was worried about playing us on Saturday. (Any kid in high school that used his middle initial had to be a nerd, right?) He conveniently neglected to say that Wedgewood had won fifty-two games in a row and were state champs.

The girls ran in, wearing their green-and-white outfits with "CBHS" on the front, got whistled at, and tried out a new cheer. They tumbled and jumped all over the gym. Some of the more difficult routines involved throwing girls into the air. If one of them fell or was dropped, everyone went from cheering to laughing.

My eyes were always on the freshman girl in the corner of the group. To me, she was the only one there. She never fell, or was dropped, and unfortunately, she still had no clue who I was.

And of course, that Saturday, Wedgewood beat us so badly I have erased the final score from my memory.

One of the best things about being in high school, even if the football team was bad, were the dances. They were held Friday nights and gathered about three hundred kids in the gym. The best bands would come and play for three hours. Catholic and public school kids came together to dance, talk, and have fun.

As a freshman, it was also your first opportunity to check out the girls you would hang out with for the next four years.

The first dance was the third Friday in September. My mother wanted to make sure that my first high school dance would be special. She also wanted to make sure I looked good while attending it. One night when I walked in the door after practice, she asked me about my plans for the dance.

"You are going to dance on Friday, aren't you?" she asked me.

My Friday nights up until this point in my life were usually spent sitting on the couch next to my dad watching "The Rockford Files" and hoping he wouldn't fall asleep before we could order a pizza from the Pizza Villa.

"The Rockford Files" was my favorite detective show because it wasn't like all the rest of them on television at that time. Every week

James Garner got beat up, complained about how much he hated his job as a private detective and working for only $200 a day plus expenses. And most weeks his clients lied to him, which usually led to some kind of a run-in with the police.

Rockford also drove a cool gold Firebird that he seemed to wreck chasing the bad guys in each episode. It was the perfect show for a teenage boy to watch with his dad.

And if it was a good week, and my dad didn't start snoring on the couch next to me, we ordered a pizza and picked it up just after ten. John, the owner of Pizza Villa, made the best pizza I have ever tasted. He hid the pepperoni and anything else you wanted on it under the cheese. I have never seen any other pizzeria with a recipe like that!

I lied to my mom and asked her, "What dance are you talking about?"

"You're going to that dance Friday at school, and I'm taking you to Pantastik after dinner to get an outfit to wear."

As I was dumping my homework on the dining room table, I yelled into the kitchen, "Mom, how many times do I have to tell you that men don't wear outfits, they just wear clothes!"

"Do you want some new clothes for free, from a cool store or not? Then close your mouth and leave me alone. I'll call it what I want! Or I'll let you wear that ugly graduation suit from the Sample your dad bought you in June. You remember that green leisure suit, don't you?"

I never wanted to wear that suit again (if I did, I would no doubt have caught some sort of polyester disease). So I kept my mouth shut and went upstairs to get ready for dinner.

I knew that there must be a string attached to this sudden interest in my social life, but being the unemployed teenager that I was, any offer of new clothes and the opportunity for free transportation to a dance was not going to be turned down.

Pantastik was a store on Elmwood where all the cool kids shopped. It had dress jeans, jackets, and vests. You could buy clogs, shoes, and all the latest disco wear. No one over the age of twenty-five ever shopped there. As you entered the store, the music was loud, and a disco ball spun from the ceiling. It was quite the shopping experience. The girls that worked there all looked like the girls from ABBA and must have gotten a commission on every sale because they swarmed around you, treating you like a celebrity as you walked in.

My mom went right to work picking out a pair of dress jeans, a jean vest, and what would be best described as a hippie shirt. She also bought me a pair of Bastad blue clogs. My jeans were Faded Glory. They had beige leather patches and had no pockets, and my vest was a match to the jeans.

Mom really took care of me that night. As we left the store, the string I was waiting for was revealed. Mom broke the news to me that she was going to be a chaperone at the dance.

"Mrs. Stephens asked me to help at the dance, and I couldn't say no."

"Mom, you can't do that to me! It's high school, and I can't have my mother hanging around cramping my style at my first dance."

"From what I see, you don't have much style, except for the clothes I just bought you, and anyway, you don't really want to spend the rest of your high school Friday nights sitting next to your dad on the couch watching TV and hoping he orders you a pizza, do you?"

When it was put to me like that, I knew I had to just keep my mouth shut and go along with her plan. It was true that I really didn't have any style to speak of, but I had to say something. I knew, especially after spending all that money on me, that this wasn't going to be an argument I would win.

But I quickly made up a simple set of rules for the dance that my mom would have to follow.

"Mom, you are only allowed to go under certain conditions," I said when we were getting into the car.

My mom guaranteed that she wouldn't do anything to embarrass me, so I reluctantly agreed to the arrangement and hoped for the best. She loved being around kids, and I knew she would probably have as much fun at the dance as I would.

(Looking back, I am glad she went to all the dances and that she enjoyed herself so much. All my friends loved my mom, and they were able to talk to her about anything. It remained like that until she passed away in 2005.)

The night of the dance, we picked my cousin Ronnie up. He thought it was funny that his aunt would be at his first dance too.

"Aunt Lizzie, you're not going to be watching and reporting to my mom all the girls that chased me around, are you?"

"No, I've already been told the ground rules by your cousin: walk in five minutes behind the two of you, not to talk unless spoken to first, not take any pictures at the dance, and most of all make no eye contact with any of the girls you might be talking with—"

I had to interrupt and add one other thing, "Mom, you forgot one other condition, you can't talk to any of our teachers either."

We were dropped at the front door as agreed and walked in as my mother parked the car. I saw hundreds of kids wearing all the newest in disco wear. There were pretty girls everywhere, and everyone was trying their best to look cool and fit in. Groups of kids were scattered around the hall and the cafeteria all talking and waiting for the band to begin playing.

The doors to the gym were still closed until eight o'clock sharp, and then they swung open as ABBA's "Dancing Queen" was inviting everyone in. Ronnie and I went from the cafeteria to the gym. The first girl I saw was Stephanie. She was standing with her brother, and what appeared to be her sister, in a group of kids from North Buffalo that I didn't know.

"She's right there, go over and talk to her," Ronnie said, pushing me in her direction.

"Talk to who?" I quickly shot back, hoping he wouldn't say any more to me. "She doesn't even know my name. I just can't walk over to her and start talking. Her brother is there, and he will kill me, remember?"

"Go and ask her if she still has black and blue marks form you tackling her at tryouts. You're never going to find out unless you try, and if her brother starts beating you up, scream for your mommy. She's here and can defend you!"

Just what I needed, a comedian and my mother crashing my first high school dance.

The gym was decorated like a large disco and was so dark you could barely see your feet. The band National Trust started playing, and for the first time, I was part of the disco world of loud music, dancing, and whirling mirrored disco balls. I will never forget how cool it felt seeing all that and the feeling of being grown up for the first time.

I tried to watch the crowd and find Stephanie. The only time I saw her was during the "Bus Stop" dance that was played between the band's sets. The lines of kids dancing and having fun is still very clear in my mind, as was the realization that I would never be able to dance like that.

Of course, I didn't dance (I didn't know how) and was too shy to talk to most of the girls. I spent the night holding up the gym wall under the basketball hoop. I have to admit, in my dress jeans and vest I did look cool, but it was really too dark in the corner to be seen by anyone except the teachers chaperoning that were sneaking around looking for kids that were making out to throw out of the dance.

My mother held up her end of the bargain and didn't talk to me until the end of the night when we were leaving to go home.

"Did you two have fun?"

"It was all right," I responded

"I must be getting old because that band was so loud that I had to put toilet paper in my ears!"

"Ma, you are old."

She was right. Both Ronnie's and my ears were ringing too!

"Henry's for some hamburgers?" Mom asked as we piled into the car.

Henry's was next to the school in the Kings department store parking lot. We never would refuse that offer. The neon sign in front proclaimed "ten-cent hamburgers" (but since the oil shortage, the price went up to twenty-five cents), and they had the best milkshakes ever made.

We went in and ordered six burgers, three fries, and three large strawberry milkshakes.

It was loud, and most of the place was filled with kids from the dance and their parents. Henry's featured a three-foot-tall fiberglass hamburger character with a big red *H* on it in the corner next to the cash register. The floor was black and white with a checkerboard pattern. There were booths that had small jukebox remotes hanging from the wall.

Ronnie and I stuffed in a few quarters and waited for our order to arrive. The songs "Disco Duck," "Play that Funky Music," "Lowdown," and anything by KC and the Sunshine Band were played over and over as we waited for our food.

When the order finally came, I looked around and saw all the kids from the dance at a hamburger place enjoying a special, innocent time with their parents.

High school is such a confusing period of your life, but right then and there, it was perfectly clear to me about my feelings for my mother and cousin sitting with me.

This is what it's all about, I told myself.

I also told myself that if you take the time notice, all the really important things in life are within your reach if you remember to take hold of them.

I made my mind up to grab ahold and never let go of the feelings that were most important to me.

And at that moment in a noisy hamburger joint, I decided I didn't care if my mother crashed all the rest of my high school dances. In fact, I thought it was kind of cool to have her around.

We ate our food, tried as hard as we could to suck the thickest strawberry shakes known to mankind through our striped straws, and listened to great disco songs. We dunked our fries in ketchup and vinegar, and most importantly spent time talking with each other like we always had.

But right then, it all seemed a little different. Something had changed me for the better. I was starting to grow up and realize the important things for the first time.

After we dropped Ronnie off, and just before we pulled up in front of our house, I told my mom the "rules for the dance" were canceled and that I was no longer embarrassed to have my mother at any school dance I went to. I also told her I was sorry for making the dumb rules up in the first place. She hugged me, started cry, and told me how much she loved me.

What I wouldn't give to have just one more Henry's hamburger with my mom right now.

CHAPTER 6

My mother was standing at our kitchen sink cleaning up the dinner dishes. We had her favorite dinner that night, "pigs in a blanket." I'm not sure, but I think the "pigs" were leftover meatballs from Sunday's sauce, and I know for sure the "blankets" were cabbage.

Doesn't sound very good, does it?

Our kitchen was very small with a table and four chairs. It was painted an olive green with a sunflower clock that ticked way too loud. But it was big enough for me when this dinner was served to slip our dog sitting under the table as much of the "pigs" and "blankets" from my plate as possible. Humphrey was the only dog I've ever met that would eat anything that fell on the floor or was fed to him by a kid trying to be excused from the table.

My mom had a schedule for dinners—Sunday – sauce, Monday – meatloaf, Tuesday – TV dinners, Wednesday – sauce again, Thursday we ate at Aunt Pat's, Friday – some sort of fish or "pigs in a blanket," and Saturday – steak. Mom had to have her routines. She said it kept her sane, and she always told me how much she didn't like to cook. But since we didn't have a lot of money, going out to dinner as a family didn't happen very often.

So she reluctantly cooked for us almost every night.

Her favorite night was Tuesday because we ate TV dinners and there were no dishes to wash. Mom would buy them at Twin Fair on shopping night, which was usually Mondays. They were eighty-five cents and were made by Swanson, Banquet and Hungry Man. The TV dinners were aluminum foil trays with some of the worst assortment of meats and vegetables known to mankind. The dessert was a kind of pastry that usually burned before the main course was cooked.

You had a choice of turkey, German-style beef and red cabbage, fish and chips, fried chicken, and my least favorite, meatloaf. The vegetables were carrots, beans, and peas that tasted like wax, as did the fat-based gravy that was slopped on the meat.

The best part of the dinner was that the entire family ate on flimsy metal TV trays in front of the television set in the living room. After you were done eating, you folded the trays up, put them back in the storage rack, threw out the aluminum tray and the plastic forks, and just like that dinner was over.

This was a major advancement for the moms of 1970s families!

But tonight was a Friday night, and it was movie night. So we had to finish dinner quick and get ready to leave for the show. Tonight we were meeting my aunt and uncle at the show. I was probably a little strange compared to most of my friends because I enjoyed doing things with all of my parents' friends and my aunts and uncles.

I now realize how lucky I truly was to have all of them in my life. Each of them was special to me in a different way. All of them had grown up in the depression, lived through World War II, and become successful in one way or another.

"Liz, the movie starts in an hour!" my father yelled from the living room as he was looking through the movie section of the *Buffalo Evening News*. "I called Joe and told them to meet us out in front at seven," he continued.

"It would be nice if someone, once in a while, gave me a hand after dinner, you know, clear the table, wash the dishes, dry the dishes, feed the dog!"

"A woman's place is in the kitchen, not a man's!" my father would always shout back without hesitation.

I was coming downstairs and listening to the conversation that I had heard about two hundred times before and laughed every time. Most nights, dad, as soon as dinner was done, left the table and took his usual position on the couch watching Walter Cronkite. Mom stayed in the kitchen, cleaned up, and got ready to assume her spot on the "barcolounger" next to dad for the rest of the night.

Looking back, in the seventies the roles of parents were so much more defined than they are now.

I was happy we were going with Uncle Joe and Aunt Charlotte. Uncle Joe had been my father's friend since they lived next door to each other when they were three years old on Jersey Street in the early 1930s. And Aunt Charlotte had become like a sister to my mom. Uncle Joe was larger than life and the center of attention at every party. Aunt Charlotte, on the other hand, was movie star beautiful, quiet, refined, and barely five feet tall.

Every summer as a kid I measured my height compared to my Aunt Charlotte, and with much fanfare, I finally passed her in fourth grade.

I walked into the living room, and my dad told me, "One of the guys at breakfast today already saw the movie and said that *Rocky* could have been about me."

Mom, just completing her kitchen duties, laughed. "Nick, there haven't been many five-foot-five heavyweight champs from the West Side!"

"If your grandma hadn't talked me out of turning pro, I could have made it to the top, you know. My trainer was Tommy Paul. He knew how to win. He was a winner, world champion in 1928!"

I had heard his boxing story many times. He was tough; there is no doubt about that. Maybe he could have been a great fighter. At various times in his life, he had shown me how tough he was. My father had been knocked down, but like all great fighters, he always got back up and continued on. It was a trait that he always told me I needed to have to be successful in anything I tried.

"Nicky, come on, we are leaving!" Dad yelled from the front foyer.

The entire family assembled in the front hall and started to walk out onto the porch.

Dad turned to Humphrey and told him, "Watch the house while we're gone, boy," and then locked the door.

It was really great having a dog like Humphrey that liked "pigs in a blanket" and understood his responsibilities as a watchdog. It always amazed me how people talk to their dogs and think that they understand them. He was a great dog, and my father loved him a lot, but I have to believe that he had a limited understanding of the English language.

We walked down the porch stairs toward our station wagon for our night at the movies. We were on our way to the North Park Theater. It was a neighborhood movie on Hertel Avenue in North Buffalo. It was built in the 1920s, had a beautiful marquee and large brass doors.

When you entered, the carpets were plush. There were lobby cards announcing upcoming movies, and best of all, the smell of fresh popcorn with butter that invited you with warmth that new movies only wish they had.

"Dad, there's Aunt Charlotte waiting," I said as we pulled up in front.

"Go on, Uncle Joe must be getting the tickets. I'll park the car," Dad said, motioning toward the marquee with red letters spelling out "Rocky," flashing lights, and what looked like a mile of neon.

"Lizzie, leave Nicky in the lobby with my ticket, and get to the concession stand so we aren't late for the movie."

Mom rolled her eyes got out of the car and mumbled something like "Yes, sir, you'd think this is the first movie I ever went to!"

She hugged my aunt and walked inside. My Uncle Joe and my father weren't related. They were *Goombahdis*, which means the best of friends in Italian. I have seen it spelled many different ways, but it always means the same thing: best friends.

They were such good friends in fact that when they thought they were going to be drafted into the Korean War, they enlisted in the National Guard together. By doing this, if they were activated, they would go together and be able to protect each other.

They never were activated, but they did spend two weeks a year for five summers defending Fort Drum from attack by the ever-present threat from the Canadians just north of them.

Uncle Joe had the tickets as the three of us walked into the lobby. He gave me two and told me to "wait right here for your father."

At the North Park, the upcoming movies were always prominently displayed in the lobby showcases. As I stood there alone looking at them, I heard a couple of girls laughing behind me.

When I turned around, it was Stephanie and her older sister that I had seen at the dance.

Here I was again, face-to-face with her with nothing to say. I don't know what divine force kept putting us together, but it was definitely giving me *every* chance to get to know her.

I was close enough to hear their conversation. It was Thanksgiving time, and they were talking about all the relatives that had come to their house for turkey and dressing.

When my father walked in, he had one thing in mind, get to our seats, and as soon as possible.

"Nicky, Nicky. Hey! What are you doing? Let's get to our seats," my dad said to me as he headed for the usher taking tickets at the entrance. "I don't want to miss a minute of the movie, let's go!"

We walked in, and Mom and Aunt Charlotte were still in line at the concession stand.

My father was getting nervous that we would miss the start of the show, or even worse for him, get seats too close to the screen.

"Come on, Liz, what's taking so long?" he asked mom.

"Do you want hot popcorn or some that was made a month ago?" she asked him, shaking her head.

My Aunt Charlotte grabbed me and whispered in my ear, "Honey, don't worry, there will be five coming attractions before the movie starts."

I guess my mom had had enough of my dad's questions because she told him, "Go sit with Joe, did you forget he was with us? He is saving us seats."

My dad and I walked into the auditorium and found him very quickly. I always hated when people held seats for people that weren't there, but it didn't bother Uncle Joe. He got five great seats in the middle halfway down.

As the previews started, the theater got very dark, but no mom, no Aunt Charlotte, and no popcorn yet.

I had seen the trailer for *Rocky* a few times, and it looked great, and I had heard a lot about it from friends that had seen it too. I knew my dad was going to love it. It was about a down-and-out boxer from Philadelphia that lived in an Italian neighborhood named Rocky. He was given a shot to fight for the heavyweight title.

My father had fought for the Golden Gloves championship of Buffalo in the 1940s. He lost, but wanted to start to fight professionally, but as I mentioned before, my grandmother talked him out of it. She told him to continue to sing, that "God gave you a beautiful voice, and that is what you should concentrate on." (He did take my grandmother's advice and sang professionally until he was in his seventies.)

My mom and aunt finally arrived, just in time to see the previews for some movie that was coming in the spring called *Star Wars*.

There were two seats available directly in front of us. As the previews continued, two people walked in and sat down in those seats.

Of course it was Stephanie and her sister. With the way things had been going lately, there was no doubt she would sit down directly in front of me.

So there I sat with my mom and aunt on one side of me and my uncle and father on the other side.

There was nowhere to hide if anything went wrong tonight! I had to convince myself to stop overthinking all these situations I constantly found myself in and concentrate on what was important right here and right now.

The only problem was I didn't see anything positive in the situation I was in currently. Then it hit me. At least Stephanie wasn't at the movie with a boyfriend. Maybe, just maybe, she would someday be at the movies with me.

I couldn't believe it, first the dance with my mother as a chaperone, and now at the movies with my extended family. How embarrassing.

I was sweating bullets hoping that I wouldn't spill popcorn, cotton candy, or root beer on Stephanie or her sister as they were passed to me.

I couldn't help but laugh to myself that I was continually running into this girl. What put her at Ronnie's party, on the cheerleading team, the dances at school, and now just three feet from me at the movies?

The *Rocky* story was fantastic. My father kept elbowing me, telling me that he knew someone that reminded him of every character in the movie. I, too, saw similarities to many people I knew. And Uncle Joe liked it, so much in fact that he was talking to the movie screen, telling Mickey, the trainer, how to work Rocky out.

I quickly came to the realization that my dad and uncle lacked proper movie etiquette, but there was nothing left for me to do but hope that some old lady behind us didn't start telling them to "shush" or "shut up."

"Mickey is just like my trainer Tommy Paul, that gym looks like the one I trained in, you know I could do ten one-armed pushups," my dad whispered to me as the movie progressed.

"You couldn't do ten regular pushups, who are you kidding?" Uncle Joe told him.

"Can you two be quiet? We're trying to watch a movie," Aunt Charlotte said to them.

At that point, all I could do was laugh, because my father and uncle were very funny without even realizing it most of the time.

In the movie, Rocky was too shy to ask the girl named Adrian who worked at the pet store for a date. I knew what it felt like to be shy with a girl, especially the one sitting right in front of me.

It was fun watching how shy Rocky was and how shy she was. When they finally went on a date, it was ice-skating. He had to pay the rink attendant ten dollars for the use of the rink. I hoped that someday I would be able to go ice-skating too with the girl sitting in front of me.

I thought the night would end without any further incidents until Rocky was fighting Apollo Creed for the championship belt. All of a sudden, my father started to yell at Rocky like he was actually watching a live fight and he could hear him! Uncle Joe jumped in too.

"Hit him!" my dad yelled.

"Hit the SOB!" Uncle Joe yelled.

"Left jab, move right, hit the bum!" all came out of Uncle Joe's mouth as the fight scenes continued.

"Get up, don't let him win," Dad screamed when Rocky was finally knocked down.

At that point, he should have been telling me to get up too, because I was on the sticky floor covering my face, hoping the girls in front of me weren't turned around watching the performance taking place in the two seats to my right.

At the end of the movie when the decision was announced and Rocky lost, dad yelled, "Rocky, you got jobbed!"

I slid down in my chair again in sheer horror. I don't know if Stephanie and or her sister turned around. But everyone else in the movie did!

How much more embarrassing could it get for me?

I grabbed my dad's arm and pleaded with him to lower his voice.

"Dad, stop. It's only a movie, he can't hear you," I kept telling him.

When the movie ended and Rocky was screaming for Adrian, my mom and aunt started to cry. The reaction from the audience was great.

As the credits started rolling and the house lights came up, I was putting my jacket on. Stephanie was looking right at me, putting hers on too. I couldn't muster a word to say to her or her sister. My heart was beating way too fast.

Out we walked right behind them into the bright lights of the lobby. We stopped under the huge marquee for a few minutes talking about the movie. It was unanimous. We all loved it.

Stephanie was there too, talking to some people nearby.

"How long until *Rocky 2*?" my uncle asked.

"No way, this is the end of *Rocky* story," my father said. (What a great prediction that was!)

We said our goodbyes, and my dad went to get the car.

I had stood outside of this theater so many other times waiting to be picked up, but this time something was different. I noticed things that I had never noticed before. The sounds, the smells, and the lights were all a bit more vivid. Maybe it was because Stephanie was there.

All the blinking lights, the neon, and snow gently falling made it look like I was part of a magical snow globe. I turned and watched that special girl walk away from me until she disappeared from sight.

Rocky didn't win that night, but in some way, I felt like I had.

CHAPTER 7

As the fall gave way to winter, it was time for hockey season. Hockey was definitely my favorite sport. I liked football and baseball, but I *loved* hockey. Cardinal Brennan was just beginning a varsity program, and as it turned out, my former coach was hired to coach the team.

"I was talking to Mrs. Chamberlin today, and she told me Bill was hired to coach the team at Brennan."

"Mom, I'm a freshman, no way will I make the varsity."

The tryouts were very difficult if you were a freshman goalie. The seniors shot much harder and quicker than anything I had ever seen. My first shot at the tryouts was from Ray Busch, who had gone to my grammar school. He was a senior and was captain of the team. It was like a laser and made me look like a bum. I eventually got the timing down and started making some saves. But I knew the two older goalies were better and more experienced than I was.

"Nicky, you made the JV and can dress for the varsity games," Coach Bill told me.

I was happy to just be part of any team and knew my time would come in the following years.

Being the third goalie on a hockey team was a pretty bad position to be in. You know, unless a bomb goes off, you won't get to play, and in practice, you are a target for older guys who try to kill you. The varsity and JV teams practiced on the same ice. I did get to play net for most of the JV games. It was fun playing on that team. We won most of our games.

As luck would have it, Stephanie's brother Dan was on the varsity team. He was a great player and very well liked. He didn't say much and was cool in an "Arthur Fonzarelli" kind of way. He was a great athlete and had all the girls following him around. He called me "Freshman" a few times. (I guess he wasn't the only one in his family to not know my name.) I did sit next to him in the locker room on a few occasions, but the most I got out of him was that he wanted to borrow my shampoo after practice.

I spent most of the varsity games trying to stay warm and laughing as I watched my dad nodding off to sleep in the stands. My mother loved hockey and never missed a JV or varsity game. She happily drove me to the games or practices and had a good time whether we won or lost, even if it meant nearly freezing to death watching a team lose its fifth game in a row.

After a particularly embarrassing loss, I asked my dad on the way home, "Tough staying awake tonight, hah?"

"Hey, I have been working almost every night plowing. This winter has started out really bad. I need a few nights of good sleep."

What an omen for the future that was!

My father did work hard. All summer he cut lawns and did landscaping jobs, and in the winter, he plowed. At night Dad sang at various bars and restaurants around Buffalo. All to make sure we had what we needed. He sang the classics and had quite a following. But my father always made it clear to me that I was going to college so I wouldn't have to "work like a dog" the way he did.

The varsity team was bad, really bad. The best player on the team was Danny. I soon found out that Stephanie liked to watch her brother play and was at almost every game. I'm not sure, but I think that actually once she looked at me and smiled. I also noticed one time at a game she had figure skates flung over her shoulder and a Johnson Skating Club jacket on when she sat down in the bleachers.

During one game as I looked in the stands to see if my father was sleeping yet, I saw my mother talking to Stephanie, who was seated next to her. All sorts of crazy things started going through my mind. Knowing my mom, she was probably telling her how cute her son was, pointing to me sitting on the end of the bench trying to stay warm, that I had new dress jeans, what a great goalie I was, and that I would someday be the president.

"Mom, who was that girl you were talking to in the stands?" I asked in the lobby of the rink after another loss.

"She was cute, wasn't she? Nice girl, I asked her about being a figure skater and if her boyfriend was playing in the game. She laughed and told me her brother played for Brennan. We also laughed some more at how bad your team is."

I just shook my head. My mother had now talked to Stephanie more than I had. How much more awkward could this get?

At least she didn't ask mom if she liked my dad's performance at the *Rocky* movie!

I made up my mind to go and watch her skate. After all, she had watched me sit on the bench on the football team and the hockey team. It was now time for me to watch her.

Our team was off for a couple of weeks during the Christmas vacation. We had a great holiday and spent Christmas night at my grandma Carnavale's house. She lived in an old mansion that was a hotel for the Pan-American Exposition held in Buffalo in 1902.

We went to grandma's house every Sunday for "sauce." Her house had a huge chestnut tree in front, a welcoming front porch, and a double front door with stained glass. When you walked in, the house was loud and filled with love. She had an old dog named Tammy that would greet you at the front door with a friendly "woof."

Every holiday found the house loaded with our family and friends, and the smells of Italy in the air. The presents were stacked to the ceiling, and everyone was dressed in his or her best clothes for the trip to grandma's for the party. The front hall had coats and hats hanging everywhere and rubber boots all over the floor. So many, in fact, that you would trip over them as you walked in.

The next few steps brought you into the loudest room in the house, the living room. Chairs were stationed around the room, making it easy to communicate with anyone in it. That is where the real action was. When a room is filled with that many Italian men trying to make their point, it had to be loud.

My father made sure that I would go around the living room kissing and hugging all the adults seated around the perimeter. With eight brothers and three sisters it could get confusing just who was who, but I always got through it. There were so many of them that I didn't know most of their names! But I obediently did it without saying a word to my father.

My favorite uncles were usually clustered together in one corner of the room arguing about one thing or another. My Uncle Pat I would go to first. He had a laugh that was contagious and always seemed to be happy to see me. My Uncle Paul would always be right next to him. He was the Frito Lay Potato Chip truck driver for the West Side. His truck always had some chips waiting for me. And if my Uncle Charlie was there, he greeted me with a big stogie in the corner of his mouth and a joke from his time as a vaudevillian comedian.

My mom would go right to the kitchen with whatever she had brought in her Corelle pan and put it in the oven and warm it up.

The dining room table was the largest I had ever seen. It looked to a little kid to be able to seat an entire football team. The mantle had pictures of all my uncles in their World War II uniforms and a picture of President Kennedy still front and foremost.

We would then make our way to Grandma's bedroom to put our jackets on her bed. Her bedroom looked like a grotto. On her fireplace were rosaries and candles burning in small red holders honoring every Catholic saint.

I loved that magical old house. It had a beautiful Victorian staircase that seemed to be filled with a hundred cousins playing on it when you walked up it. A trip into the basement saw us scared of the octopus furnace with its giant tentacles reaching for us. Or even better was a trip to the attic into one of the bedrooms that Mark Twain supposedly slept in when he visited the Expo.

But best of all, the air was always filled with love, laughter, and the smell of sauce cooking. Grandma's old dog always barked until you scratched her stomach. And after you did, she would keep watch right next to grandma wherever she went.

Nothing had changed in the house since the 1930s when my family moved in. Grandma had just turned eighty-seven years old and still walked to church every morning. I can't explain how, but it was a house that just made you feel like you belonged.

Because my father had eleven brothers and sisters, it was standing room only on important holidays like Christmas. Grandma had an aluminum tree that spun as a multicolor light turned it all sorts of amazing colors. Big red lights lit up the porch to welcome all of us, and the front window had Rudolph and Santa lit up like a department store.

My cousin Frank would dress up as Santa Claus and come into the house for pictures with all the kids. One year, my cousin Billy was looking out the front window and saw him leaving his car dressed as Santa. He marched in the middle of the living room and proudly announced that "Santa drives a yellow MG like cousin Frank!"

The adults had a momentary look of terror on their faces that was priceless before they burst out laughing. Frank managed to pull his Santa routine off for one last year, and just as quickly, all my uncles went back to their loud holiday discussions as all the aunts cooked, set the table, and yelled at the kids to not get their "good clothes" dirty.

Grandma bought us one gift. She had to buy seventy-six gifts for all the sons, daughters, daughter-in-laws, son-in-laws, grandchildren, and great-grandchildren. A trip into her back bedroom would mean seeing the entire room filled with presents, each with a name tag written by her telling us something special about ourselves and telling us how much she loved us. It didn't matter to us that we only got one present because she gave us many things more important than a gift.

As school began in January of 1977, it was time to go and see Stephanie skate at the Johnson Skating Club. Because of my schedule, it took a couple of weeks for me to finally make it over there.

There was only one rink in Buffalo where her group skated. It was the Gannon Rink, and I had to find a way to get there. I also knew that some of the girls skated in the morning before school and that some skated right after school. My first guess would be that she skated after school.

I was eating my Quisp cereal for breakfast when I told my mother that I would be late for dinner that day.

"I have to stay after today to get ready for a report that is due next week."

"Why didn't you do your homework on the weekend?" she asked.

"Mom, weekends are for fun and recovering from the week. You don't do homework on the weekend!"

I really didn't like lying to my mother, but I had two things going for me at that point. It was really a "white lie." My mom told me many times that if you lied for a good reason, it wasn't "whole lie." It was a "white lie." And second, Father Joe from church told us that altar boys gets a few "get out of jail" passes for white lies for their service to the church.

The plan was simple: use my bus pass after school to make my way to the rink. When I arrived, there were a bunch of girls that were about to go on the ice. There was one girl there that was different from all the rest. Her skates weren't as expensive as the other girls, neither was her outfit, but what I saw when she skated was amazing.

The first thing I noticed was most of the girls were a bit distant to her, and Stephanie seemed to be alone in the crowd. I saw that they really didn't include her in their conversations before and during the practice. She skated by herself and talked only to her coach. The same grace that made me notice her the first time I saw her made it difficult to take my eyes off her as she skated.

The rink was very old and had a huge sign on the wall that lit up, naming all the types of ice dances. It was noisy, smelled musty, and was cold. The stands were concrete and not very comfortable. I sat up there trying to act like I belonged.

The one thing I learned from this experience was, when you try to look like you belong, you always look like you *don't* belong.

When it was her turn to skate, the music started and she went out to center ice. She was graceful, fast and smiling, and light on her feet. Her movements were like she was on a cloud with angels.

After watching her skate, I wondered why she would ever waste her time cheerleading and wouldn't spend all her time at the rink perfecting her moves. I only stayed a few minutes because I didn't want to draw any attention to myself. But I had seen enough to know that aside from being the prettiest girl I had ever seen, she was very talented too.

As I walked out of the rink, I thought about the *Rocky* movie, and how the down-and-out boxer went on his first date with Adrian at an old rink like this one, and how hard it was for him to work up the courage to talk to her. I really understood how he felt. Here was a guy that wasn't afraid to fight the heavyweight champion but couldn't ask a clerk at a pet store for a date. How ironic that was.

As I slowly walked toward the bus stop, it started to snow like I had never seen before.

Snow, Snow, and More Snow

As I took the bus back home to the West Side, the snow blew around like the dust bowl of the Depression. In fact, it kept snowing for the next seven days.

It was the start of what was to be called the Blizzard of '77.

At first, we didn't mind because everything was shut down and we didn't have school, but very quickly it became very dangerous, and many people lost their lives because of the snow, wind, and cold.

On the first day of the blizzard, we didn't realize how bad it was going to get, and my mother actually drove me and two of my friends to hockey practice. The rink was in Fort Erie, Ontario. Canada is very close to Buffalo, and we visited there often in the winter and summer.

When we left the rink, we couldn't see to the end of the car.

It was the first time I ever heard the term "whiteout." As we went over the Peace Bridge on the way back into the US, it was like we were floating in a cloud snow. My mother was not the best snow-storm driver and was very nervous as we passed through the customs booth and back into Buffalo.

We took the exit toward Niagara Street, but because of the conditions, the car slid off the road into a guardrail and ended up in a snowbank.

We got out of the car to look at the damage. My friend, and the other goalie on our team Sam, quickly took control of the situation.

"This isn't good, not good at all," he kept saying out loud. "We are going to freeze to death here. This isn't the way I want to go out!"

Directly in front of us was Lake Erie and the Niagara River, or at least it should have been there. Instead all we saw was a wall of snow that was blowing at us like a tornado.

"Mrs. C, we will have to rock the car back and forth to get us out," Sam told my mother.

Back and forth we went, but not before some of the funniest interactions I ever witnessed happened. Sam was by far the shortest player on the team, had red hair, and was funny without even trying. (And after that day, my mother always said Sam was her favorite of all my friends, and that drive in the Blizzard of '77 was the most she ever laughed in her life.)

He kept yelling at my mom to "put the car in reverse, forward, reverse, forward" while we tried to push the car and rock it back and forth out of the snow mound.

It was so cold, and the snow was blowing so hard; our feet and hands were numb. The car wouldn't move and kept sliding further into the snow bank.

After about ten minutes of this chaos, Sam finally yelled at my mom to "slide over and let someone that knows what they are doing get us out of here."

He was totally covered in snow, and with his red hair, he looked like one of Santa's elves on a snowy Christmas night. It didn't matter that he didn't even have his driver's permit and had obviously never driven in the snow. He was determined to get the car out of the drift.

As he was knocking on the driver's side window, my mother rolled it down and told him, "Sammy, your feet won't even reach the pedals in a car this big!"

I was laughing so hard that I fell into the same snowbank we were stuck in.

He did get in, and eventually, we got the car out of the snow pile and back on to the road. We managed to safely drop everyone off and made it home. When we pulled in front of our house, the transmission in the car blew. I guess all that rocking back and forth was too much for the old car.

That night the wind howled and the house shook as the snow continued to fall at a record pace.

The next morning my mother was up very early and told me, "Dad's been out all night plowing."

I didn't know how to answer her, so I stood at our front window looking out into what could be best described as an image from a snow globe. Swirling piles of snow everywhere, and the wind was dropping inch after inch more without an end in sight.

"How long has Dad been gone?" my mother asked again.

"It seems like I haven't seen him for two days. He's okay, I know he is," I told her.

It did get worse. The snow on the lake was whipped and blown around day after day, creating conditions that had never been seen in our region before.

We were snowed in, virtually trapped in our house. We couldn't do anything except look out the front window and watch the snow. The drifts were nearing the first-floor windows on most of houses on the street. Cars parked on the street were now little more than speed bumps.

The entire city and suburbs were buried. Thousands of people were unable to leave their houses for days, some were stranded at work, and others took shelter in public buildings.

I listened to hourly calls by my mother to my aunts and both my grandmothers to make sure they were okay.

The third day of the blizzard I walked around the corner to see my friend Jimmy. It was like walking at the North Pole. The snow was drifted onto the porch of the Caples house at the corner of Bird and Richmond. The mailboxes at the corner were unrecognizable, and the streets were nothing more than snowdrifts.

Walking back from Jimmy's house, I decided that I should be helping my father. That night I waited up for him to come home. When he walked in, he looked exhausted and cold.

"How bad *is* it out there, Dad?" I asked.

"Like nothing I have ever seen. I have nowhere to push the snow anymore. The streets are nearly impassable, gas stations are out of gas, and delivery trucks can't make it to the supermarkets. There are cars abandoned in the middle of almost every street, and if I didn't have a 4×4, I wouldn't make it ten feet."

The next day, I got up early and told my father I wanted to go to work with him. He reluctantly told me yes.

When we walked to his garage around the corner, my father told me, "The streets are filled with cars that stalled and were abandoned. People are starting to get desperate. This is a very dangerous situation. I even saw a dog sled going down Forest Avenue!"

A lot of his customers were doctors, and it was his responsibility to get them dug out first. Everywhere we went people were flagging us down wanting us to plow them out.

My father kept telling them, "Sorry, I have to take care of my customers first."

When I left the truck to start shoveling that first day, the quiet was the most surreal thing I have ever seen or felt. When it snows that much, it becomes very quiet. Your footsteps are silent. You only hear your breathing. It's as if you are all alone in the world. It was very spooky, to say the least.

After convincing my father I could do the job of his helper, I worked with him for three weeks. I shoveled porches and opened gates as he plowed. The snow in some places was drifted as much as ten feet high. We would open up the driveways, the wind would start blowing again, and in an hour, it would look like we had never been there.

Eventually a state of emergency was declared, and cars were banned from the streets. The only vehicles allowed on the road were 4×4 trucks, which was what my father used to plow. In the customer's driveways, the snow was so high we had no place to put the new snow. Most of the time my father's International Scout hit the snowbanks and bounced off.

At home we were running out of food. While we were out working, my mother bundled up, took a toboggan out of the attic, and went on an adventure to the Potomac Superette.

My mother should have learned after our adventure the first day of the blizzard that she should leave the snowstorm activities to the men in the family.

When she returned, she told us she thought she was not going to make it back home alive.

"Where were you?" my dad asked when Mom came home bundled up like an Eskimo.

"Nick, we are out of everything. The snow stopped, and the sun came out. I thought it would be okay to walk to the corner store.

Boy was I wrong. The butcher was out of meat. The store had no bread, butter, or milk. When I started walking back, I was pulling what groceries I could get in the sled. Then all of a sudden, the wind started howling and blowing, the sun disappeared, and I couldn't see five feet in front of me. I have never been so scared in my life. I thought that I was going to freeze to death before I got home. I stopped at Muller's house to get warm. I waited for the snow to stop and then walked the rest of the way home."

"Liz, I'll do the shopping from now on."

Mom looked at him and without missing a beat told him, "That would be the first grocery shopping you've done since we got married in 1959!"

We all burst out laughing for the first time in a while!

About the only thing good that happened during the blizzard was my father bought me my first car. We were in a dark driveway of one of his customers when he told me to go in the garage and check out the car parked in it.

"Mrs. Marsh had told me she wants to sell her car," he told me. "You've been working very hard for me. You proved that you're growing up. Go in the garage. If you want the Corvair in there, I'll buy it for you, and you can start driving it when you get old enough."

I walked into the garage on Lincoln Parkway, turned on the light, and the Corvair was a mint 1967 Camaro. The car had 12,000 miles on it, was turquoise, and was every teenage boy's dream car.

I walked up to the car like I was having a dream. I opened the door and sat in it. The smell of the car and the feel of the seats were like brand-new. It even had air-conditioning. It felt like the car had been sent from heaven to me. I knew that all the good things I had done in my life had finally been rewarded!

I ran out of the garage as fast as my snowmobile boots would let me to the truck.

"Dad, that's a Camaro!" I yelled at him through the falling snow and his closed window.

"Camaro, Corvair, Cutlass, they're all the same to me. Do you want the car or not?" was all he said.

The answer to that question was a definite yes! We bought the car for the unbelievable price of $500. Mrs. Marsh even stored the car for me for two years until I was allowed to get my license. (That car is still as cool today as it was in 1977, and in fact, I still have it after over forty years.)

When the snow finally stopped, the city was still paralyzed for weeks. The plows couldn't get down the side streets because of the broken-down cars and the drifts. Tow trucks were dragging cars off the streets so they could get plowed. What a mess the entire city was. President Carter declared Buffalo a disaster area.

Eventually the streets were cleared, school went back in session, and life got back to a normal. My friends and I did enjoy the snow that was left. The snow was so high in my neighbor Joey's backyard that we sledded off his garage roof. In another backyard, I was able to lie on my back and dunk a basketball on a ten-foot hoop!

The snow piles stayed around until May, but the memories have stayed with anyone that lived through the Blizzard of '77 to this day.

CHAPTER 8

During my freshman year, I had made friends that lived all over the city. Visiting all these neighborhoods made me feel like I lived in the whole city instead of just the West Side. It was a whole new world to me.

As most teenagers do, I wanted to be as far away from my house at night as possible. My mode of travel was my ten-speed bike. I bought it at Twin Fair with some of the proceeds from my graduation party.

Having a bike was a liberating experience, to say the least. The only rule I had was to be home at eleven.

When June came and the weather started to feel like summer was finally here, I began to leave the friendly confines of my immediate neighborhood. The freedom that my ten-speed bike gave me was amazing. In fifteen minutes, I could be anywhere I wanted to be. No parents were driving me and, most importantly, knowing where I was and who I was with.

It was the teenage freedom we all wanted.

My mother was not very thrilled with my newly found independence. Every night I left the house the same questions came from her. I knew what was coming and was ready for it.

"Where are you going tonight? I wish you would stick around here so I don't have to worry about you. Who are you going to be with? Make sure you are home by eleven!"

My response wouldn't vary much from "I don't know, mom."

Dad would then tell her to leave me alone and let me grow up, because after all he had a full-time job already when he was my age.

"When I was his age, I was a busboy at the Towne Casino every night. That's where I met Sinatra."

He would tell us that story as much as the "I could have been a contender if your grandma would have let me continue boxing" story. Then he would tell me to "be careful and be home when the streetlights come on!" with a wink and a laugh. That was one time where I think dad remembered what it was like to be a kid trying to get some freedom away from his parents and was looking out for me.

Okay, so I know you'll want to hear how dad met Frank Sinatra. My father was working at the Towne Casino Restaurant when Francis Albert came in after a concert downtown. According to my dad, all the waiters and hosts just stared at him when he walked in. My father wasn't afraid and walked right over to his group and led them to a table and started to fill their water glasses. Sinatra asked him what his name was. My father said, "Nick Carnavale, sir." As soon as he heard that his name was Italian, he told him, "You're my busboy for the night." Dad stayed at the table and took care of them.

When he left, he gave my father a twenty-dollar bill and said, "Thanks, Nicky."

As a result, we had what my mom called the "Sinatra shrine" in our living room. My father had hundreds of albums with opera and other types of music, but most important to him were his Sinatra albums. He must have had over fifty of them arranged in alphabetical order waiting to be played at a moment's notice. His record player was used so much that he had stacks of needles in a drawer next to his piano ready to be used at a moment's notice too.

Whenever we had company, the first thing my dad would do was put on a Sinatra album to set the mood.

When July started, one sad thing happened. Jimmy left our the neighborhood. He moved to the suburbs so his father was closer to work. That day, I got up early in the morning to help Jim and his family finish packing. I was very sad when the final load of belongings was put in the back of the family station wagon.

Jimmy was holding the last thing to go into his car, his golf clubs, as we stood at the curb looking at each other not knowing what to say.

What a horrible feeling, not knowing what to say to your best friend. We were both trying to act tough and not show the other one how upset each one of us was.

His father finally broke the silence when he said from the other side of the car, "It's time to go, boys."

"We're still going to be best friends, aren't we?" I asked him.

"Of course, we are," he quickly responded.

"Where's North Tonawanda anyway? Can I ride my bike there?"

"Nope, it's too far," he said, holding back tears.

We stood there awkwardly looking at each other. We gave each other a hug, and he jumped into the back seat of the Vista Cruiser with his clubs on his lap. I slammed the door shut, and when I turned to walk back home for the last time from his former house, I saw his mom crying in the front seat of the car.

I have never told anyone, but I cried all the way home too.

It is the worst feeling, losing your best friend when you are a kid. After all, you only have one "first best friend." And you feel like you'll never have another best friend again. Suddenly, it makes you feel like you're not a kid anymore. But with time we make new friends and the hurt slowly fades away.

I was now entering a new part of my life with friends from school and not so much from my neighborhood. It was a big adjustment for me.

When I got home, my mother told me that my Uncle Sam was on his way over to pick me up. Uncle Sam was married to my mother's friend Aunt Serena. They were one of a large group of my parents' friends that were not really related to me but I still called them "Aunt" and "Uncle" anyway.

I always felt calling someone Aunt or Uncle when they really weren't was the ultimate compliment you could give to them. I loved all my aunts and uncles the same, whether they were related to me or not.

Aunt Serena and my mother became friends on my first day of kindergarten. It seems I was crying when my mother was dropping me off that first morning. So was Aunt Serena's daughter Maria.

Our teacher, Mrs. Sally, pushed both of them into the hallway, telling them, "They'll be okay as soon as you two leave. Now leave!"

And just like that, two young moms started talking to each other and decided to go and get a cup of coffee to calm themselves down. The result was a friendship that lasted forty years.

There was something very special about my Uncle Sam, and I always felt very close to him. He had two daughters that were like sisters to me. The girls and I went to school together, played and argued like we were family. I went to the beach, amusement parks, and cookouts with them almost weekly during the summer.

And my Aunt Serena, she was my mother's closest friend without a doubt.

"Why's he picking me up?" I asked my mother.

"He needs your help."

Having something to do temporarily took my mind off Jimmy moving away. The best part about doing things with Uncle Sam was he made me laugh with his colorful stories about what happened when he was younger or his adventures with the men he worked with. All of his friends had cool nicknames like they were characters in an old James Cagney movie.

He worked for the City of Buffalo. Last summer, I told him that I wanted old bikes to work on in the garage. Before I knew it, our entire driveway was filled with bikes that had been put at the curb all over the city.

Some of the bikes were easy to fix, and I gave them to my friends to ride, and once the word got out that I had spare parts for bikes, it seemed like the whole neighborhood came by at one time or another looking for parts for their bike.

My friend Jay helped me put a bunch of bikes together, but he never needed any parts. He had the coolest bike any fourteen-year-old has ever seen, a Western Auto purple Stingray. That bike was the dream of every boy around, and Jay treated it like it was made of gold. But of course, I was the only one allowed to ride it besides him.

My mother put an end to my bike repair business because she said our driveway was starting to look like a bad episode of "Sanford and Son." So I regrettably put all the bikes back at the curb for some-one else to use.

When Uncle Sam pulled up, he told me to "jump in." I soon realized why he had dropped all those bikes off at my house the year before. It was time for some payback.

"Nicky, do you remember the bike Maria got for her birthday last week?"

"Yep, I do, the one with the handlebars on wrong, the fenders on wrong, and wheels that were ready to fall off, that one, Uncle Sam?"

"Ya, that one!" he said with a wink and a smile.

The week before at Maria's party, I looked at the bike and couldn't believe that someone could put a bike together with so many mistakes.

I had to ask, "Who put that bike together?"

"I did," he announced proudly.

I proceeded to tell him all the things that were installed incor-rectly. He quickly grabbed the bike, and me, and into the cellar we went as fast as we could.

"Can you fix it?" he asked me with a look of panic. "I'm not very good at this kind of stuff, ya know."

"Sure, anything for you, Uncle Sam."

I walked over to his workbench in search of the tools I would need to correctly put the bike together. From what I could see, my uncle's favorite tool was a butter knife that substituted for every other tool known to mankind.

Up the stairs and back outside I went. I asked my father for his toolbox he kept in the trunk of the car.

"Dad, I need the tools so I can fix Maria's bike before she wants to go for a ride and the wheels fall off and then she dies on her birthday."

My dad brought the box in the basement, and after about twenty minutes, the bike returned from the cellar with all the prob-lems fixed without anyone knowing the truth.

"Maria's bike got stolen today. Grace Ann left the gate open, and someone stole it! Can you believe it?"

The first thing I thought of was that maybe if I hadn't fixed it, the thief would have left the bike in the yard because he felt sorry for the girl that had to ride a bike that messed up.

"We're going to get her a new bike."

When we got to the Two Guys on Niagara Falls Boulevard, things started to get really funny. We walked in and went to the bike section where they were on racks stacked two high.

A zit-faced boy walked over and asked if he could help us.

"I want that pink bike right there," Uncle Sam said, pointing to the exact bike Maria got the week before.

"No problem, sir," the kid responded.

He walked a few steps to a shelf and started to pull a large box out with a picture of the same bike on the side of it.

"Kid, you don't understand, I want THAT BIKE RIGHT THERE on the upper rack," he said, gesturing emphatically.

"But, sir, this is *that* bike."

"No, you're not listening to me. I WANT THAT BIKE RIGHT THERE!" he said just a bit louder.

I knew that he wanted the assembled bike so he wouldn't have to try to put another one together again. And I figured that I was the insurance policy if he had to get an unassembled bike.

But the kid had no idea what he was saying.

"Where's the manager?" Uncle Sam asked him.

"I will get him, sir."

A few minutes later, he returned with an older man with a name tag that said "Manager" on it.

"Can I help you, sir?" he politely asked.

"Yes, you can, you see my daughter's bike got stolen. I have to get another one. My nephew here had to put that the last one together because I put it together all wrong. He missed part of the party because he was down in the basement with me fixing the bike. I don't want him missing any more parties because of my daughter's bike, I don't like putting bikes together, and I'M NOT PUTTING THIS BIKE TOGETHER! Are you getting the picture yet? Now do you understand?"

Uncle Sam said all that without taking a breath.

"No, sir, I don't. In *that* box is *that* bike," the manager said, repeating what the kid had said again.

Uncle Sam was standing there holding his head like it was ready to explode. I was almost ready to fall on the floor laughing. I had to say something before Uncle Sam blew his stack right there.

"Mr. Manager, you see, we want the fully assembled bike. My uncle doesn't like to put things together. He has terrible tools. He uses a butter knife to fix everything. He has very little patience for things like that. Is it possible to buy a fully assembled bike so we don't have to put it together?"

"Well, why didn't you just say that?" the manager said.

Then Uncle Sam told him, "I said it about five times."

"Five-dollar assembly fee, is that okay?" the manager asked.

"At this point, I would pay fifty dollars to just get out of this store!"

The manager took the bike off the rack and gave it to us. We started to walk to the front of the store.

"What about accessories?" I asked.

"What do you mean accessories?"

"Uncle Sam, this bike may be put together, but it's certainly not done. It needs some more to make it cool."

"You mean like a speedometer?" he asked me.

"Uncle Sam, this is a girl's bike, you have to think like a girl. Can I take care of the rest?"

I walked over to the next aisle and picked out a pink basket, pink streamers, and a Brady Bunch–looking radio for the handlebars.

"Now *that's* a cool bike for a girl!" I told him.

We lugged the bike out of the store and put it in the back of his Oldsmobile very carefully.

"Never work in retail," he told me, shaking his head all the way to his house.

We went into the basement and put all the extras on the bike, and I have to admit; for a girl's bike, it was cool.

Uncle Sam proudly brought the bike up into the sunlight and said to Maria, "Maria, that's the last bike I'm ever buying you!"

As he dropped me off, he told me, "I'm glad I took an interpreter and a bike customizer with me today!" He laughed and shut the door of that big, old black car and drove away.

Uncle Sam made me laugh so much that day. The worst of the sting from Jimmy moving away was now over. With Jimmy gone, the rest of the summer was spent with two friends from Brennan that lived out of my immediate area.

My trusty Kia ten-speed made that all right, and because Uncle Sam had nothing to do with its assembly, it served me well from the first day.

A typical summer night had me riding to Jack's house. Jack had a younger sister named Lisa that sometimes tried to come along with us. The number of excuses we used to not let her could have filled an encyclopedia. After we got away from her, it was usually on to Andy's house.

Our bike adventures were just beginning because Jack had a crush on a girl named Debbie. The three of us rode by her house about one hundred times that summer. We never saw her, but I think a lot of the neighbors thought we were looking for hubcaps to steal and watched us more with every ride by we did.

Andy liked to play basketball, and many nights found us at Nativity Playground watching the older kids play ball. They were great games that attracted hundreds of people to watch. It was funny because the referees were all from the West Side, and it was pretty obvious they wanted only West Side teams to win. A lot of the games ended in fights that the cops had to break up.

The nights I liked the most were when we sat on Andy's porch and listened to music on his transistor radio. Sometimes his dad would sit there along with us and pass out advice like they were M&M's. We talked and watched all the cars pass his house and tried to name the make and model as they drove by.

"Monte Carlo 1970!" Jack would yell.

"'72, different taillights!" I would scream back.

All of the neighborhood loved the Yankees of that season. The entire summer seemed to be Yankee pinstriped. They had some great players on the team—Reggie Jackson, Catfish Hunter, Thurman

Munson was the catcher, Bucky Dent, Lou Pinella, and Billy Martin was the manager.

I never rooted for the Yankees. In fact, I detested them. The Oakland A's were my favorite team. But make no mistake, baseball and summer just seemed to go together.

One night, a friend of Jack's named Victor Mangione made his confirmation. He had been telling everyone that he was related to Chuck Mangione, the musician that had a number one album at the time and was from Rochester.

Andy and Jack were altar boys for the confirmation mass. Victor said that Chuck Mangione was going to be at his confirmation party that Saturday.

Well, needless to say, word went around the neighborhood very quickly. Everyone wanted to meet him. He was always on *The Tonight Show*, *Midnight Special*, and *The Mike Douglas Show*. But only three soon-to-be high school sophomores were dumb enough to actually make a plan to meet him.

Andy's bright idea suggested that we hide in the bushes across the street from Victor's house with copies of his album and markers waiting for him to sign them. Why in the world I ever went along with such a dumb idea still baffles me to this day!

So the three of us did hide in the bushes waiting for Chuck Mangione to show up. We waited, and waited, and waited.

"This is so stupid, we're getting eaten alive," I kept telling the other two stooges I was with in the bushes.

About the only thing that did happen that night was that every mosquito on the West Side took a bite out of us. After about two hours of "hiding out," we got back on our bikes, *Feels So Good* albums in hand, and rode home in search of large bottles of Calamine lotion!

"He's probably not even related to him!" I screamed as we rode away scratching every inch of uncovered skin on my body.

Some nights if we had the money we would walk to Mr. Pizza to get a large pizza for $3.99 or to La Nova's for a sub. The pizza at Mr. Pizza was great, and they had a coupon on the box for a free T-shirt after buying ten pizzas. If we decided on subs, we waited for them outside of La Nova's on a picnic bench. It was great sitting out there watching the sand flies get zapped by the purple bug light. After getting our food, we would walk to the corner store and buy sixteen-ounce bottles of Crush.

There is nothing better than a slice of pizza, some subs, and a cherry Crush on a warm moonlit night. We would talk about girls, what new rules our parents were inflicting upon us, and what school would be like in the fall.

Some nights we would also ride over to Arkansas Street (pronounced *Ark-can-sis* if you were from the West Side) to watch the "Old Italian Guys" play bocce ball. It is a game with three different-colored balls rolled toward a mark on the lawn. The men had taken a vacant lot, planted grass, and created an authentic bocce field like they had back in Italy. The men spoke only Italian as they played. Most of them were bricklayers and concrete laborers. They would come over to their "park" right after dinner and play until dark. They would argue back and forth about scores and shots. Their gestures to each other amazed us. They actually had conversations without saying a word!

When dusk would arrive, they would walk home and water their tomato plants and gardens before going to sleep with the sounds of Sinatra in the air.

Each night that we watched them, we tried to figure out the rules of the game. As far as I could tell, the game revolved around an argument over whose ball was closest to the mark. Most of the men were dressed in dark suits and did a lot of gesturing back and forth and toward each other. We learned many Italian swear words from them as they argued with each other as they took their turns rolling the balls. They laughed and enjoyed themselves, and as the summer wore on, large glass bottles with homemade wine began to appear. They took sips of it and passed it around. It seemed like every one of them had Kool cigarettes hanging out of their mouth as they argued the night away.

I think they were betting on the games, but we couldn't tell for sure. Money and gesturing continued nightly until dark.

The final part of my summer routine involved jogging to Delaware Park each morning and lapping it once and running back home. I calculated that it was about five miles. I knew that this would get me into shape for football season. I also worked out every day lifting weights. Unlike the year before, I knew what was going to be expected of me to make the varsity football team. I wanted to make that varsity team more than anything. My cousin Ronnie was going to play too. I knew how much fun it was going to be to play with him and finally make it to my sophomore year.

During that summer, we never had any set plans. We were so free, and it seemed like we would let the wind take us wherever it wanted. What a feeling of freedom for the first time it was.

CHAPTER 9

The Brennan football practices started at the end of August. I felt confident and more relaxed as the tryouts started, and after a few days, I made the varsity team. The next end-of-summer highlight would be the girls starting their cheerleading practices on the field next to ours.

I scanned the girls' captains practice for several days.

"Stop wasting your time looking for her," Ronnie told me as we walked out of the locker room to ride our bikes home. "She's not cheering this year, concentrating on skating instead."

"Well, when exactly were you going to get around to telling me that bit of info!" I said to him while giving him a punch to the bicep.

"Nicky, there are more fish in the ocean. We're now sophomores. We will have no problem picking up chicks."

"I'm really not interested in the rest, just her," I said as I unchained my bike to ride home.

What a letdown. I spent my whole summer running around the park, lifting weights, and studying the playbook all to try to impress her. Now she wasn't there. Don't get me wrong. I still loved to play football and couldn't wait to start playing games, but it would have been better with her cheering us on.

In spite of the new cheerleading situation, football was great. Something strange happens when you transition from a freshman to a sophomore. You start to get a little respect from the older kids, and you now have the ability to look down on the freshman players. The freshmen take in the footballs, clean the locker room, and are last in the showers.

Since Stephanie was no longer cheering, I had to figure out a new way to get to know her. The idea I came up with was that since Bishop O'Malley was our sister school, brothers and sisters should at least know each other, right?

The first day of school I approached Jamie, our class president, with the idea of the brother-and-sister sophomore classes doing some activities together.

"Jaimie, how about finding out if we can plan some activities with the sophomores at O'Malley. It would be fun to plan some dances or skating parties, wouldn't it?"

He was a great kid and wanted to start a band with him as the drummer. That was perfect for him because he sat behind me in class tapping away with whatever was in his hands every day.

He thought it was a great idea. He spoke to our student council advisor, Father Bentley, about our thoughts. He said it was great idea too. My plan was starting to work.

In early October, the football team had been given Monday off because of a big win over Bishop Turner High School. Our student representatives set up a meeting with our sister class. We boarded the bus after school and went downtown to O'Malley High School.

"What is it going to be like going into a school filled with six hundred girls?" I asked Jack as we travelled down Delaware Avenue toward downtown.

"I don't know, but I'm willing to find out!" was the response from three of the boys on the bus.

We entered the old mansion that was now a school at just the right time (if you were a fifteen-year-old boy). The girls had to wear ugly plaid uniform skirts, and they wouldn't be caught dead wearing them outside of school. So they would hang jeans in their lockers and put them on at the end of the day.

We walked in the huge castle-sized doors that were the entrance to the all-girls school. Andy was leading the way.

"Don't look up," he screamed as we walked up the stairs, and the doors closed behind us with a loud thud.

Naturally, we all looked up, ignoring his warning. Imagine the looks on our faces when three hundred girls were getting changed in the hallway next to their lockers right in front of us. They were putting pants on and sliding their skirts to the ground while jumping into their dress jeans.

The six of us stood there with our mouths open for what seemed like an eternity. None of the girls screamed, although most of us wanted to. When the girls finished changing, they started walking by us out of the school like nothing happened.

Jack said, "I can die now!"

"Will someone pick Dominic up off the floor," Jaimie said.

"That was like a freakin' movie," I said to the group as we started moving through the hall shaking our heads, trying to act like we hadn't seen a thing. "Now that was a sight I will never forget!" I said to group in the echoing hallway.

After the initial shock of entering the building wore off, we got down to business. We went into the office and asked to see the principal.

"Hi, we are from Cardinal Brennan, and we are here to see Sister Mary Francis," I told the secretary.

"She'll be right out," she said without looking up as she continued typing away.

When Sister Mary Francis came out, she looked us over like we had just joined the army. The nuns that ran O'Malley were the same nuns that ran my grammar school. They never spared the rod when they felt there was a need for it. The rod usually was an aluminum yardstick to the hand or back of your head. After the inspection, she called another nun to take us to the library to begin the meeting.

The advisor to the girls was a nun that had to be two hundred years old. She shuffled into the office with the speed of a snail. She took us to the library only after she, too, looked us up and down. We must have passed her test because she actually left us alone in the library with some of the girls that were waiting for us when walked in. There were about five girls from both the North Side and West Side waiting for us. I knew two of the girls, Marybeth and Maureen, one from my grammar school and one from my neighborhood. Maureen and I were very close growing up and was like a sister to me during my grammar school days. Marybeth lived around the corner, and we knew each other for years. They both seemed happy to see me and immediately started talking about the plans the girls were going to suggest.

More girls continued to file into to the library until they outnumbered us about two to one. In the last group was Stephanie, and she sat down right next to me. Maureen introduced me to her, and I tried to act like I'd never seen her before.

The meeting was great. We planned a bowling party (Jamie's father owned Grant Am Lanes), a roller-skating party, and a dance. My idea had actually worked.

The two-hundred-year-old nun returned with some RC Cola for us to drink. She actually was very sweet and told us we seemed liked "fine young men." Wow, a compliment from a nun. Now that was a rare thing.

"You play hockey, don't you?" Stephanie asked me as I opened a can of pop.

Her question broke the silence at the end of the meeting. I nearly put the pull-tab in my mouth instead of drinking the pop while simultaneously almost falling out of my chair. She actually did know that I existed!

"Football and baseball too," I responded with pop nearly coming out of my nose.

"Didn't I sit with your mother at the hockey games last year?"

I knew what was coming next. She was going to tell me that my mother said I would be president someday, or the next Sabre's goalie, or some other embarrassing thing.

"I think you did. Was my father snoring very loud in the stands during the games?" I asked.

She laughed, and then there was silence. I had to keep the conversation going. But I couldn't think of anything more to say.

Here was my first chance to make it sound like I was a jock and try to impress her, and instead I'm worrying about what my mother might have said to her.

Now that I knew she recognized me, I was happy that she didn't ask me if I liked the *Rocky* movie or remembered me running her over at football practice!

"Didn't you use to be a cheerleader?"

"I did last year, but I am a figure skater, and I have to concentrate on that now, not enough hours in the day."

My brain was going a mile a minute. I was finally talking to the girl that I had thought about for over a year.

Keep talking. Keep talking, stupid, I kept telling myself.

"When do you skate?" I asked.

"I'm skating at 6:00 a.m. before school this year, and I catch the bus to school by seven thirty."

Just then Sister Two Hundred Years Old said the meeting was over.

What terrible timing!

Keep talking, keep talking, I repeated to myself over and over again.

The meeting then broke up. We stood and walked out of the library toward the front doors and out of the school. I could take one of two buses. I waited to see which one Stephanie was going to take, and I took that one home.

I hoped that our conversation would continue while standing at the bus stop. When we got there, I tried to get close to her to continue the conversation. But I just couldn't get close enough to talk to her.

I then thought, *Sit with her on the bus and continue the conversation.* When the bus came, Andy got on first, Stephanie second, and I got on third, and the rest of the kids followed. We all walked toward the back of the old silver Metro Bus. When we reached the back, Andy sat down, and Stephanie sat right next to him.

All I could do was sit across the aisle and watch and listen.

Andy was a good friend. And he didn't know that I liked Stephanie. He had this strange effect on girls. For some reason, all the girls liked him. None of us could figure out why. He was loud and had a strange way of making fun of himself that the girls thought was funny. He was working his magic on Stephanie with me watching from across the aisle.

I started staring out of the window because it was obvious what was happening. Andy wasn't afraid of talking to *any* girl he was interested in. And he talked away the whole ride home to the girl I had been thinking about for over a year.

I could tell by her body language that Stephanie liked him.

I felt like I had been kicked in the stomach.

CHAPTER 10

The next few weeks were awful. Even a trip to Pantastik with my mom for a new pair of dress jeans didn't work. I had to go to school and play football with the guy that stole my girl. Let me express to you that every time Andy touched the ball at practice, I hit him hard, real hard. And the more he bragged to everyone about going "steady" with Stephanie, the harder I hit him! I guess it really wasn't very nice to do this because after all he didn't know I liked her. The only one that knew was Ronnie.

"Too bad she's dating that goof Andy," Ronnie said to me at the end of one of our practices.

"I finally get to talk to her, and five minutes later she is dating one of my best friends, just my luck."

"Girls are crazy. That's why I play the field. I'm too good-looking to waste myself on just one girl!" he told me.

That was the best thing about Ronnie. I knew that no matter what, he was always going to look out for me. He knew that I would always be looking out for him too. I think all the nights sleeping over at each other's houses watching Vincent Price's "Friday Fright Night" horror movies had made us that close. We slept with the lights on because we were so scared, and we would talk until 4:00 a.m.

I have never had anyone that I felt as close to as him.

I decided that maybe it was time to change my look to get the girls. I made a bold move. My hair still looked like my fourth-grade picture. Parted on the side and slicked down. No more grammar school look for me, I told myself. It was the seventies. No longer would I be one of the guys that got his haircut at the corner barber-shop for three bucks. I had to change with the times.

I looked no further than the music we were listening to support my thoughts. The most popular group of this time (at least in my neighborhood) was KC and the Sunshine Band. KC had a shag haircut, and he got all the girls to "Shake Their Booty," so maybe it would work for me.

I went to Gino's on Grant Street. He was a nice guy that resembled Dom DeLuise. The salon was called Gino's Hair Styles. During the day, he catered to old ladies with beehive hairdos, but one night a week, Wednesday, he gave "fashion cuts" to men.

He even had the audacity to charge five dollars for a haircut.

Upon entering the salon, the first thing I noticed was the smell. It smelled like an indoor swimming pool. Bleach everywhere. *Ah*, I thought, *this is how we have so many Italians with blond hair on the West Side*. He also had pea green chairs and sinks to finish off the look of the salon. He had an eight-track player with Dean Martin and every other Italian singer playing. And one other thing, he had those hair dryers that looked the engine off a World War II plane.

"Can you make me look like KC?" I asked him.

"KC who?" he asked me.

The lead singer from KC and the Sunshine Band, hair parted in the middle and feathered back. (If I had asked him for Al Martino's hairstyle, I'm sure he would have known what to do immediately.)

"Coming right up, one shag haircut!"

Gino did a lot to earn that five dollars. It was probably then that my hair began to thin, because he washed my hair, made me sit under one of those space helmet dryers until my scalp burned, then cut my hair, wet it down again, and used a blow dryer the size of a cannon to dry my hair again. All that wear and tear couldn't have been good for my scalp.

Nevertheless, I emerged as a Harry Casey look-alike after about an hour and a half.

I had new Faded Glory dress jeans, Bastad porthole clogs, a jean vest, and my hair parted in the middle. I was ready to go. Being all dressed up with nowhere to go was an understatement, to say the least.

That was until Ronnie called me.

"Do you want to go to He and She's on Sunday?" he asked.

He and She's was still a wildly popular disco that all the cool older kids went to and the one that I couldn't go to during the summer of my broken nose.

"How would we ever get in there?" I asked him. "How will we ever sneak into a bar? We don't look eighteen, and we have no way to get there."

"Hey stupid, it's on Sunday, and they are closed."

"Why would I want to go to a closed bar?" I asked.

"You idiot! They have a special teen dance because Monday is Columbus holiday and everyone is off the next day. Junction West is playing, and we can catch a ride with them in their van."

Junction West was the most popular band in Buffalo at the time. Ronnie's older brother Harrison was the lead singer and the coolest guy I ever knew. They were so popular that girls would sit outside of Ronnie's house waiting for Harrison and the other singer, Joey, to come home after practice. How cool that must have been to have girls chasing after you like that.

One time I was getting my school pants shortened at the seamstress Mrs. Vignerri's house. Harrison was there with Joey getting fitted for their wild white disco jumpsuits. When I left with my mom, there were girls hiding on the side of the house waiting to ask them for their autograph when they came out!

Junction West had a horn section and played the best R&B and disco you would ever hear. They wore their white jumpsuits that would have made the Ohio Players jealous and were paid handsomely for a dance because of their large following. If they were playing, it was a guarantee that every available pretty girl would be there strutting their stuff.

I figured it was now time to start acting like a big shot and use my family connections to meet girls. My mother drove me over to Ronnie's to get ready for the big night.

"Come on in, and sit down," Ronnie said as I knocked on his bedroom door. "You ready to get down tonight?" he asked.

"I guess so."

"There's that 'I'm not going to get the girl' attitude again," Ronnie told me. "Tonight you're going to dance with a girl, if I have to ask her for you! Here, try on this mood ring I just bought. What color did it turn?" he asked me.

"Black," I said.

"Oh-uh, it works. Black means 'love I lack.'" He started laughing so hard at me he had water coming out of his nose. "You better try some of this Hai Karate cologne. The girls can't resist it. Tonight you are going to have fun whether you like it or not!"

Well, there it was. Even before I made it to the dance, I was "lacking love" and resorting to cheap aftershave in a feeble effort to attract girls.

The night really didn't start out that great. Since we went with the band, we had to go early, real early. We were stuck in the back of a van surrounded by speakers and amps. When we finally got out of the van and went in, we were already sweating. He and She's was the first bar I ever walked into. It had a large disco ball in the center of the room. The entire old warehouse was painted black. The walls, ceiling, stage, and even the floor was painted black.

Ronnie and I, as payment for the ride and sneaking in for free, got stuck setting up the speakers, microphones, and the lights. I now was a very well-dressed, sweaty, hair-parted-in-the-middle roadie!

"This is really cool, isn't it?" Ronnie kept asking me.

"Anything you say, cous'. When does the crowd start coming in?" I asked.

"Not until seven thirty, but it will be worth it. I heard from my brother that more than two hundred tickets were sold to girls from O'Malley. You know what that means—she'll be here!"

"Yep, and she'll be here with someone else!" I screamed back over a sound check.

That was just great, I thought. *I'm now all sweaty and will be rewarded with watching Stephanie dance with Andy all night.*

Ronnie had a smooth way about everything he did and with the girls. He was very distant with them, which they seemed to like.

All this boy-girl teenage stuff just confused me so much. Andy could act like an idiot and the girls liked him. Ronnie was cold to them, and that worked too. And here I was with no plan and no girl.

I knew it was going to be a rather big challenge to find my own angle to attract the girls. I couldn't help but wonder what would work for me.

When the doors finally opened, in the first group of kids were two familiar faces. Maureen and Marybeth were walking right toward me. They walked over and gave both Ronnie and me a hug.

Not a bad start to the night, I thought.

"Act like you don't care, it works every time," Ronnie whispered to me as we stood uncomfortably looking at each other with the girls standing in front of us.

"But they have been my friends since I was five."

"Now it's different. We're in high school, and we have to act cool," Ronnie told me.

I didn't take his advice. I talked to them the same way I always did. After all, they were my friends. We had danced the "Locomotion" together in fifth grade, and I wouldn't change the way I acted toward them. But I did start to look at Maureen. I had never realized how pretty she was. Her shoulder-length blond hair gave her a farmer's daughter look. Marybeth was pretty too.

Wow, this teenage stuff was weird. One minute you are talking to friends from your kindergarten class, and the next second you are looking at them like they are pretty almost-sixteen-year-old girls.

I thought about the time in seventh grade when Maureen asked me to "couples skate" with her at our CYO party at Arena Roller Rink. I had never held a girl's hand before. I had skated with her mom lots of times at our parties, but never with her.

Wow, did that feel good, skating with a pretty girl in my class—awkward, but good. I wondered if she would she dance with me now.

I also started to remember that I turned tomato red when she asked me to skate. The song that was playing, it was "Don't Go Breaking My Heart" by Elton John and Kiki Dee. I was so nervous as we skated around holding hands. The only thing that I could have broken that night was my ankle because I kept tripping over Maureen while we skated. She was so easygoing that she just laughed and never mentioned it to me.

Junction West started the dance with "Love Machine" by the Miracles. The disco ball started spinning, lights were flashing, and I was officially part of the disco scene. I was in the Buffalo version of Studio 54.

And you know what? It was pretty cool.

The band played away, and I stood and talked to Maureen and Marybeth. They went up and danced to "More, More, More." Things were looking good until Stephanie walked in with Andy. They were holding hands off to my left. The music slowed, the lights went low, and to this day I don't know what came over me.

I walked up to Maureen and asked her to dance with me. She said yes and looked at me with a very shy look on her face.

The song was "Three Times a Lady." I danced with her and held her close. But there was no spark. My heart didn't skip any beats like it did when Stephanie came close to me. I just kept looking over the pretty girl I was dancing with and at Stephanie dancing with Andy.

Then I started thinking, *Hey, you're with a very pretty girl. She didn't say no when you asked her to dance. It didn't matter that you've known her just about your whole life.* She was pretty and she was dancing with me. That had to count for something.

When the song was over, we walked back to the same spot, and both Ronnie and Marybeth were just looking at us. It was another strange moment, to say the least.

Maureen blushed and did what all girls do when they need to talk. They grab their purses, grab the nearest girlfriend, and walk to the bathroom together.

"You did it!" Ronnie screamed.

"Did what," I replied.

"You broke the ice."

"What ice?" I asked.

"The girl ice, you stepped out on the frozen lake and didn't care if you fell in, that's great."

"But it was only with Maureen," I said.

"That girl is gorgeous, every boy in here would want to dance with her, and she danced with YOU!" he screamed to me. "She could have said no, she danced with you. And by the way, we are going to get my sister Jen to help you with your dance moves. They are pathetic!"

He was right. She did dance with me, and she didn't say no. Maybe it was a major accomplishment. (And I did know that my dancing could use some help.)

Junction West continued to get the crowd up and dancing for another couple of hours. The disco ball continued to spin.

And I had to watch Stephanie kissing Andy as the night went on. Even with my newfound confidence that still bothered me.

But when the dance ended, and Ronnie and I walked to my mother's car, I realized that I had changed a lot of things about myself by doing a simple thing like asking a girl to dance. Maureen realized that I wasn't little Nicky anymore, and she wasn't little Maureen anymore either.

I went to my first disco bar, and most importantly, I wasn't that same shy kid anymore.

"You guys want some Henry's Hamburgers," my mom asked, driving away from the front door and past the Blue Whale Car Wash.

"Mom, if you only knew how good that strawberry shake is going to taste *tonight*!"

CHAPTER 11

The football season came to an end shortly after my life-altering disco experience. We finished the season with a loss to St. Michaels 14–12. I remember this game because it was written in the newspaper that we shouldn't even play the game. Michaels was ranked number one in the state. They had beaten Wedgewood to end their winning streak at sixty games. A bunch of kids from that team were going to Division 1 schools on football scholarships, and we didn't have any.

It was also the first varsity game I started.

We scored a touchdown to bring us to within two points as the clock was running out. On the conversion, our quarterback was sacked on a sneak trying to tie the game. So I guess someone forgot to tell our team we weren't worthy of playing them.

On the last play of the game, we lost. Maybe St Michael's took us a little too lightly, or maybe a bunch of our players had the game of their lives. I would vote for the latter.

What a way to end the season.

The end of football season meant that winter wasn't that far behind. Hockey season would be coming soon. This was the fall of 1977, and we all remembered very clearly what happened in the winter of 1977. We prayed that we wouldn't have to deal with ten feet of snow ever again.

"And our final announcement is, don't forget the sophomore bowling party Friday night at Grant Am Lanes," Father Williams mentioned as he finished the morning announcements.

We were sitting in homeroom waiting to go to our first class when we heard the reminder. My entire homeroom started talking about the party on Friday.

"Who's goin' to the party?" our homeroom teacher asked.

A bunch of the guys said, "If there are girls, I'll be there."

Our bowling party was now the talk of our class. Because it was November, none of us were riding bikes anymore. It was too cold. The plan was to somehow get to one kid's house and pile into their mom's station wagon for the ride to the lanes. Station wagons were great. Most of them could fit about eight people. We would all jump in the car and fight over the rear-facing seats. If you were lucky enough to be in a Vista Cruiser, you could stare up at the sky through the glass roof and flash peace signs to the cars behind you.

As it turned out, it was my mother's turn to drive. She always enjoyed having the kids gather at our house. When they walked in, they were given Hawaiian Punch and chocolate chip cookies. Mom talked to every kid like she was his or her best friend. She used snacks and the Hawaiian Punch truth serum to get all the gossip from them without realizing it. By the time she was done, she knew who was dating whom, who liked whom, and who just broke up with whom, by supplying some sugar and by asking a few questions.

My mother would then use that information to interrogate me either later that night or first thing the next morning. Most of the time I just said, "Mom, no comment."

"Mom, can you drop us at a house in North Buffalo? We'll walk the rest of the way."

I purposely didn't tell her whose house it was. Knowing my mom, she probably would have invited herself into her friend Stephanie's house for coffee and doughnuts.

"Okay, who will be driving you home?"

"Andy's mom is driving us home."

Andy had set it up so that we were meeting at Stephanie's house. All the boys and girls we hung around with would meet there and then walk to the bowling alley in one big group. When we got to the house, there were a few kids standing in the driveway talking. As we got out of the car, another car pulled up and dumped out a bunch of boys. There were now about fifteen kids in total.

"Let's get moving. I told my dad we would be at the lanes about eight thirty. We've got to get going," Jamie said.

Since his dad was letting us bowl for free, everyone started moving. He also was going to let us be the first ones to play the new Elton John "Captain Fantastic" pinball machine. Playing pinball and using the jukebox were what teenagers liked to do the most. So the group started moving away from the house in a hurry.

"Let's go. I'm not waiting for her anymore!" Andy yelled as he walked out the side door of Stephanie's house.

I just shook my head as he walked past me and continued talking to the group. All the kids fell in behind him like he was the Pied Piper and walked toward Hertel Avenue. It was always so strange to me how kids will follow other kids without thinking for themselves.

At that point in my life, I wasn't going to follow the guy that was making my life so difficult. I didn't plan it, but everyone walked away except me. I was standing in Stephanie's driveway alone. Her house was large with a huge porch and a long driveway that was lit by a light above the door.

It looked warm, inviting, and was decorated for Thanksgiving. I stood there staring at it. I don't know why, but it felt like I would someday spend a lot of time there.

As I was standing at the end of the driveway staring at the house, I was startled by a horn attached to an orange Plymouth 'Cuda with a black stripe trying to pull in the driveway. I jumped out of the way as it pulled in the driveway right up to the garage.

A man got out and walked toward me.

"Are you tryin' to get killed, kid?" a voice asked.

It was dark, but I knew the voice. It was Stephanie's brother Danny.

"Can I ask you a question? What are you doing standing in my driveway?

"Hi, Danny. It's Nick, the goalie from the Brennan hockey team, remember?

"Oh, ya, I shot you a few times in the head last year, didn't I?" he replied.

Well, at least he remembered me, kinda, I thought.

"Sorry, I was meeting some kids here to go with them to a bowling party. They all just walked away and left me standing here by myself."

"Is my sister going with you?" Danny asked.

"I haven't seen her yet tonight," I replied.

All I could think of was what the varsity football players told me freshman year, about what Danny would do to anyone that went near his sisters.

"A bunch of Brennan and O'Malley kids are going to Grant Am Lanes, some left already…"

He turned and walked away before I finished what I was saying.

"Come on, I'll see if she is still home," he replied.

I walked up the driveway slowly because I still didn't trust him. Was he going to kill me because I was there to see his sister like all the guys said?

We entered through the side door, and I stopped just short of the top of the stairs. Danny was taking off his sneakers and jacket while sitting on the top stair. He was sizing me up, there was no doubt about that, but all of a sudden, he didn't seem as intimidating sitting in a spot he had sat on since he was a little boy.

"Steph, I found this kid standing in our driveway and almost ran him over!" he said with a laugh, pointing back toward me.

When I looked up, Stephanie was looking down at me as Danny walked away. She had on a blue sweater and a pair of Levi's and was so pretty that I just stared at her and didn't say anything.

"Just ignore my brother, he thinks he's funny," she said.

Danny pushed past his sister and walked toward the refrigerator in the kitchen.

"He wasn't lying. He almost did run me over!" I said.

"He's on 'Donny and Marie' tonight, you know," she said to me as she walked toward the back of the house.

"Who's on 'Donny and Marie'?" I stuttered.

97

"Andy Gibb, and my boyfriend, Andy, doesn't want to wait to see him, but I do," she continued. "He doesn't like to do anything I ask him to do. Will you wait a few minutes with me until he comes on and then walk with me to the lanes?"

I thought I died and went to heaven, and she didn't have to ask me that twice.

"Isn't he the Bee Gees' little brother? He has that song 'Love Is Thicker than Water,' right?" I asked.

"Yep," she said as she turned and walked away toward the family room.

"Come on, I'll introduce you to my family."

I followed her into the kitchen. The kitchen smelled like a freshly baked apple pie. I had made it into the house, talked with her brother, and was now about to meet the rest of her family. *Pretty good progress so far*, I thought.

"Mom, ah this is…" She hesitated for a moment and then said, "Nick."

She did remember my name after all!

Danny was drinking something leaning against the counter while his mom was cutting a piece of pie. He looked at me out of the corner of his eyes. I knew what he was doing, and he knew I knew what he was doing.

I walked through the kitchen and saw her mom standing at the sink cleaning up. When she turned around, I knew where Stephanie got her beauty. Her mother was a stunning woman with that same friendly smile.

I walked around the kitchen table and extended my hand to her.

I said, "Hi, Mrs. Pacifico, nice to meet you, my name is Nick Carnavale."

"That's a nice Italian name. Are you as excited to see Andy Gibb as the girls are?" she said with a laugh.

"More," I said as I walked away toward the family room.

"Honey, would you like some pie? It's still warm."

"No thank you, I'm fine," I replied.

I just kept thinking this was great. Danny didn't kill me, and now I met her mother, and she even offered me a piece of pie. What was next?

What was next wasn't much fun.

In the family room Stephanie's three sisters were sitting on the couch. Two were younger than her, Cindy by a few years, and her baby sister, Katie, was about five years old. Stephanie's older sister, Gina, was there too.

The two older sisters were staring at me. Katie was playing with a doll. Gina looked me up and down. She inspected me more than "Sister Two Hundred Years Old" did.

"Who are you?" Gina asked.

"I'm Nick. Who are *you*?" I asked.

"I'm Stephie's older sister, the one that watches over her," she said right back. "What are you doing here? What school do you go to?" she continued asking me.

"We are going to a bowling party, and I go to Brennan," I answered.

"Do you know who my brother is?" she asked.

"I play hockey with Danny" was my answer.

Then a voice from the kitchen said, "Leave him alone, he's okay." It was Danny to the rescue.

I knew what she was saying without saying it. "Stay away from my sister" was the bottom line. I knew that Gina would be the one to give me a hard time in the future, but I also knew she did it because she loved her sister. I had to admire her for that.

I also couldn't help thinking, *Here she is giving me a hard time, yet she allows her sister to date a guy like Andy? Does this dating stuff ever make sense?* I asked myself.

"He's on next!" Cindy yelled to her mom.

Donny and Marie had just finished singing a song to begin the show. They announced that Andy Gibb was on next.

Mrs. Pacifico came in and sat on the couch right next to me. We watched Andy Gibb joke with Donny and Marie. Andy called Donny "Donald," so Donnie called him "Andrew." A few other dumb jokes followed, but when he sat down and started to sing "Love Is Thicker than Water," anyone could see that he was going to be a star.

He wasn't much older than we were at the time, but with the Bee Gees writing songs for him, the sky was the limit. (Looking back on it now, what a shame it was that he didn't reach his thirtieth birthday.)

"Wow, he is *so* cute, I'm in love. I have to go to Record Theatre and buy his album right now!" Cindy said.

We laughed and got up off the couch and walked back toward the kitchen. Danny was sitting at the table eating something, trying to act like he wasn't watching too.

"Have a good time, and, Stephanie, don't come home too late," she said as we walked out the side door.

Stephanie and I walked to the bowling alley. I don't remember what I scored, whom I bowled with, or who was at the party. I do remember that I talked with her like I knew her my entire life. She laughed at my jokes, and I laughed at hers. We talked about school, and we talked about nothing.

I had never met anyone like her before. I knew, more than ever, how very, very special she was. And thanks, Andy Gibb, I do owe you an awful lot!

Chapter 12

In the next few months, many of my friends got their licenses. What a great feeling it was not asking your parents to drive you around anymore. I had to wait awhile before I got my license. I was told in no uncertain terms that I was not allowed to get my license until my seventeenth birthday.

But one of my friends, Tim Tucci, didn't have to wait. He got his license a few weeks after his sixteenth birthday. Tim had complete control over his aunt's 1971 Plymouth station wagon. It was yellow, huge, and had fake wood on the side. (I still don't understand why people in the seventies thought it was cool to have contact paper wood on the sides of their cars.) Tim was a public school kid and an excellent mechanic. He could fix bikes, cars, and motorcycles.

He also was an expert at sneaking out of his house and taking that old wagon out for a ride without getting permission.

Tim was the first person to get me interested in muscle cars. He had a 1968 Camaro RS that he was trying to put on the road. It was the first car I ever did any work on. It was a big brother to the Camaro my father had bought for me. After helping Tim with his car, I couldn't wait to put my Camaro on the road.

I also made a few more appearances at Stephanie's house. I went most of the time with Andy and Jack. We would get dropped off and walk to the movies or roller-skating, or just get a pizza and hang out.

I got to know more of Stephanie's family. Every time I saw Mrs. Pacifico, she was friendly to me, and she must have thought I was too skinny because she wanted to feed me whenever I got near her kitchen. Most of the time I took her up on her offer. Her Italian cookies were amazing, and so was her spaghetti sauce. Many times I was in the kitchen with her while everyone else was watching TV in the family room.

I finally got to meet Stephanie's dad while sitting on the porch one day. He was a construction worker with concrete on his boots and hands like stone. He pulled into the backyard and came to the front of the house to talk to Stephanie.

"Hello, Mr. Pacifico, I'm Nick Carnavale, it's nice to meet you," I said to him as he came around the corner.

Most of the other boys sitting on the porch looked the other way and didn't say a word to him. The girls all said "Hello, Mr. P" to him.

He had eyes that looked right through you, and he gave me the "don't mess with any of my daughters" look I was so used to by now. I know why he did it, but at the same time, I could see that he loved his family, worked hard to provide for them, and had a kind side that he didn't want anyone to see.

But growing up in my family, I recognized what type of man he was. He was like my own father—proud, hardworking, and honest.

As he walked away from me, he told me that he went to high school with my dad. When he told me that, I knew he was made of the same stuff my dad was and that we would become friends.

"He was quite a football player. I've also heard him sing many times," he said as he walked into the house.

I also started to get to know Danny better. At hockey practice, we talked and sat near each other in the locker room. He was now the captain as well as an "All Catholic" player. He told me that I was getting better at every practice and to keep working hard.

Most Friday and Saturday nights were now spent with our growing group of friends. On a couple of occasions, Maureen and Marybeth and their friends from Bishop O'Malley were with us. I introduced Jack to Marybeth, and you could tell they liked each other. Jack was shy, and so was she. They just kind of fit together.

Maureen and I hadn't talked since the He and She's slow dance. I was standing with Ronnie at the box office window of the Colvin Theater when he saw her walking up behind us.

"Be cool," Ronnie whispered to me.

"About what?" I asked as I turned around.

"With the girl." He pointed toward Maureen.

Marybeth and Maureen stood behind us in line. I knew that Jack would want to sit with her, and I would probably sit with Maureen.

"How is school going?" was about all I could think to say to her.

"Okay" was all she said.

"Come on, let's go get some popcorn," I told her as we walked away with our tickets.

"Hey, wait for me!" Ronnie yelled as we walked away from him.

The movie we were seeing was *American Hot Wax*. I sat with Maureen, Jack, Stephanie, Marybeth, and Ronnie. I shared my popcorn with Maureen. Here I was again with this very pretty girl that obviously liked me, but I was more interested in the girl sitting behind me. More than one time, when I looked back, she was kissing one of my friends.

This was just another weird situation, and I couldn't wait for the movie to end.

I talked with Maureen through the entire movie. She was a great girl, but I just couldn't get past the fact that I used to cheat off her in sixth grade math, was in the class play with her in first grade, and shared my lunch with her for nine years.

There was another movie that would create a completely different situation a few weeks later. At the beginning of December, the world of every teenager was turned upside down. That movie was *Saturday Night Fever*, starring John Travolta as a kid working at a hardware store that became a disco heartthrob every Saturday night. The music from the movie became the soundtrack of the late seventies. Everywhere you went you heard the songs, especially the Bee Gees' music. And everywhere you went, people wanted to dance and act like John Travolta. Overnight John Travolta and his dancing became a sensation.

One night Tim called me and said he could get his aunt's car and take us to the movies. He didn't have his night license because he hadn't taken driver's ed. But that didn't stop him. He picked me up,

Jack, and Dominic, and we went to Andy's house to get him. When we got there, he told us that Stephanie was going to come along.

"What? It's just the guys tonight!" Jack screamed at Andy.

"Are you kidding me, one girl and five guys?" Tim said.

"Just drive, everything will be okay when we get over there" was Andy's response.

I knew we were in trouble. Andy couldn't even think quick enough in algebra class to tell Mr. Gagne what 7 times 7 was. How was he going to explain to Stephanie's family the boy-to-girl ratio dilemma that was now facing us?

Great, I thought to myself, another night watching Andy and Steph, while I sat there hoping someday to take his place. Then I did what I usually did, started to think too much. The way I saw it, we had at least three problems that needed our immediate attention.

1. We were driving with an underage driver.
2. We were going to try to enter an R-rated movie. (In the seventies, no one under seventeen meant no one under seventeen.)
3. How would it look when we picked up a girl with five guys in the car.

After I announced our three potential problems, I was told I'm going to die young because I worry too much, just lighten up, and a great seventies term "loosen up."

It was at that point I came to the realization that my friends were going to have many issues with solving the simplest of problems as an adult. I shook my head and stared out the window the rest of the way.

When we pulled up to the house, we had to think fast because Gina was on the porch waiting with Stephanie. She stared at the car and marched right up to us with an extreme attitude. She bolted right up to the driver's side window and did the "roll down the window" motion.

"Who are you?" she asked Tim.

She was starting to be famous for that first question.

"Tim" was all he said.

"Tim who, and what school do you go to?" she asked, pointing in his face.

I felt sorry for Tim because I had gone through this same line of questioning a month earlier, and he didn't have Andy Gibb to save him the way I did.

"Tim Tucci. I live down the street from Nick, and I go to McKinley High School," he replied.

"Are you old enough to drive at night?" Gina continued.

"Yes, I am. I really should be junior, but I have a late birth date, and my parents held me back in kindergarten." Tim said.

What, she believed that lame answer? Tim could lie with the best of them. He just kept leaning over and changing the station on the radio as the questions continued. He was cool as a cucumber under the cross-examination.

"How come there are no other girls in the car?"

It was now time for me, with my newfound courage, to get involved.

"Gina, the girls are all at Dominic's girlfriend's house, and if you don't stop interrogating us, we are going to be late for the movies. We're fifteen minutes late to pick them up already."

She took a step back and shook her head.

"Can we go now NOW?" I asked.

Stephanie winked at me and got in the car.

"*Saturday Night Fever* is an R-rated movie, how are you going to get in?" Gina continued.

"Haven't you heard? There is PG version starting tonight. We'll see that one," I said.

Tim put the old Plymouth in drive before the cross-examination could continue.

"I can't believe that worked!" I said, looking back at Gina as we drove away.

Problem 3 was solved.

Stephanie turned to me and said, "I don't know many people that could handle my sister the way you just did. You know she is only looking out for me. She thinks that is what a big sister is supposed to do."

I think a few of the guys actually thought I held my own with her too. Here I was stepping up to make sure Steph could go with us, and Andy didn't say a thing during the whole conversation. What a doofus. The doofus that gets the girl. I hoped the movie we were about to see would have a better plot than that.

But then I started to think, *Why did I bother doing this? For me? For Andy? For Stephanie?*

The answer was me. In some way, I was coming out of my shell, and it was because of Stephanie and all the crazy situations she put me in.

We had to go to the suburbs to see the movie. The Holiday Six was one of the new style movies with more than one screen and lacked the ambiance the old movies had. We were used to our neighborhood movies that dotted the city of Buffalo with only one screen, a dusty smell, and very large screens.

When we walked in, we used the "stand with an old person and make it look like you're with them" approach for the tickets. We made it through the first hurdle pretty easily. The second one looked a lot harder. There was a police officer standing near the usher taking the tickets.

How would we get by him?

As we got closer, the cop leaned over and told the ticket taker he had to go to the can and would be right back. We timed it perfect, and the pimply-faced kid taking the tickets didn't even make eye contact with us.

Problem number two solved.

From the opening credits, the soundtrack and the images in the movie mesmerized me. If only I could walk down Elmwood Avenue with a can of paint like Tony Manero, dance like Tony, and fight like Tony. The clothes, music, and dancing defined the era.

But the strangest thing that happened that day was that the girl Tony was in love with, her name was, you guessed it, Stephanie!

If a guy as cool as John Travolta couldn't get a girl named Stephanie, how much of a chance would I ever have with one too?

Aside from that coincidence, it was simply one of the best movies of our time.

When we left and were driving home, KB1520 had on the top ten hits of the day. All ten were from *Saturday Night Fever*. We all agreed we had just seen something that we would never forget.

And we made it home without being stopped by the cops.

Problem number 1 solved.

CHAPTER 13

The winter of 1978 was nothing like the year before. I played hockey and actually began to start a few games. The more we won, the more fans came to watch us. Stephanie was at almost every game. She sat with my mother most of the time. We talked after every game, and she was the first person to congratulate me after I won my first game.

"Great game. I had to hold on to your mother at the end because it was so close," Stephanie told me in the hallway outside the locker room.

I couldn't help but think how weird our relationship was. I was friends with her entire family, she sat with my mother at my games, I covered for her goofy boyfriend all the time, and her mother was always trying to fatten me up.

But she was just my friend.

Any guy knows that is the kiss of death. If a girl thinks you're her friend, she would never date you. In any event, we continued to hang around almost every weekend.

Andy was on the Brennan basketball team. Our whole group went to the home games and sat together in the last rows of the bleachers in the gym. The home games were usually on Friday night. After the games, more often than not, we went to a restaurant called Casa Di Pizza. At "The Cas," as we called it, you could eat pizzas on a chrome stand, subs, and chicken wings. My favorite item was the "Super Assorted Sub." It had a week's worth of cold cuts piled on it with a roll the size of a loaf of bread.

Most of the time, we were met with a less-than-enthusiastic middle-aged waitress that hated her life and really hated teenagers even more. But it was always fun in spite of her. When you walked in, it felt like you were eating at one of your great-aunt's house for sauce. The food was always good, and you got plenty of it.

After eating our pizza, all of us would rush home to watch *Rock Concert* and the *Midnight Special.* It was the only way we could see the bands that we were listening to on the radio. I can recall clearly seeing ABBA, Wild Cherry, Pablo Cruise, Blondie, and the Ohio Players for the first time on the *Midnight Special.*

As spring grew closer, baseball practice started. Our practices were held in the gym until the weather broke. The coach told me that I made the varsity team after only a week or so. Since I was a sophomore, I was eligible to play on both the JV and varsity teams. The juniors and seniors were the only ones allowed to go to Florida for spring training. I stayed behind and practiced with the JV. We had a very good player on the team named Danny Smith. He was big, strong, could hit and pitch like no one I had ever seen. Danny was also a hockey player, and I had gotten to know him pretty well. He was a good kid and never acted like he was better than the rest of us. There were so many Major League scouts at our games that they had their own section in the stands. They probably laughed when I got up to bat, but they didn't when Danny did. He eventually was drafted by the Yankees and played in the minor leagues until an injury ended his career.

The season was great. I played a few games in left field. The juniors and seniors on the team were very good and more experienced. Our coach, Mr. Quigley, was a Buffalo fireman and a great coach. He made baseball fun for all of us. He told Andy, Jack, and I, the only sophomores on the team, to play summer ball to get ready to start on the varsity team next year.

We had a winning season for the first time in three years. Our baseball season came to an abrupt end with a must-win game to make the playoffs. We lost, and our season ended.

At the conclusion of sophomore year, the first annual Cardinal Brennan Lawn Fete was held. All the students were expected to volunteer for it. It was supposed to be a lot of fun. Andy, Ronnie, Jack, and I worked all three days at various jobs. Jack was in the food tent.

Andy was picking up garbage. And I got what I thought was a great job, working at the Flyin' Bobs ride collecting the tickets. Ronnie got stuck making cotton candy.

My assignment had me working with a carny who was in charge of the ride named Clayton. He was tall, had arms that hung down to his knees, large spaces where crooked teeth used to be, sandy brown hair in a ponytail, bell bottom Wrangler jeans that were covered in axle grease, and a Stars and Stripes bandanna. He also had about a fourth-grade education and the peculiar habit of whistling and fluttering his lips while he waved his hand in front of his mouth before every sentence he mumbled.

All I could understand was take three tickets from every rider, which I happily did. The ride was a bobsled that spun around, down, backward, and forward. The problem was that the only song he played during the ride was "Slow Ride" by Foghat.

I heard that song for what seemed a thousand times that weekend. It was a very fast ride, and I couldn't understand why he wanted to play "Slow Ride" on a fast ride.

Maybe it was the carny's favorite song!

The most interesting thing that people were winning at the fete was a plastic baseball hat. They were cheap imitation batting helmets of Major League teams. I won a San Diego Padres helmet. (I wore it every day that summer. I thought it was a great addition to my summer look.)

On Saturday night while I was taking the tickets wishing that Foghat had broken up in the sixties, I saw the younger sister of one of my older Front Park Hockey teammates. Her name was Michelle. She had grown up to be a pretty petite blond with curls and big green eyes. I guess she didn't get sick of "Slow Ride" because she talked to me across the fence for over an hour while I took the tickets.

And without the usual effort, I easily asked her for her number and told her I would call her during the week.

She shyly smiled and quickly wrote down her number and walked away with her friends.

Wow, I thought, that was pretty easy, almost too easy.

I called Michelle on Thursday night and asked her if she wanted to go to the movies.

"Ah no, Nick, I don't want to go," she said coldly.

"Do you want to do something else?" I asked.

"No!" was all she said, and she hung up.

That had to go down as one of the strangest telephone calls I ever made. I don't know why she acted like that. Maybe her brother told her she couldn't date one of his teammates, maybe she had a boyfriend that she was trying to get jealous at the lawn fete, or maybe she was just shy. In any event, that phone call led to nothing but a dead end.

The last day of school felt great. The sense of freedom and "It's finally over" prevailed. We cleaned out our lockers, went to the gym, and did the same. I walked around and said goodbye to my teachers and went to the bus. As strange as it may seem, I actually felt bad knowing my sophomore year was over, and half my high school career too. (My father said to me many times that high school would be the most fun you'll ever have, and enjoy it while you can, because real life and all the responsibilities associated with it is no fun.)

When I squeezed through the front screen door and dropped my stuff in the front hall, the smell in the air told me something special was happening later that night. It wasn't coming from the kitchen. It was coming from upstairs and making its way down the staircase into the foyer.

My mother had been talking about the concert she was going to with my Aunt Serena on the last day of school for a few weeks. Every summer Tom Jones came to Buffalo and performed at Melody Fair in North Tonawanda. It was a summer concert place that was round, and the stage spun as the performance was happening.

To be honest, I had forgotten that the concert was that night. But when I smelled the Aqua Net in the air, I knew something important was happening. (The Aqua Net was only broken out for such occasions.)

My mother only went to the top shelf for that big pink can of hair spray when she was going somewhere important.

"Mom, are you and Aunt Serena going to throw your old underwear on the stage tonight?" I yelled upstairs.

"I don't think your dad, or Uncle Sam, would like it if we did that. Will you go into the hi-fi and get the Tom Jones Live in Vegas eight-track?"

I walked into the living room and got the eight-track for her and walked back to the stairs. Mom was on her way down, and she was dressed to the nines with a black sequined dress and her hair teased up.

"I'll take that. Uncle Sam's new Delta 88 has an eight-track player that actually works in it. Aunt Serena and I will be singing along with 'Tom Live' all the way down Niagara Falls Boulevard!"

When I saw her, I smiled knowing she was going to have a great time. Aunt Serena and my mom did everything for their families and hardly ever did anything for themselves. They were best friends and about to "go out on the town," as my mother would put it.

I smiled as the screen door shut and Mom made her way down the sidewalk.

I yelled "Tell Tom I said hi" as she got in her car.

"Don't wait up" was all she said as she drove away.

That summer was also the first summer that I had a real job. A group of us got Summer Youth Program jobs. Andy, Jack, and I, as usual, along with a bunch of juniors and seniors, were the crew. We were hired to work at Brennan cutting lawns and cleaning the school. Mr. Nixon was our boss, and he was fun to work with. We rode our bikes to school every day unless it rained and worked from 8:00 a.m. until noon.

One of my first week assignments was to trim the grass around the entire school and football field. Mr. Nixon took the three of us out to the field and gave us each a weed wacker and told us to get to work, and that he would see us next week when we finished.

"Boys, take the whip and get to work," he told us.

That was great, I thought. *He doesn't even know the name of the tool that we are going to be using the next few weeks.*

"I don't want to see you until the entire football field, fence, stands, trees, and building are completely clean." He shook his head and laughed as he walked away, spitting tobacco on the sidewalk as he left us to fry in the July sun.

None of us had ever seen a weed wacker before, and we had no idea how to start them.

"Choke it," Jack said.

"Pull the string and see if that does it," I said.

We eventually got them started and worked for days doing the entire football field, the bleachers, around every one of the hundred trees, and what seemed like a mile of fence surrounding the field and school. All without safety glasses and wearing shorts. Most of the days I came home with plastic stuck in my legs and a really bad sunburn.

At the end of the second week, we had to go to Buffalo City Hall to sign for our first paycheck. All the kids that had never worked in the program the year before had to do this.

"Who has a license?" Mr. Nixon asked.

Joe Lamarca, a junior, raised his hand. Mr. Nixon threw him the keys for the old Brennan window van. It was an early 1960s Dodge van that looked like the Mystery Machine on Scooby Doo.

"Get there, and get right back. Take the sophomores and don't get them killed," he told Joe.

When the four of us got in the van, it was obvious that Joe had no idea how to drive. He went around the first corner so fast that the side doors swung open and we nearly fell out. The three of us sat in the back hoping that all the praying we did while serving mass every Sunday was going to keep us alive.

"What the hell was that?" Joe screamed as we had cars honking at us after he drove through a Stop sign on the way downtown.

"It was a Stop sign. How did you ever pass your road test?" I asked.

"I didn't, barely passed my written test," he said as we sped down Niagara Street.

"You lied to Mr. Nixon?" Jack said.

"Sure did! He can't send me to the principal's office, it's the summer, can't keep me after school, no school, what can he do to me?"

"He can kill us, if you don't kill us first!" Andy screamed from the back seat as he rolled from side to side wishing old vans had seat belts.

We did make it back alive, and we eventually finished our weed-wacking adventure.

After the Brennan baseball season ended, we took Mr. Quigley's advice and continued playing baseball. A group of the sophomore players entered a team into the BEN PAL baseball league. (It worked out great with our work schedule because the games started an hour after we finished work.)

However, we didn't have a coach. Since the games were during the day, none of our fathers could coach the team. We needed a college-age kid to coach us. We decided to ask Danny to coach us. It was actually Andy's idea to ask him to coach. I didn't think he would do it because he was playing MUNY ball and going to college in the fall to play baseball.

To my surprise, he accepted and became our coach.

Practices were the hardest baseball practices I ever endured. He worked us, and we practiced all the time. Danny added a couple of players from his street to fill out the roster. Both of them quickly became very good friends of ours. Charlie and Victor were their names. Their older brother, Matt, was our assistant coach.

The team had kids from the West Side and North Side, were from public schools and Catholic schools. We played up an age division and did very well. We lost in our first playoff game to the team of older kids that eventually won the Buffalo City championship.

We also had three of the prettiest fans at any baseball game at Delaware Park that summer. Stephanie, Gina, and Cindy were at most of the games. It was at this point that my group of best friends for the next few years was cemented. Bobby, Charlie, and Vic were added to the group that hung out with us all the time.

And something else happened. A bunch of kids from different neighborhoods, and different schools, all became friends because they played on a summer baseball team. That friendship thing never ceases to amaze me.

Since none of us had our license yet, we were still riding our bikes to meet our friends. All the West Side kids rode over to North Buffalo every summer night. We ended most nights on the Pacificos' front porch. We talked and listened to the top ten at 10 on WKBW 1520 AM. Our summer youth jobs provided us with all the money we needed for our frequent trips to the ice cream stand, movies, and any pizzeria we could find.

All our activities stopped at ten thirty as we hopped on our bikes and rode like crazy home because our curfew was 11:00 p.m.

Our trip home was always an adventure. It started with a race down Great Arrow Street. It was filled with empty warehouses where the Pearce Arrow cars were built in the 1920s and '30s. The huge factory had been empty for years and was filled with hundreds of broken windows. If any place in Buffalo looked haunted with the ghosts of dead factory workers, it was this place.

There were also very few streetlights, which made shadows that appeared to move as you rode by the broken-down factory. For the most part, no one would say anything as we pedaled as hard as we could down the center of the street.

"What was that sound?" Andy would scream, trying to scare us.

Jack and I would take off like a bat out of hell. I had to hang on to my plastic baseball hat and try not to lose my clogs because we were riding so fast. I didn't want the ghosts from the second shift to get me! If I dropped anything on that street, even my hat, I wouldn't have stopped to pick it up.

That was only the beginning of the scary ride home.

We also would cut through the State Psychiatric Asylum to get to Richmond Avenue. The buildings were built in the late 1800s and looked like giant gothic castles. They had been abandoned in the 1950s when the newer hospital was built. Each section had huge windows that made it look like ghosts of the dead patients were staring out at you.

We never looked up as we rode by them because if anyplace was haunted, it was those old buildings. We had been told that there were still dungeons in them. And we were in no hurry to be the next occupants of those dungeons.

In the newer section of the "Nut House," as we called it, the patients were in barred rooms with porches that faced the road we used. They would scream at us to get them out, and some told us they were going to kill us if we didn't break them out.

As we rode out of the main entrance of the hospital, the three of us would breathe a sigh of relief every time we reached the relative safety of Richmond Avenue knowing we were almost home. I would then happily turn down Bird Avenue safe and sound knowing that no ghosts had gotten me or my friends that night on the scary ride home.

Hollywood Comes to the West Side

During the spring of 1978, our neighborhood was filled with movie cameras and, more importantly, movie stars. James Caan came to Buffalo to film a movie called *Hide in Plain Sight*. The true story revolved around a man from Buffalo trying to find his children who were put in the witness protection program.

I was determined after my last attempt at meeting someone famous (see Chuck Mangione in chapter 8) that I was going to meet and get James Caan's autograph at any price.

My favorite movie of his was called *Rollerball*. My parents liked him because of *The Godfather*.

In any event, I watched "Eyewitness News" every night to see where they were filming. It was a big story because there hadn't been a movie filmed in the Buffalo area since Marilyn Monroe made a movie in the fifties in Niagara Falls.

They filmed all over the West Side. I spent countless hours watching them from across the street at the Stadium Post on Ferry Street. I was fascinated by the lights, cameras, and all the preparation it took to film a scene. I watched and waited for the stars to come out to catch some fresh air. Every time that James Caan walked out onto the huge front steps, everyone started to scream and clap. He always waved and seemed genuinely flattered by all the attention.

The police had a roadblock set up, and we couldn't get anywhere close enough to get an autograph. It was still okay because I felt like I was in the movie too.

After they finished at the Stadium Post, the next scene had them driving down Grant Street toward Ferry. I staked out a spot on the corner of Bird and Grant. The car with the actors went up and down the street at least twenty times.

There were multiple cameras strapped to the car as they drove past us. The cameramen were in chairs bolted to the bumper of the old red Galaxie 500. The most interesting thing to me was that a man was sitting on top of the car spraying water on the windshield to make it look like it was raining. The Buffalo Fire Department was spraying the street and sidewalk to make it look like it was raining too.

Because of all the different camera angles, we also had to move from one side of the street to the other as they changed the shots. James Caan was close enough to us that we could hear him directing the actors.

But I wasn't ever able to get close enough to get an autograph.

In the movie, the family's home was on Breckinridge Street, and it was there that I was finally able to meet James Caan and get his autograph. I was standing about half a block away watching everything going on.

As the crew was setting up the 1960s-era cars on the street, Mr. Caan walked to the corner of Baynes and looked down to see how it looked from that perspective. I was standing alone on the corner staring at him.

He smiled at me and said, "Hello, son."

All I could get out was "Hi, Mr. Caan."

As he walked away, I ran up to him with a pen and paper. He took the paper from me and signed his name on the top of one of the vintage cars.

I told him, "Thank you, sir."

He smiled and walked away.

What a thrill that was to meet a real movie star!

A few weeks later, my father was hired to entertain the cast and crew at the Armory Tavern on Connecticut Street. The entire family went along to watch him perform and for a chance to "go Hollywood." Dad sang with a quartet, singing Italian songs for the entire evening.

My mother just kept repeating "I can't believe I'm in the same room with Sonny Corleone!" while we ate. My dad kept telling her to be quiet and eat her pasta fazool.

The actors and actresses were great, and some of them sat at our table. I remember Danny Aiello sitting with us and joking about the blizzard. Joe Grifasi, an actor who was from Buffalo, sat with us too. He defended Buffalo and our snowy climate and said what a great place it was to live.

The night ended with my mom telling Mr. Caan he was even more handsome in person than in the movies! He smiled and gave my mother a hug.

We all laughed at my starstruck mom and starting loading up the station wagon for the ride home. "I can't wait to call Serena and tell her that Sonny Corleone gave me a hug. She is going to be so jealous!"

CHAPTER 14

During that same summer, John Travolta became the most popular actor in the world. He had been on the cover of *Time Magazine*. The headline read "Travolta Fever." John's portrayal of Tony Manero in *Saturday Night Fever* made every one of our group into polyester-wearing disco kings. We all had to have a red leather jacket like the one Tony wore. We had to have the shoes he danced in, and we all thought we could dance like him too. One thing I knew was that I had to have that jacket.

If you lived on the West Side like I did, you shopped on Grant Street. On Grant Street there was a men's store called Phillips Brothers. In the front window was a copy of Travolta's leather jacket that cost fifty-nine dollars. I'm not sure, but I think I spent my confirmation money to buy it. I also bought a few gold necklaces and a pair of black polyester pants to complete my disco closet.

I also went to Russo's Men's Shop to buy my *Saturday Night Fever* shoes. It was located on Chippewa Street. It was not the best area, but my cousin Harrison worked there when he wasn't singing with the band.

When I walked in, he was spraying Lysol all over the store because the last shoe customer had smelly feet!

"Harrison, I need a pair of shoes like Travolta wore in *Saturday Night Fever*. You got anything like them?" I asked.

He got me a few to try on, and I settled on a pair of platforms with a one-inch heel that matched my leather jacket for $15.99.

We all were ready to try out our new clothes by going to the Elmwood Village teen night. It was every Sunday night. The bar was up a long staircase to the second floor. The slogan for the bar was "It's the only place in Buffalo you have to go up, to get down."

My friends went to teen night, and we also started to dance with girls. I began to notice that the guys that danced had the most girls talking to them. I gave it a shot a few times and decided that the world would be a safer place if I continued to hold the wall up near the pinball machines.

It was at one of these dances that everyone began talking about the new Travolta movie that was about to open. It was called *Grease*. I had never heard of the musical called *Grease*.

"How about all of us going Saturday to see *Grease*?" Stephanie asked me.

"Sure, what's it about?" I asked

"It's about a girl and boy that like each other, date each other, break up, make up, and end up together in the end. It's set in the fifties."

As planned our group of about fifteen converged in the movies to see *Grease*. Andy and I sat down with Steph in between us. I sat back in my chair thinking that the movie was going to stink. I was wrong. I enjoyed every second of it. Olivia Newton John was perfect as Sandy, and John Travolta made everyone forget about Tony Manero and now think about Danny Zucco.

When Sandy walked out of her house and began to sing "Hopelessly Devoted to You," it was like I was singing the song to the girl sitting next to me. She didn't know how I felt and at that point even had the nerve to be holding Andy's hand.

Our group went three days in a row to see *Grease*. The *Saturday Night Fever* songs were now being replaced on the radio by songs from *Grease*. And by the third night, we all knew the songs by heart and sang along in our seats. I actually did sing "Hopelessly Devoted to You" while the girl I was hopelessly devoted to sat right next to me.

At the start of the summer, Stephanie had a job babysitting a little girl from across the street from her. The little girl loved going to the Buffalo Zoo. It was within walking distance of her house. Andy, Jack, and I rode our bikes to meet Stephanie and little Rachel at the zoo.

While we walked around in the beautiful sunlight, I looked at Stephanie and saw how pretty she really was. No makeup, nothing fake about her. Her smile lit up even the smelly Gorilla House.

She was also so nice to that little girl. I started to think about how great a mother and wife she would be. Then I was suddenly startled out of my daydream.

"Wipe it off!" she screamed.

I looked at her and started laughing. One of the monkeys threw poop on her arm. The three of us looked at each other and laughed some more. The chimpanzee was laughing and pointing at us too!

"In my purse, Kleenex!" she screamed again.

I immediately grabbed her purse from the back of the stroller she was pushing.

"Where's the Kleenex," I said, still laughing.

"In the bottom!" she yelled again.

Without thinking, I grabbed her arm and wiped it off. For the rest of the day, we laughed about what had happened. I also realized how hard it was going to be for me if I continued to hang around her under these circumstances.

That night, we were all together again doing what all kids eventually do, go to a party at a house where the parents weren't home. The party happened at Victor's house, just down the street from Stephanie's. His older sisters and brother threw the party. We all went.

It was fun to go to a party without any parents around. There were the usual girls crying on the front lawn because their boyfriends had broken up with them; the bad kids were sneaking in liquor and beer into the party.

And Styx was playing too loud on the record player.

"Do you want a beer?" a boy I didn't know asked me as I entered the house.

"No thanks."

Ronnie was with me and said that we should grab a beer and hold on to it because it would make us look cool.

I told him no because I knew that somehow my parents would find out.

Ronnie, as usual, called me out.

"Nicky, let me get this straight, you are afraid that someone, who is underage, is going to tell on you, that you were drinking at a party where everyone was drinking, and that he was at, so that means he was drinking too?"

I really hated it when he was right. I knew my parents would kill me if I started drinking. I promised my mom many times that I would not start till my eighteenth birthday.

That was one promise I thought I would never break.

It was easy to see how these parties could quickly get out of control. I'm sure that half the kids at the party didn't even know who was throwing the party. I saw kids passed out on the floor, puking in the driveway, and making out in every corner of the house.

One of the girls making out was Stephanie. She was sitting with Andy on the couch. I looked at them and just shook my head.

What is she doing with him? I kept asking myself.

The more I thought about it, the more aggravated I became. After all, what was wrong with me that none of the girls seemed interested in me?

I decided right then that no matter how much I enjoyed hanging out on her porch, how much I enjoyed her family, how much it meant to be her friend, I couldn't do it anymore.

I wanted to tell her my true feelings, but I never did. I wanted to tell her how pretty she was, that I would treat her better than anyone else, and that I loved her. Yep, I loved her, but I couldn't.

I can't do this anymore, I told myself.

I found Jack and told him, "I'm leaving. Tell your mom when she comes to pick us up I got a ride home with someone else. I'm leaving right now."

He looked at me with a stunned look on his face and said, "Okay, I guess."

Ronnie was watching the whole scene and grabbed me and pushed me into the back hall and up against the wall.

"What are you doing? You're not going anywhere. I saw you looking at them. There are twenty other girls here that you could be talking to."

123

"But they're not *her*," I said.

I walked past Stephanie and Andy. They were still kissing on the couch. I pushed my way through all the mayhem and loud music on the way to the front door without saying another word to anyone.

I walked out and all the way home to the West Side in silence.

CHAPTER 15

It was a long, quiet walk home. The good thing about quiet walks is that you can think. No one is distracting you from what is rolling around in your head. I just couldn't figure out what this girl had that made me so confused.

When I got home, I felt terrible. Why didn't I just walk up to her and tell her my feelings? Why was I worried that you don't stab your friend in the back over a girl? All this rolled around in my head as I fell asleep.

I decided that I wouldn't go back to her house. That would be easy to do since the summer baseball season was over and football was about to start. With the summer quickly coming to an end, I hoped that football would put my mind on other things.

One night on the way home from Ronnie's, I rode my bike past Marybeth's house. She was on her porch with a bunch of kids. I decided to stop to see what was going on. Jack had starting dating her a few months before, and I thought he might be there doing what we always did, hanging out on the porch.

I put my bike in the garage and walked around the corner to see what was happening. When I got to her house, there were a few girls that I didn't know and two boys. I knew both of the boys from grammar school. Willie and Mike were good guys. In addition to school, I had played baseball and hockey with them.

Willie introduced me to his girlfriend. She was a classmate of Marybeth's. Her name was Janet.

"Football start yet?" Willie asked.

"Next week."

"What position are you playing this year?"

"Wide receiver, I think."

Willie was a good athlete and had five brothers. He went to Washington High School. Mike was a hockey player, talked way too much, and went to McKinley High School.

Both were in my class from kindergarten through eighth grade. Since we went to such a small school, we picked right up as if we were still seeing each other every day.

"This is Janet," Willie said to me.

"And these are her friends, Carla and Dee.

Carla was a pretty girl with blond hair. I started talking to her, and she seemed very easy to talk to. She went to O'Malley and said her father was very strict and didn't let her out much. That's why I had never met her before.

Dee was very pretty too. She had dark hair and dark eyes and a laid-back California style. She knew a bunch of my Carnavale cousins because they lived across the street from her.

"Where is Maureen?" I asked.

"She is at Crystal Beach till school starts again," Marybeth responded.

I had only seen her a few times since we danced at He and She's. I hoped that she would be the one that would make me forget about Stephanie. But I guess that would have to wait until school started.

When football practice began, I was now one of the veterans on the team. During my first two years, I had played almost every position except quarterback. I decided that I had good hands and should try for wide receiver. I was not fast, but I could catch the ball.

Our coach, Mr. Nixon, had other thoughts.

"Nicholas, I think you're a tight end. You're your too slow to play receiver, but you're a good blocker."

"Anything you say, Coach" was all I said.

We continued to practice twice a day until school started. This allowed me to have an excuse when I was asked to go to North Buffalo and hang out. I had to get up early for practice in the morning, and that seemed to work.

As school started, the Diocese of Buffalo stated that they were going to "reassess the number of Catholic high schools in the district." We thought nothing of it and got ready for our first football game. It was against the Gannon School. We had our usual pep rally before the game. The cheerleaders were there, and no one got killed when they tried their new Brennan pyramid.

The game against Gannon was at their home field. The smell of fall was in the air, and I was ready for my first game as a tight end. We won the game 16–6. I looked up in the stands to see if I knew anyone. My dad was up in the corner of the bleachers with his binoculars.

And I hoped that Stephanie would have been there too. She was not.

One other thing happened. I caught my first touchdown pass! It was about a ten-yard pass I caught over the middle. When I hit the ground in the end zone and realized I had scored, I jumped up into Mark Damon's arms. I think he was as excited as I was. That pass gave me the best feeling I ever had playing sports up to that moment.

After the game, my dad was thrilled too. He was waiting for me as we ran to our bus after the game.

"Great catch, did you save the ball?" he yelled to me.

"Dad, you're supposed to act like you've done it before. I didn't even think about grabbing the ball."

My dad had been a star player in high school and had even played semipro football for a time. I wore his number, 19. I had to go back on the bus to Brennan to shower and change after the game. I caught a ride home from Danny Agro, our assistant coach. Danny was as excited as I was over my first touchdown.

I rushed to get home and talk about the game with my father. I knew he would compare it to a game he played in the forties that was "just like" the game I had just played. But even so, I couldn't wait to talk to him about it.

I walked into the house and it was quiet, very quiet. No TV, no radio, no Saturday Sinatra, not a sound. I walked into the living room. My mother was sitting in her favorite chair. She was quietly crying. I knew something was very wrong.

"Sit down, Nicky," she said. "There is no easy way to say this except, Grandma died this morning."

CHAPTER 16

My grandmother was eighty-nine years old. She came from Italy with little more than the clothes on her back. She was sixteen in 1904 when she came through Ellis Island and married my grandfather, Nicholas Carnavale, that same year. They had twelve children that survived to adulthood. There were six children that died at birth or shortly thereafter. She was born in a house with a dirt floor, had never gone to school, and came to America with her three sisters looking for a better life without knowing anyone. She taught herself to read and write without any help, and raised her family with love and wisdom that comes from getting everything the hard way.

What an amazing woman she was.

It's hard to imagine the changes in the world my grandma saw. She had no electricity as a child and lived in a house with no plumbing. Yet she and my grandfather provided for sixteen people during the Great Depression. They sent four sons to World War II and at last count had over seventy-five members of their extended family. They had children, grandchildren, great-grandchildren, and even great-great-grandchildren.

That old house she lived in held over forty years of memories for our family.

My grandma died quietly in her sleep. I knew as soon as she passed away heaven got an angel that was going to watch over all of us.

She was the first person that was close to me that passed away. When you are a kid, death is so strange. You really haven't started to live yourself. You don't realize how good you have it. You have people taking care of you and watching out for you. And when death strikes, you really don't know what to say, how to act, or what to do when it touches you.

Our family's wakes were always held at the same funeral parlor. It was in an old mansion on Mansion's Row in Buffalo. The wake was two days long. The first day hundreds of people came. I stood there in my green leisure suit amazed at all the people my family knew. Mayor Sedita came. Judges, prizefighters, policemen, and firemen all came to pay their respects to my relatives.

It seemed as if the entire West Side came to comfort us.

I was proud that my family was so well liked, and though my grandma wasn't rich, she was very wealthy when it came to people loving her. Everyone said the same thing—she put her family first and herself a distant second. She was beautiful inside and out, and all her children had become great in their own right. With that they said she died a very wealthy woman.

On the second day, with everyone in the community that had come to pay their respects, I realized that none of my friends had come to do the same. I think a lot of them were scared of wakes. Scared of death.

I know I was.

Maybe some of their parents thought they were too young to go because they wanted to protect them from what we all sooner or later have to face. Maybe they didn't come because they didn't know what to do or say.

I felt sad and alone as I walked upstairs to talk to my cousins. The second floor of the funeral home had a smoking room. The room had a cloud of gray smoke at the center. After a conversation about O. J. Simpson and how great the Bills were going to be this season, the room emptied out.

I sat there alone for quite a while thinking about my grand-mother. I thought about the emptiness that was going to be there for all of us without her being around. I thought about my Aunt Vera switching the hot pepper labels with the sweet pepper labels every time we got together at the house, and how everyone would wait for the first person to eat a hot pepper when they were expecting a sweet one.

It is funny. The little things that don't seem to matter when they happen, those are the things you remember when someone dies.

The laughter and the love, that's what I was going to miss the most.

It's strange what you think of when someone dies. There are no set rules for any of this, whether you're an adult or a confused kid like I was.

I suddenly had the feeling that someone was watching me. I looked up, and a girl was standing in the doorway. It was Stephanie.

"Your mother sent me up," she said quietly.

She was in a dark dress that made her look so pretty I had to turn away from her. I hadn't seen or talked to her in almost a month. But she always had the same influence on me, even at my grandmother's wake.

I didn't know what to say. I just sat there and stared ahead.

"I am sorry about your gram," she said, walking toward me.

"Thanks, it's been really tough on the family. My mom and dad are taking it so bad. I don't know what to say to them. Most of the time they don't show much emotion, and I don't either. No more Sunday sauce, no more Christmas parties with her at the center, no more grandma. I am going to miss the sounds of that old house of hers. I learned one thing the last few days, that death is so final."

It was then that I started to cry for the first time since my grandma died. Stephanie walked over and hugged me. I now knew that in some way she had feelings for me, but as usual, I didn't know what kind they were.

She sat down next to me, grabbed my hand, and held on to it. As I sat there holding her hand, I asked myself, *Why can't you see how I really feel about you?*

She told me that she was now working at Burger Chef on the weekends and was sorry she missed my touchdown in the first game. We talked about skating and why I should come and watch her. She said nationals were coming up and that she had to go to Lake Placid to compete. She also told me what everyone in the group had been doing and that it wasn't same without me around.

"I miss you. Everyone misses you. You need to start hanging around with us again. You're the one that organizes everything. You're also the one my parents trust the most. I want you to promise to call me when all this is over and tell me what is going on in your life. You know, Nick, it is so easy for me to talk to you."

"Stephanie, it should be very obvious to you how important you are to me" was all I said without looking at her.

"Stephanie, do you know anyone that has died?" I asked her.

"My grandpa died when I was a little kid, but I don't really remember him at all."

"I am going to miss her so much, and it hurts really bad," I told her.

She hugged me again, and I didn't want to let go of her. There were a few moments of silence before we stood up and walked to the top of the ornate staircase.

"Come on, I need to go back downstairs," I told her.

I was still holding her hand as we walked out of the smoking room.

Just before we went down the stairs, she told me, "You're my best friend, and I miss you very much," and she kissed me on the cheek.

I turned to her and stared into her eyes. I wanted to kiss her and tell her all my feelings right then and there, but I just couldn't. Not at my grandma's wake.

What a girl, I thought. She had the guts to come to my grandmother's wake all by herself and to tell me how important I was to her. It was so innocent. She didn't mean that she wanted to cheat on her boyfriend with me. She just wanted to tell me how important I was to her. She was convinced that she could have a boy as her best friend.

It takes a special girl to think that that was possible. I knew I was in this for duration of whatever this crazy relationship was. It was like riding the Wild Mouse at Crystal Beach backward. I never knew what was coming next, and the twists and turns were going to be many. I really didn't care where this ride was going to end, as long as she was there with me.

We went downstairs, and I introduced her to the rest of my family. Ronnie smiled when he saw us coming down the stairs.

He walked over and whispered to me, "You're probably going to marry that girl someday."

C H A P T E R   1 7

The rest of the football season flew by. I never did catch another touchdown pass. But it didn't matter. We played tough and ended the season at 4 and 4. We had two great freshman players that made us look forward to next year and hopefully a winning season.

I started hanging around with Stephanie and the old group of friends because of my conversation with her at my grandmother's wake. I spent a lot of the fall cheering for Steph as she competed to get ready for her skating nationals. Sometimes I went with Andy, sometimes with Gina, sometimes with her parents.

I made my mind up that I would be there for her the way she was for me when I needed her most. My father seemed to not understand my relationship with "that girl Stephanie Pacifico."

"Is that girl your girlfriend or what?" he asked me one day as we sat watching TV.

"No, she is Andy's girlfriend."

"But she is at all your games, and you're always going to watch her skate and talking to her on the phone."

"Just friends, Dad, it's the seventies. Things are different than when you were a kid. We actually have phones and like to use them!" I told him.

"It just seems to me you spend an awful lot of time with her," he continued.

"Leave him alone, Nick, it's time for 'All in the Family,'" Mom said, saving me from any further questioning.

My mother knew what was going on and was clearly covering for me. She was really so cool when it came to relationships and the nightmare of being a teenager. Without saying anything, she told me what I was doing was okay.

At Stephanie's meets, she excelled at the figure 8s. Her jumps were great, and it was worth it to see her smile as she kept winning the competitions.

Ice hockey season was here too. I was the finally the starting goalie on the team after sitting on the bench for most of my first two seasons. I also had a fan at every game, and she was sitting up there with my parents.

Christmas of 1978 was very strange. It was our first without my grandmother. We had nowhere for our huge family to go. My Uncle Harrison and Aunt Vera volunteered to have everyone come to their house. We did, and they had us over for the next twenty-five-plus years. Their house was warm and inviting and filled with the sights and sounds of whatever the season. When you opened the door into the house, you never knew who would be sitting there. Aunt Vera invited everyone she knew to her house for every occasion. Uncle Harrison enjoyed it too. He would sit at the end of table and laugh at how many people filled up his house for every holiday.

She was as good a cook as grandma, made as many Italian cookies as grandma, and I loved her as much as grandma, but it still didn't feel the same as the childhood memories of that old house on the West Side. Maybe those memories are left, at best, behind us.

Our whole family was now going to make new memories in a new house at Christmas and every other holiday with Aunt Vera in charge. She had the biggest heart of anyone I have ever met. And before I knew it, she had become our new grandma.

On New Year's Eve, the group decided to go and see the movie opening that night called *Ice Castles*. I should have learned my lesson about not going to the movies with the group. It always seemed that the movie was in some twisted way about my relationship with Stephanie. This particular movie was about a figure skater that loses her eyesight. She dumps her hockey player boyfriend and ends up dating an older man. Then she realizes that the hockey player was the best thing for her and starts going out with him again, and naturally wins the skating competition.

I'm not sure, but I think Ice Castles was the first chick flick I was ever dragged to. The story line was all too familiar—hockey player falls for a figure skater.

Now that's a subject I knew little about.

January brought the annual Brennan Winter Dance. The band was going to be my cousin Harrison's band, Junction West. Ronnie and I decided to volunteer to run the dance and use the opportunity to meet girls.

Our dance committee consisted of Ronnie and a senior named Tony Lincoln and me. (Tony's older brother, Al, was one of the players that killed me during my first football practice with equipment.) Our moderator was Mr. Cavaretta, my homeroom teacher. We never admitted it in school, but Mr. C's brother was on my little league baseball team, and our parents were friends. (He was a great guy and one of the best teachers I ever had, and in fact, he inspired me to become a teacher myself.)

It was our job to organize and advertise the dance. We made posters and posted them at every Catholic high school around Buffalo. Tony and I made sure that it was our job to deliver the tickets to all the girls' schools.

"Best way to meet girls is to dance," Tony said as we traced letters onto the dance posters in the cafeteria.

"Quit talkin'. Let's just get this done. I can't stand the smell of these markers anymore!" Ronnie said as he plugged his nose with paper towels at the other end of the table.

We had no copy machines. All the posters had to be made by hand. We traced around the letters and then used markers to color them in. Ronnie and Tony were both wrestlers. I stayed after school until they finished practicing and organized the materials until they finished.

We spread out poster board and traced the letters on twenty posters in the cafeteria.

Brennan High School Dance
Friday, January 17
8:00–11:00

135

Featuring Buffalo's Best Band
Junction West
(The baddest group from East to West!)
Tickets $6

Tony didn't miss a beat and ignored Ronnie.

"Girls really love the guys that can dance. Watch the jerks that end up with the pretty ones when they dance. Someday I'm going to take a dance class to meet a pretty ballerina! I might even marry her."

"There aren't many blind ballerinas. That's the only one you could ever get!" Ronnie shouted back.

I wanted to tell him the world wasn't ready for me to start dancing yet. But I kept my mouth shut and listened to the other two going on and on. They were really funny without trying.

Tony was a great talker and could probably sell ice to an Eskimo. He sold our principal, Father Williams, on the idea of us personally delivering the posters and tickets to the girls' schools.

Father Williams entered the cafeteria to monitor our progress and walked over to the table filled with the completed posters.

"Nice job, you boys might have a future as billboard artists," he said.

"Father, the tickets and posters might get lost in the mail, so we need to personally deliver them to the schools, and we'll need to use the Brennan van to do it," Tony said with a straight face.

(My last ride in the Brennan van during our Summer Youth Program summer job was eventful, to say the least, and I was in no rush to *ever* take a ride in that jalopy again.)

"Mr. Lincoln, you can take the van after school tomorrow. I'll have the secretary call the schools and let them know that you'll be there after three."

Father Williams started to walk away and said one final thing over his shoulder, "And ah, oh ya, the girls do like the ones that can dance better!"

All three of us laughed as he walked away. We all agreed that our principal was pretty cool for a priest. I called Stephanie that night and told her to meet us after school in the office.

When we got to O'Malley, I gave her the tickets and a poster for the hallway. I could tell something wasn't right with her.

"Hey, what's wrong with you?" I asked as we hung the poster up. "Stephie, I have to get to three more schools today, what's wrong?" I asked again.

Tony walked out of the office and said, "Let's go, we have to hit Holy Angels next."

"If you want to talk, call me later."

She didn't call me, and I never gave it a second thought.

We got in the infamous Brennan van and drove to the other schools. (Tony was a much better driver than Joe Lamarca and actually *had* a license.) We got back to school by five.

On the day of the dance I was excited and didn't even mind that my mother was chaperoning again. My "mom at the dance" rules from freshman year had been discontinued, and I enjoyed talking to her about her funny observations of the dance. (I knew she wouldn't miss this dance. She never admitted it to anyone, but my cousin Harrison was her favorite nephew, and she loved to watch him perform.)

That day the usual things happened. I waited until the last minute to start getting dressed, and as usual, I couldn't find the clothes I wanted to wear.

"Mom, is my blue silk shirt still in the wash?" I yelled downstairs as I was getting ready in my room.

"In the dryer, it will be up in a minute" was the reply.

We had to get to the dance an hour early because the three of us were working the front door. Ronnie, Tony, and I had one thing in mind: use this opportunity to meet girls. Mr. Cavaretta was right there with us watching everything that was going on.

We made change, sold tickets, and made sure that Junction West had their required cans of Pepsi on the stage.

The hallway was packed with kids ready to have a good time. The smell of Aramis cologne and Body on Tap shampoo was all around. Everyone was dressed up and ready to dance in their best polyester. There were so many Farrah Fawcetts and Tony Maneros that we knew it was going to be a great time.

Father Williams sneaked up behind us as we were sitting at the front door counting the ticket money and asked us, "Remember, these guys are charging $1,500 for this dance, are we going to break even?"

"We've got it under control, Padre. Go out and look at the circle. It's filled with parents dropping off their kids. Look at the pizza line in the cafeteria, and look at the line at the foosball table."

I told him, "It's a sellout!"

The three of us had done it. We had pulled off a great dance, made money for the school, and were slowly edging toward "big man on campus" status.

I had on a silk shirt, polyester pants, my initial necklace, and my platform shoes from Larusso's. (Tony Manero should look this good, I kept telling myself.)

After we sold our five hundredth ticket, we were allowed to leave the front door. Five hundred tickets at six dollars each, it was huge success. We sent the off-duty policeman, who was our security guard, to the parking lot to tell everyone that didn't have a ticket that we were sold out.

"No ticket, no dance" was what he kept repeating as the cars entered the circle in front of school.

With my newly found status, both Ronnie and I went into the cafeteria to get a slice of pizza from my mother working at the counter. I saw Janet and her friend Carla talking in the cafeteria. Carla watched me the whole time. I walked over to her and bragged about the success of the dance. We went to the gym to dance. I attempted the "Bus Stop" and the "Freak." It was fun, and nobody seemed to care if you couldn't dance. It also helped that the stage was the only thing that was lit, and it left the audience in near darkness.

The thumping beat, the lights, and the mood was perfect for a teenage disco crowd.

My cousin Harrison was in a white jumpsuit, as was Joey, the other singer. The horn section sounded every bit as good as Earth, Wind & Fire on every song.

The party was on!

When I was leaving the gym, Ronnie started taking Tony's advice about dancing. He was in a group of girls that were staring at his moves. He was pumping his fists up and down like Travolta in *Saturday Night Fever*. But his gyrations were not even close to the beat. It was hilarious watching him. But as Tony predicted, his rather weak rendition of the dance was enough to get him a few slow dances later.

About halfway through the dance, Harrison and his band were about to take a break when he called Ronnie, Tony, and I onto the stage. We jumped at the chance to go up during the "Love Rollercoaster" jam they were playing. He introduced us as his brother, his cousin, and his new best friend and thanked us for getting such a great crowd together that night.

On the stage with Junction West with everyone watching, I had struck disco gold!

In one corner of the hallway outside the gym, Stephanie and Andy were arguing. They were doing this most of the night. She finally walked away from him and ended up hanging out with Ronnie and me. Andy stood alone by the bleachers the rest of the night.

When the dance was about to end, and it was slow dance time. I got brave and asked Carla to dance. She accepted. When the dance was over, we headed over to the Casa Di Pizza for some food.

But as we walked out the door, a little bit full of ourselves for all the success of the dance, Mr. Cavaretta grabbed us and said, "Hey big shots, you *will* be here at eight tomorrow morning to help me clean up right? I will drive all of you home, and remember to wear your old clothes!"

"Gee, thanks a lot, Mr. C" was about all I could muster.

Since my mom was at the dance, she offered to drive us. At that time, she was driving the 1967 Camaro my father had bought for me during the Blizzard of '77 (the car eventually became mine). She packed eleven people into that little sports car!

I can try to describe it as best as possible. Mom in the driver's seat, two on the transmission hump, two on the front passenger seat, three sitting in the back seat with one person on each available lap, for a total of eleven.

"Oh my god, the perfume stinks in here!" Sissy kept saying as we bounced up and down in the car on the way to the restaurant.

We laughed while we were squeezed into the car, the windows kept steaming up, and as expected, someone farted.

Eleven people all shouted at the same time, "Who cut the cheese!"

(My best guess was, Johnny Porkchop did. I had smelled that odor many times during Mr. P's biology class.)

The windows were opened, and every time my mother hit a bump, heads hit the roof, legs got squashed, and arms went numb, and because no one wore seat belts in the seventies, people nearly flew out of the car.

What a memorable ride that was! (Even now when we get together, that ride is always brought up.)

When we got to the restaurant, there were fifteen of us. We put the tables together in order to squeeze all together. The girls sat on one side and the boys on the other. Andy didn't make it to the restaurant but Stephanie and her younger sister Cindy did.

One of the best things, besides the food, at "The Cas" was the jukebox. It was a neat sixties Seeburg jukebox with crazy blue and orange neon lights showing a street scene from New Orleans. The names of sixties dances blinked on and off as it was playing. It was "three plays for a quarter," and each one of us picked three songs. It didn't matter if the same songs were continually picked. When you heard your three songs played, the rule was you had to scream "My three."

We had the same mean old waitress we always did.

"Separate checks, I suppose," the waitress said sarcastically. "Don't you know how hard it is to write separate checks? Last time you guys were here, someone skipped out on a bill that had two slices and a Coke. They deducted the $1.97 from my check. That's not going to happen this time. Aren't you kids from Catholic schools? You should really know better."

We didn't know if she was serious or not. We laughed at her as she frisbeed the menus on the table and waddled away.

140

"Do you think that I'll be like her when I get older?" Stephanie leaned across the table and asked me, smiling for the first time that night.

"I think you'll probably have to work really hard to grow a mustache as thick as hers," I replied.

When the nasty waitress returned with our rolls and butter, she dropped them on the table without saying a word and grumbled something about being back soon to take your orders.

I stared at her as she walked away. *What a horrible life she must have. She has to get up, come here, and hate her job. And do it over again the next day.*

"We have to come up with a name for her," I said.

"Who?" Jimmy asked.

"The waitress."

"She's a Matilda," Dee said.

The whole table laughed, and Matilda it was.

At our table, everyone was involved in some sort of conversation with someone else. We must have been as loud as a cafeteria at a middle school. When our songs started to play on the jukebox, we had officially taken the restaurant over. As Baker Street's sax solo started to play, we were teenagers, doing what they do the best, being loud and acting stupid.

All of it was so innocent. Laughing, playing music, and eating with your friends was just about as good as it could get for a sixteen-year-old.

While all this was going on Jack was still trying his best to impress Marybeth. He was doing his best tough-guy "Dirty Harry" and was leaning back on his chair while talking to the girls. He lost his balance and fell backward just as Matilda was walking behind him with our pitchers of birch beer. Jack hit the floor. Matilda hit the floor, and so did about a gallon of pop!

We all laughed so hard we were crying as Jack lay there doing his best turtle-on-his-back imitation. He was getting madder and madder by the second as the pop dripped off his face onto his patterned polyester disco shirt.

From my side of the table, all I saw was a pair of platform white disco shoes sticking up in the air and one irate waitress on the floor screaming for Joey the manager. It still makes me laugh to this day when I think about that one-in-a-million chain reaction accident.

No one got up to help either one of them to their feet because we were laughing so hard. Jack was really embarrassed when he finally rolled onto his side and tried to get up.

Matilda called him a few choice words as she rolled on her side too and struggled to get up. I knew that she was going to do something to get even with our group. She probably spat in our next two pitchers of birch beer or put some hair in our pizza.

"What's so funny?" Jack with his face beet red, getting really aggressive for the first time since I had met him.

"Good move, slick," I said, still laughing.

"Well, at least I can spell!" he shot back.

"What are you talking about?" I asked.

"That cheap initial necklace you have on, it's backwards," he said.

I pulled up my necklace. The letter N was on backward.

"I put it on looking in the mirror, and it looked okay to me," I said, still laughing.

I could see that he was getting really mad at me for no apparent reason.

"Yep. It was on backward, but it is a lot more expensive than that chair you just broke when you fell back," I said to him.

He came at me and threw a punch. It missed.

Then Johnny grabbed him and said, "What are you, stupid or something, isn't he supposed to be your friend?"

The girls got in between us before anything else happened. Jack walked out of the restaurant and called for a ride home. I laughed it off, but in the back of my head, I said to myself, *Don't trust him anymore. A friend doesn't act like that.*

As Matilda put the chrome pizza holders with our pies in front of us, our conversation turned to a new song that had just come out. It was called "Heart of Glass" by a new wave group called Blondie. Jaimie, being the musician in the group, had played the song on the jukebox. He told us that she was better looking than Christy Brinkley.

At that point, none of us understood what new wave meant, but it sounded different, and we liked it. We also found out that Blondie was going to be on the *Midnight Special* after Johnny Carson that night. After hearing that she was going to be on TV that night, it was decided to hurry up and get home to watch her.

Our pizza was great as usual. We paid our separate checks to Matilda and started looking for a pay phone to call for our rides home. There was a long line outside the restaurant's phone booth.

Stephanie and I walked out into the wintertime darkness to find one out on the street. We walked down Elmwood Avenue toward Utica Street.

One phone had no handle. One booth had no phone at all. We finally found one that worked at the corner. As Stephanie made her call to her brother to pick us up, we looked at the high-rise apartment building at the corner. I had the feeling that someone was looking at us from one of the porches. Both Stephanie and I saw the glow from a cigarette attached to the scariest-looking woman (with no teeth and greasy hair) that I had ever seen. She was leaning over the railing and staring at down at us only from only a few feet away.

"What are you kids looking at?" she screamed at us.

We did what all spooked teenagers do. We started to back away and run toward "The Cas". Stephanie screamed, and I think I did too. As we were running, she grabbed my hand and whispered in my ear, "I broke up with Andy."

CHAPTER 18

When I went home that night, my dad was asleep on the couch with the TV on. I quietly walked in and changed the channel. He never heard a thing and kept sleeping.

I watched Blondie on the *Midnight Special*. Debbie Harry was beautiful and had "it." I don't know how to describe the new wave sound other than it wasn't disco, but it was definitely cool, and she was definitely beautiful.

I couldn't believe that Stephanie was now free and able to date anyone she wanted. I hoped her next boyfriend was going to be me. I was not sure about the rules of dating your friend's ex-girlfriend.

I went to the best person I could for advice on this subject—Ronnie.

"Hey, who broke up with whom? Did she break up with him, or did he break up with her?" he asked.

"What does that matter?"

"Well, if he broke up with her, he didn't want her anymore, and he didn't like her anymore—so then it's okay for you to date her, but if she broke up with him, and he still likes her—then it's not okay for you to date her. Got it?"

"What you just said was so complicated. I'll have to wait for college to figure it out," I told him.

"Or you could just not care, and then you do whatever you want!"

"Thanks, Ronnie, as usual you gave me one of your confusing answers to what I thought was a simple question."

"The sooner you figure out that girls are the most confusing subject you'll ever study, the better off you'll be. Look, you have been waiting around for Stephanie since my eighth grade graduation party, we're juniors now, how much longer can you wait? Ask her out. If she was dumb enough to date Andy for a year, she might be dumb enough to go out with you too!"

I could see where this conversation was going—nowhere. I convinced myself to take it slow and see where it would go.

Stephanie and Gina were now both working at Burger Chef on Delaware Avenue. I went to visit them as often as I could. The two of them looked kind of funny in their brown pinstriped uniforms. For some strange reason, Gina was starting to be nice to me. She always gave me some extra fries or a Super Chef for free with my order.

My English teacher, Mr. Boland, moonlighted as the night manager at the restaurant. He always had some smart remark when any of the Brennan kids walked over to Burger Chef. No doubt he was embarrassed that he was flipping burgers at night to make ends meet. He actually was a pretty cool guy, and I enjoyed his class because we read a bunch of books that were great reads, and for the first time, I actually enjoyed reading. Teachers during this time were paid very little, and they all worked second jobs.

I'm sure he knew what was going on with the free stuff, but he never said anything to me.

I took the bus to the fifties-era Burger Chef to meet Stephanie after she finished her shift on Saturday afternoons. I would sit in the restaurant with a strawberry shake and wait for her to finish. Then we would walk down Delaware Avenue toward her house. I would tease her about smelling like french fries, and she would tell me I was about to start smelling like cigarettes.

My job at this time was setting up and taking down the bingo tables at school. We had to set them up in the gym in the morning and come back at night to take them down. The pay was twenty dollars. We thought that was great money. The worst part of the job was cleaning after the games were over. Most of the time there was a huge cloud of smoke in the center of the gym because of all the smokers puffing away during bingo. Cleaning the aluminum foil ashtrays was disgusting, and most of the time we just threw them out.

Jack, Andy, and I were the main workers along with a sophomore named Mike. One of our mothers would drive us in the morning to set up. At night we would hang around, eat the leftover pizza and pop, and start to remove tables as soon as bingo was done. While we were taking down the tables, the parent volunteers would get hammered on the kegs of beer the school supplied!

Wow, how things have changed.

The Brennan hockey team was finally starting to win games. I started most of the games in net that season. Our coach started to recruit good hockey players. Most of them I had played with since I was younger. Front Park was an outside rink where most of the kids on the West Side skated. We practiced late on Friday nights and early on Sunday mornings. Our games were always during the week.

I started to talk to Stephanie on the phone almost every night. Nothing major, just small talk. She was training very hard for her skating finals in Lake Placid again. She got up at 5:00 a.m. every morning and went skating. I don't know how she did it. She also got up early on the weekends starting at 6:00 a.m. at Burger Chef.

The priests from my school were French Canadian, and most of them played or liked hockey. They had two season tickets for the Buffalo Sabres. The games were always sold out. It was nearly impossible to get tickets. When a pair wasn't going to be used by the priests, they would mention it on the morning announcements. Usually, a group of kids would run down to the office and say they wanted to buy them.

One Friday morning, Mrs. Major, the school secretary, made an announcement that if anyone wanted to buy tickets for the game on Sunday, they were available in the office. I ran down as fast as I could.

"Are they still for sale?" I asked her.

"They sure are, this Sunday, Minnesota North Stars, twelve dollars each for a total of twenty-four dollars."

"I'll take them. Can I pay you on Monday?" I asked.

"Sure, here they are, have fun, are you going with your mom?" she asked.

"I hope not!" I answered as I turned and walked out the door.

CHAPTER 19

I had managed to save about forty-five dollars the last few weeks. Paying for the tickets would be no problem. I knew whom I was going to ask to the game. It would be the first time I was going on a real date with a girl.

But would she go with me?

"Stephanie, do you want to go to the Sabres game on Sunday?" I asked nervously on the phone after school Friday.

"How in the world did you get tickets?"

"From school, they couldn't use them, so I bought them," I answered.

"That would be fun, how are we going to get there?" she asked.

"We'll figure that out tomorrow. Right now I have to get ready for hockey."

All during practice I don't think I stopped a puck. I didn't focus, and that was a dangerous thing considering I had people shooting pucks at me. I couldn't believe that after all this time I was finally going to be alone on a date with her.

But getting there was going to be difficult. My parents bowled on Sunday nights. They wouldn't be able to help. I couldn't ask Stephanie's parents to drive us either. How weird would that be?

I decided that we would take the bus back and forth to the game.

When we were setting up for bingo the next morning, it felt strange. Andy, even with all his faults, was my friend. I kept thinking, What would he think if he knew that I was going on a date with his ex-girlfriend? And what would Jack have to say? I put it out of my mind and figured that no one would ever find out.

"Gina isn't working today," Mr. Boland said as I walked into Burger Chef after setting up for bingo.

"I'm here to walk Stephanie home."

"She is on the burger board till one, and she isn't working the counter," he told me.

"I'll wait" was my response.

It was the first time I had seen Mr. Boland act like that toward me. All of a sudden, he acted like he was embarrassed to be working there. I started to feel sorry for him again. He was a very smart guy, college graduate, and a great teacher, but he still had to work at Burger Chef at night and on the weekends.

As I said before, his lessons were fun, and the books we read in his class were great. They weren't the classics all the other teachers made us read. They were actually interesting. My favorite book we read in his class was *The Pigman*. It was a sad story about an old man named Mr. Pignati that couldn't accept the fact that his wife had died. He made friends with two teenagers that liked each other but couldn't admit it. The kids make a huge mistake, and Mr. Pignati dies a lonely man. (Yes, I had managed to find another story where the boy and the girl couldn't admit they liked each other.)

As I walked home with Stephanie, we were both so excited to be going to the game. She had never been to one, and I had only gone to one game in 1973.

"We are going to have so much fun tomorrow, I can't wait!" she said to me.

"But getting there could be a bit of a problem for us."

"Nick, you worry way too much about everything. We'll be fine. We'll walk if we have to" was all she said.

We decided that we would bus it and leave at about five. I would have to leave my house at about three thirty, take two buses to North Buffalo and two buses to the auditorium for the game.

At bingo that night, Andy brought his new girlfriend. Her name was Kelly. She was a pretty girl that didn't say much. She sat there on the bleachers in the gym as we worked. She went to O'Malley and was in Stephanie's class. So I decided that it wasn't worth it to worry about Andy and his feelings for his ex-girlfriend. He had already moved on with his love life.

As usual, Jack had a few remarks to say about Andy bringing his girlfriend.

"Why is *she* here?" he asked me.

"Don't know, don't care" was my only response.

"I can't believe he broke up with Stephanie to go out with her," he said.

"She seems nice enough to me. She is pretty too. Who says he broke up with Stephanie to date her?"

"Stephanie's much better," he told me as he walked away and started cleaning a table.

Wanting to change the subject as quickly as possible, I told him, "Let's stop talking and get this done as soon as we can. I'd like to get home before midnight. I have practice in the morning."

"All right, I'll keep my mouth shut and work," Jack said as he stacked a bunch of chairs onto a dolly and rolled them away.

Getting up early the next morning was difficult. But the excitement of the date later in the day made practice fly by. My mother drove to practice and as usual picked up a bunch of the players from the neighborhood. After she dropped off the last kid, there was a strange silence in the car.

"Ah so, what's up for the rest of the day?" my mother asked.

"I'm going to the Sabres game."

"How in the world did you get tickets?"

"From school," I answered

"Who are you going with?" she asked.

As I mentioned before, my mom had a way of getting information without you knowingly giving it up. I was ready for this line of questioning. The best thing to do was not really answer her.

I just looked at her without saying a word.

"Is it a *girl?*" she asked.

"Mom, you have to promise not to tell anyone."

"Your secret is safe with me, but who is it?"

"Stephanie," I said.

"She is such a sweet girl. How are you going to get there?" she asked.

"Bus," I answered.

"I can probably drive you to her house and get you to the game before bowling," she told me.

"Mom, if you just take me to her house, I'll take it from there."

My mom did keep the secret. She never told my dad, or anyone else. She dropped me at Stephanie's at about five. It was just starting to snow as she drove away.

I rang the doorbell, and like most Italian houses, the smell of sauce was in the late Sunday afternoon air.

"Nick's here," Cindy said as she opened the door and walked away.

I walked into the kitchen, and the entire family was staring at me. It wasn't like I hadn't been to their house fifty times before. Now it seemed a little different. It was probably my imagination, but that's the way it felt.

"What are you guys doing?" Gina asked.

"Sabres game," I said.

"Big shots, huh?" Danny said.

"Sit down and have something to eat," Mrs. Pacifico said to me.

"You know how much I love your sauce, but we have to get going to the game. I will take one of those cookies on the counter," I said.

Mrs. Pacifico was always so nice trying to feed me. Mr. Pacifico didn't say anything as he twirled his spaghetti on his fork and spoon. He just gave me the "be nice to my daughter or else" look as he started to drink some of his homemade wine.

Stephanie came walking down the stairs and into the kitchen. Again I couldn't believe how pretty she was. She wasn't wearing her Burger Chef uniform anymore, just Levi's jeans and a button-down shirt. She didn't have to try to look pretty. She just was.

My heart was beating, and I'm sure I was blushing. I just kept thinking, *What is* that *girl doing with me?*

"How are you getting to the game?" Stephanie's dad finally asked.

Before I could answer, Stephanie told him, "Nick's mom is taking us. His father is bringing us back."

I mean it was one thing to lie to Gina about *Saturday Night Fever*. It was another to lie to her dad about a hockey game. We walked out the side door into the fresh snow.

"Are you trying to get me killed?" I asked.

"My dad will be asleep by eight tonight. Trust me, you'll live to see another day."

We walked down to Colvin Boulevard and caught the bus. It took us downtown. We told the bus driver that we were going to the game and asked if he could tell us when to get off as close as possible to the Aud. He did and said we had about a mile to walk.

"Down that street over there," he said, pointing toward the arena.

"Thanks, sir, have a good night!" I said as we jumped out into the snow.

Downtown was pretty dark at night, and we moved fast. It was as scary as a walk on Great Arrow Street and walking through the nuthouse all rolled into one.

"Kinda scary, isn't it?" Stephanie said.

"We'll be okay, just keep moving."

As we approached the arena, we saw many people, and it didn't seem so scary anymore. The sights and sounds of the old Aud were amazing. There were peanut vendors, scalpers and hot dog salesman all yelling different things into the winter air. They were all trying to get our attention as we made our way toward the huge front doors.

"Peanuts, popcorn, need a ticket? Hot dogs?" was shouted at us as we crunched through the snow toward the front door.

We went through the turnstiles, and girls were selling programs, and the concession stands were everywhere. People were smoking in the halls, and the smell of popcorn was in the air.

"Tickets please," the usher asked.

We were sitting in the "reds" right at center ice. As we walked to the seats, I thought to myself, *I have the prettiest girl in the Aud sitting with me tonight.*

We watched the game, talked, ate too much junk food, and had a great time. I remember the score, 3–2. Buffalo beat the Minnesota North Stars.

Walking out of the arena, the snow was falling hard, and the crowd was moving quickly toward their cars. Everyone was happy after the big win, and people scattered in every direction as they passed the huge brass doors.

There were buses lined up outside when the game ended. Neither one of us had a clue which bus to take home. I saw the Utica bus. I thought it would take us to Delaware Avenue to get home. We ran over, jumped in, and walked to the back of the bus.

I was wrong. It took us to the worst area of Buffalo.

"End of the line," the bus driver said.

As we walked to the front of the bus, we realized it was the same driver from earlier in the night.

"Doesn't this bus go to Delaware Avenue?" I asked.

"No, it ends right here," he said.

By this time, we were the only riders left on the bus.

The driver looked at us and said, "Didn't I drive you two on my last run earlier today?"

I took a gulp and told him, "Yes, sir. I think we're lost. In fact, we are lost. It's late, and it's snowing. We can't get off here."

"Where are you trying to go?" he asked.

"North Buffalo, we are on the East Side, right? It's Sunday night, and the buses will stop running soon, right?" I said.

The driver looked at us, shook his head, and mumbled something about being young and dumb once himself and that he would help us out.

"Sit back down. I'll drive you to Delaware, and you can catch the bus north, okay?"

"Thanks," we both said at once.

The driver dropped us on Delaware and waved as he drove away.

"Your parents are going to kill us," I said.

"We will be okay. The next bus will get us to my house in ten minutes. Relax."

We boarded the bus and were in fact at her house before ten thirty. When we walked in the side door, the house was quiet, unlike when we left a few hours before.

"I still have to get home now. I guess I'll have to walk," I said.

"Call your mom, she'll come and get you."

"It's too late," I said.

"It's also too late for you to walk home in a snowstorm," Stephanie said.

"Okay, I'll call her."

When I called my house, my mother answered on the first ring.

"Are you okay?" she asked.

"Mom, I need a ride home from Stephanie's."

"You are going to owe me for this one" was all she said as she hung up.

While I was waiting, Stephanie sat next to me at the top of stairs near the side door. We talked about our adventure and decided we would never try that again. When my mother beeped, we both stood up and faced each other. I didn't know what to do. We just stood there looking at each other. I gave her a hug and stared into her brown eyes. It was the closest I had ever been to her. Close enough to feel her heart beating.

Stephanie closed her eyes, and I was just about to give her a kiss when Gina opened the door and asked, "Stephanie, is that you?"

CHAPTER 20

The next few days in school were great. I had a smile on my face, and no one, and I mean no one, knew why. At the end of the day on Thursday, Father Williams got on the loud speaker and told us to make sure that we, along with our parents, were watching the six o'clock news.

On the bus home, the guys were wondering why he said that. It didn't take long before we all felt as though we had been chopped in two.

The opening story on all three stations was the same: Bishop to close four Catholic high schools. Cardinal Brennan was the first school listed.

"What the hell did he say?" my father asked as we sat down on his favorite couch.

"The bishop has announced at a five o'clock news conference that four Catholic high schools would be closing in June. Cardinal Brennan, Bishop Mindzety, Bishop Neuman, and DeSales High School—all will close in a cost-cutting measure," Irv Weinstein reported.

What a sick feeling that was. I had put my heart and soul in my school for the previous three years. It had welcomed me from the start, and it all was ending a year early.

I wouldn't get to graduate with my friends. I would never have my senior picture hanging in the school hallway like everyone else that graduated from Brennan did. No senior skip day, no senior prom, no senior appreciation day, no final senior football game, no final senior hockey game, no senior final baseball game, and most of all, no Cardinal Brennan High School diploma.

My mother quickly got on the phone to other mothers of my classmates.

"We aren't standing for this!" my mother said to any other mother she could get hold of.

Within an hour, she had most of the other moms ready to fight the bishop's decision to close Brennan. She scheduled a meeting for Monday night in the gym. She called the newspaper and all three TV stations.

The message was the same: "We will not go down without a fight."

When Monday came, the meeting was loud and boisterous. A spokesman from the bishop was shouted down every time he tried to speak.

"Don't close our school!" the kids yelled.

"We have a right to a Catholic education!" we shouted.

"We will make every effort to place all the boys at another Catholic school," the spokesman said.

"My son has gone to Catholic schools since kindergarten. You can't do this to him. My three other boys all graduated from Brennan," a mother said with tears in her eyes.

I stood silently along the wall taking it all in. I kept thinking, *How could they do this to me?* There was no way I would go to Wedgewood or St. Michaels after competing with them for three years.

The only alternative was to go to a public school. I had gone to Catholic schools my entire life, and that transition was not going to be easy.

"What is your reaction to what you're hearing?" a TV reporter asked me.

I had never been that close to a reporter or a video camera before.

"It's just not right. I've been in a Catholic school my entire life. Now this. It's not fair. I will most likely be getting a public school diploma. I feel like I've been cheated" was the last thing I said.

My interview was used on the eleven o'clock news. It didn't make me feel any better. My school was closing, and my life was about to get very complicated.

CHAPTER 21

The next few weeks were very challenging. All the meetings the parents had didn't matter. The bishop didn't budge. The schools were going to close in June.

Since I was sixteen and a half, I finally was able to convince my father that it would be okay to start driver ed classes at school. The excitement of learning to drive and having a 1967 Camaro waiting for me did take away some of the pain of losing my school. Jack, Andy, and I took the shortened course so we wouldn't miss any spring baseball practices.

Our driver's ed teacher was Mr. Wilde. He was also my typing and business law teacher. In addition, he ran the school bookstore. He was a jolly old guy and had been in the army during World War II, but a little out of touch with our generation.

Our driver's ed car was a four-door Chevy Impala. It was a boat. We sat in the back and talked most of the time while the public school kid from our class was driving. We never really got to know him. We just called him the "public school kid." Mr. Wilde had an emergency brake on the passenger side that he wasn't afraid to use, especially when Andy was driving.

"Too fast, watch the car, oh no!" was what we heard most of the time from him when Andy was at the wheel.

"Too fast, keep right" was what was said when Jack drove.

Mr. Wilde never said anything to me except "Drive me to Mr. Donut." I had been driving the Camaro for a while and probably could have passed my road test at any time. My friend Tim also took me out driving in his aunt's station wagon many times. He would take me to the King's department store lot and let me drive the car backward around the lampposts. His reasoning was that if I could drive a car that big in reverse without hitting anything, I could drive any car in forward.

He was right.

Whenever we got anywhere near a Mr. Donut, Mr. Wilde would tell me to pull over. He would get out of the car, grab a coffee and a glazed doughnut, get back in the car, and never offer us anything. He would sit in the front seat stuffing his face and chugging his coffee, telling me to just keep driving.

"How many calories in this pit stop?" Andy asked.

"I hope enough to put him in a good mood and let us finish early," I said.

"How many doughnuts do you suppose he's eaten since the big one?" Jack asked.

"Probably enough to fill the tank he drove in the Battle of the Bulge," I said.

Our wish came true because this time he got into the car and said, "Let's get back to school. It's getting late."

With all the excitement in the last few weeks, I still talked to Stephanie almost every night. I also continued my raids on the Burger Chef whenever she was working.

When baseball tryouts came, the feeling was very strange. It was like senior year for the entire team. It felt like the end was there at the beginning of the tryouts. In spite of the terrible news about the school closing, for the first time in years we had a strong team.

We had three very good pitchers that won almost every game they threw. I had a very good year at the plate. I hit two doubles in one game and had five RBIs in another. I broke up a no hitter against St. Michaels and made many diving catches in the outfield. Baseball was a game that had always come very easy to me.

Stephanie came to most of our games and sat with my parents. After every game, I started to notice that Jack was paying a little too much attention to her.

The prom was coming at the end of May. I made my mind up that I was going to ask Stephanie to go as soon as possible.

For some reason, I thought that you should never ask a girl to the prom over the phone. It had to be in person.

All the guys at practice were telling each other about which girl they were going to ask to go. At first I kept my mouth shut and didn't say anything about whom I was going to ask to go with me. Most of the time when we were discussing which girl to ask to the prom, someone would always say "She's too pretty to go with you" and walk away, leaving them to figure out for themselves if it was true or not.

There is nothing like someone saying that to you right before you're trying to work up the courage to ask her to go with you. It was cruel, but that's just how guys are.

"I'm going to ask Stephanie to go to the prom at bingo tomorrow night," I told Jack in science class.

"Is that a fact? Do you like her or something?" he asked.

What a dumb question, I thought. He had acted very strange since he stopped seeing Marybeth a few weeks ago. I guess that teenage girls just have that effect on teenage boys.

"I like her enough to ask her to go to the prom," I responded.

I had never really trusted Jack since the night at the Casa Di Pizza when he wanted to fight me. My intuition told me something was up.

Why did I tell him that? I thought right after it came out of my mouth. Ronnie's words, "Never trust anyone when it comes to girls," came to mind immediately. I should have listened to that little voice in my head.

We set up for bingo early on Saturday morning because we had a baseball game at one that afternoon. It was a nice day, and Stephanie came to watch us at Delaware Park after she finished at Burger Chef.

When she came, I immediately got nervous. Should I ask her right after the game? Or on the walk home? When?

Being nervous must have made me play better. Jerry Sole pitched great, and I hit a bases loaded double to win the game. I played so well that I got my name in the *Buffalo Evening News* for my hits in the game.

Stephanie sat in the stands with my parents.

"Great game!" my mother told me as she hugged me after the game.

"Mom, I *always* play great," I told her.

"Played like I used to!" my father said as he patted me on the back.

"Let's go get some ice cream at Frozen Whip like we did after your little league games," my mom said.

"Sorry, I think that I'm going to walk Stephanie home instead."

"We'll drive her home," my father said.

"No thanks, we're walking," I told them as I walked away.

On the walk back to her house, there were too many people around, and the Bona brothers were with us all the whole time.

You can't ask her now, I told myself. *You have to get her alone and then ask her.* I decided that I would ask her later.

I borrowed a bike and rode home as quickly as I could. I got out of my uniform, took a shower, and rode back to North Buffalo within two hours. When I returned to Stephanie's, we hung out on her porch until dark. Her younger sister Cindy was with us the entire time.

Will you get lost? I kept saying to myself.

But her little sister wouldn't leave.

"I have to get going to Brennan to work tonight," I said several times, hoping her sister would get the hint.

She never did.

When it got dark out, I had to go to school to take down the bingo tables and do my favorite part of the job, clean the ashtrays.

"Do you want to come to bingo with me?" I asked Stephanie.

"Sure," she said.

We started walking toward school. *Here is my chance*, I thought. *I finally have her alone. Ask her now!*

"So, Stephanie, I was wondering if you would…" I started saying as we rounded the corner toward school.

Mike, the sophomore that worked bingo with us, just about ran us over as we turned onto Hertel Avenue.

Keep walking, Mike, can't you see I'm trying to do something important here? I said to myself.

"Mike, don't you want to go in and get a slice?" I said as we passed Lunetta's.

"Why would I want to pay for a slice when we get free ones when we get in the bingo hall in five minutes?" he asked me.

Wow, just what I needed, another space cadet that couldn't take a hint. And didn't he realize that three's a crowd?

Mike told me that I played great in the game that day. It made me feel like this was my day. I played the game of my life and was about to ask the prettiest girl around to go to the prom with me.

But I had one big problem, I just couldn't get her alone.

When we arrived at bingo, there were still a bunch of games to complete. The whole take-down crew was waiting for the games to finish. We walked out onto the football field and sat on the bleachers. Someone found an old football, and we started to throw it around.

It was a very weird group to say the least. Stephanie was there along with Jack, Mike, Andy's new girlfriend, and me. While we were trying to kick field goals in the dark, Jack continued to act very strange. He walked toward Stephanie who was leaning on the goal post watching our pathetic attempts at three-pointers.

"So, Stephanie, how you doing?" Jack asked with all of us standing right there.

"Okay, why?" she answered.

"I was wondering if you wanted to feel a whole lot better?"

Stephanie looked at him with the "where is this going?" look.

"I think you would feel a whole lot better if you were going to the prom with me, well, what do you say?" Jack asked right in front of all of us.

Stephanie looked at Andy and then me with a strange look. The look was like, *Nick, you're not going to ask me to go?*

Andy, her ex-boyfriend, was standing right there, and so was I. And so was his new girlfriend, Kelly. How awkward was this!

She turned to him and said, "Yes."

161

CHAPTER 22

I didn't know what to think as I walked back into school. Did Stephanie think I asked her to go to bingo so Jack could ask her to go to the prom? Did she really like Jack? Was she trying to make Andy jealous? Or was I still just a friend, will always be a friend, and was it time for me to finally walk away?

I finished putting the chairs into the storage area and walked into the foyer of school. Stephanie was there talking to Jack. Jack's mother was on her way to pick us up.

I declined the ride and walked home. It was late, and I didn't care. I walked down Elmwood Avenue alone with my thoughts. The factories I had to walk by would normally have been scary that late at night. I walked fast and didn't look to either side, and I couldn't believe what just happened.

How could Jack have done that to me? We were friends, sat on each other's porches, played ball together, rode our bikes together, were in every class together. Friends don't do that to friends. He knew I was going to ask her to the prom. And he still asked her.

I had just learned the hard way that the saying "All is fair in love and war" was true.

Someone I thought was my friend had stabbed me in the back. The way he did it, right in front of everyone, I should have dropped him right there.

What kind of a friend does that? I asked myself over and over. Was he trying to get even with me because I had laughed at him at Casa di Pizza?

But that was so long ago.

Or was he just a jerk that only cared about himself?

Ronnie's "anything goes when it comes to girls" speech started to roll around in my mind again.

I continued to walk fast and think even faster. What kind of a girl was Stephanie? Was she that dumb that she didn't realize that I liked her? I had spent the last few months talking to her every night and walking her home from work on the weekends.

Doesn't that count for anything?

Too many questions with no answers.

Or was I just a friend, her best friend? And that's all I would ever be?

More questions with no answers.

As I walked past Buffalo State College, I made my mind up to stay away from Jack. It was going to be difficult because we still had a lot of baseball games left. We were in every class together and had the same friends in common, but just stay away from him was what I had to do.

As I passed the "Nut House," I walked right through and ignored the screams from the patients. At that point, I was too mad to be scared. I knew that I had to come up with a plan to ask another girl to the prom. I was not going to be left out of the last big event at my school that was about to close.

I was making a list in my head of eligible girls. When I opened the door to my house, my father was on the couch watching the "Late Show."

"Wow, bingo went real late tonight?" he asked.

"Something like that," I told him.

"Great game today, your mom and I are very proud of you."

"Thanks, Dad, I have a question to ask you. Did you ever have one of your friends steal a girl away from you?"

"When I was a kid, people were always fighting over girls. Lots of friendships ended because of this girl or that girl. Why do you ask?"

"Got to go to bed, it's been a long day," I told him as I walked up to my room.

The next morning, I woke and had the answer to the prom question. I would ask Carla. She was pretty and always seemed to watch me whenever we were around each other.

Since it was Sunday, the Elmwood Village teen night would start at seven. I told no one my plan, or that I was going to the dance.

When I walked up the stairs to the "only place you go up to get down," Carla was standing at the corner of the dance floor. She was with Dee Dee, Janet, and Marybeth.

As I approached, she looked up and shyly smiled. The other girls seemed to, on cue, drift away from us. Before I knew it, we were standing alone and talked for the entire three hours. When the dance ended, I walked her to her dad's car that was double-parked out in front. He opened the window, and I walked around to introduce myself. I shook his hand, and he said that he knew my father and in fact my entire family. I thought that was probably a good thing.

In school on Monday, I wanted to punch Jack out as soon as I saw him. He sat next to me or near me in every class. As I walked into social studies, we almost bumped into each other.

He had a nervous smirk on his face.

I didn't say a word. I ignored him. This seemed to make him mad. I wouldn't give him the satisfaction of knowing I was upset. I bit my tongue and said to myself, *Ignore him. He's not worth it.*

Then he made a big mistake, a comment about the prom and who he was going to take. Before he got another word out, I got out of my desk and told him, "Go fuck yourself, and shut your mouth, or I will kick your ass right here in front of the whole class."

Mr. Herkart told me to sit down and asked if there was a problem. I just told him, "No, I'm not the one with a problem."

He must have thought I was serious because he never looked or said anything more to me for weeks.

I called Carla every night that week. It was not like talking to Stephanie. She seemed very quiet and reserved. I really didn't care. I was going to ask her to the prom, and that was it.

On Friday there was the Brennan Spring Dance. Ronnie, Tony, and I were in charge of the dance again. We made the posters and delivered them along with the tickets to the other schools. Father Williams gave us the legendary Brennan van to make the deliveries.

Ronnie asked me about what had happened in social studies that day.

"Can't you just forget about Stephanie and move on, forget about her, it's really not worth it anymore."

"It's not that simple. There just is something about her that I can't get out of my head. It's been almost three years. I can't just forget her. It's not that easy."

"All I can tell you is that she has made your life miserable. It's not worth it. There are so many other girls out there. Even a chump like you should be able to find one!"

I didn't know what to say because he was probably right.

"Nick, for what it's worth, I think that Stephanie is a real fox. She might be the one girl that would be worth all the crap you've put up with to get. If I didn't know her brother so well, I would want to date her too!" Tony said, laughing.

"Thanks for the support, Tony. As for my idiot cousin, oh well. Now let's get these posters and tickets delivered."

Tony was a good listener, and I knew that he was a good friend to not only me but also a lot of the other guys in school. He told me as we were making the rounds to the schools that some things are worth waiting for.

"Just take it easy, some things have a strange way of working out," he said as we drove back to school.

"Thanks, Tony, you're a great friend to have."

The dance was the perfect time to ask Carla. We were at the front door collecting the tickets and the money when she walked in. She came in with her usual group of girlfriends, and they all smiled at me when they gave their tickets to us. I almost think they knew that I wanted to ask Carla to the prom and were giving me their approval.

The usual crew was at the dance in dress jeans, clogs, and miles of polyester. The band for this dance was National Trust. It was very hot in the school that night, and kids were walking in and out of the school to cool off.

"You gotta ask her right away," Ronnie said as we walked outside for some air.

"I will. The timing has to be right."

The right time came when I saw Jack walk into the dance with Stephanie. Tony took their tickets and looked over toward me. He gestured to just take it easy.

At that point, I didn't know if I loved Stephanie or hated her. I knew one thing, that I wasn't leaving that dance without a date for the prom.

The first slow dance of the night happened at around nine. I found Carla in the crowd. She was there with her friends talking.

"You want to dance?" I asked.

"That would be nice," she answered.

We started dancing, and I blurted out, "Carla, I've been wanting to ask you something, do you think you would go to the prom with me?"

I said it so fast that I was surprised she understood what I said over the music.

Without a second to think about it, she said, "I'd love to, but I have to ask my dad if it is all right."

Well, at least she didn't say no. I would have to wait another day to get a definite answer.

"What did she say?" Ronnie asked.

"She said yes, but she would have to ask her dad's permission. He knows our family. Everything will be okay," I said.

The next day she called me and said her dad would allow her to go.

Before the prom, the baseball season was coming to an end. Our last game was against Cardinal Rooney. If we won, we would make it into the playoffs. If we lost, we were out.

Our coaches decided to play a sophomore pitcher named Donnie Maxwell in the first must-win game. He pitched all seven innings, and we won 5–2. The whole school was at the game. All the teachers, parents, and lots of the alumni were there to cheer us on.

After the first game, we didn't have much time to celebrate because we had our playoff game in two hours.

Stephanie was not at the first game. She was probably working, I thought. When she came to the second game, I looked at her, and she started to walk toward me. I turned my back to her and walked onto the field and shagged fly balls to avoid her.

As I stood in the outfield, I started to think about the last week, we went from talking every day, to not even making eye contact anymore, to now—I didn't even want to be in the same park with her or Jack.

The second game of the day was against St. Michaels. They were the champions the previous year. It was probably the most nervous I ever was when I stepped up to the plate the first time in that game.

We played them tough. Their pitcher was named Kenny Biando. He threw very hard and had a no hitter going into the fifth inning. He walked the first batter, and I was up second. I could always hit a lefty pitcher. He threw me a curve ball first pitch, and I lined it into left field. It was a double with an RBI.

The game was now tied 1 to 1. It went into extra innings, and we were running out of pitchers.

Our coach put Donnie in the game. He had just pitched an entire game four hours earlier. Don's arm was tired.

The first batter up was Kris Rebham, one of the best athletes I have ever known. He was drafted and played minor league baseball for a while. He lived up to his reputation when he drove the second pitch Donnie threw him out of the park.

Our season was over, and so was the Cardinal Brennan sports era.

CHAPTER 23

Two weeks before the prom, I walked into Tuxedo Junction to pick out my tux with my mom. We were all scheduled for our fittings the same night compliments of the Brennan Prom Committee. The flamboyant, ruffled, brightly colored tuxes were everywhere when we walked in.

We picked a tux that had pants and a vest that were brown, and my jacket was a creamy beige color. And I can't leave out the ruffled shirt with a big bow tie topped off with patent leather brown shoes. What a fashion statement I was about to make!

My mother told me I was going to be the "cutest boy at the prom" as I tried on the tux in front of the full-length mirrors. I tried not to laugh as I told her, "Thanks, mom."

When we were about to leave the store, as luck would have it, Jack and Stephanie came walking in. I made no eye contact with Jack and just stared at Stephanie. She walked over and began to talk to my mother.

"Hi, Mrs. C," she said.

They continued to talk as I walked away. My mother, Jack, and Stephanie, all standing looking at each other was very strange. It would not have taken much for me to punch Jack out right there at the front of the store. I left without saying a word.

Mom handled the situation much better than I would have. She talked to Stephanie and was friendly toward Jack. It was obvious she knew what was going on. She wisely didn't mention anything to me on the way home.

I still didn't have my license. Jamie offered to drive. I jumped at the opportunity. He had the use of his father's Buick Electra 225. It was a big old boat that was perfect for a prom "limo." His date was friends with Carla, so it was great fit.

Jaimie and I spent the afternoon of the prom washing, waxing, and cleaning that lime green Buick land yacht. He picked me up first, and we went to get Carla. She looked very attractive in a long blue dress, and her hair was curled like Farrah Fawcett's. Both of her parents and her brother were there, and they took lots of pictures.

We picked up his date, Annie, next. She was a lot of fun to be around and wasn't afraid to talk to anyone. We went back to get our pictures taken at my house. My father, as usual, took way too many pictures.

Our prom was at the Parks Restaurant in West Seneca. No one could understand why a place that far away was picked for our prom. Most of us had never even been to West Seneca! When we arrived, we quickly grabbed a table near the dance floor. They were decorated with green and white carnations and black tablecloths.

A lot of the Brennan boys had asked O'Malley girls to the prom. We walked around and talked to our friends from both schools. Strangely enough, it seemed that almost everyone was there with someone they no longer liked.

Stephanie and Jack made their entrance and sat at a table nearby. When we had to get up for our pictures, I was in no hurry. I wanted to make both of them as uncomfortable as possible. And since I was never much for getting my picture taken, I didn't mind taking it slow.

Ronnie and his date, Carolyn, were sitting at the table with us. As usual, he was as cool as could be. He also had a pint bottle in his pocket to spike the punch. We walked over to get the second round of punch for our dates when he took it out and poured the contents into the bowl. The bowl, previous to our trip, was filled with creamsicle sherbet and ginger ale.

"If we get caught doing this, we will get thrown out of school," I whispered to him.

"Hey stupid, the school is closing in three weeks, do you really think they'll throw us out now? Look over there, the teachers are all getting loaded at the bar. Who's going to notice?" he said.

I looked around, and as usual, his observations were right. The teachers were standing at the bar smoking their Marlboros and drinking, and everyone else was preoccupied with trying to get their date drunk. A streaker could have run through and not been noticed at that moment.

The punch was awful to begin with, and whatever Ronnie put in it made it worse. Our entire table was shaking their heads when we walked back with our plastic rock glasses filled with the worst punch since Prohibition.

I had to hand it to Ronnie. He sure knew how to make a good time better.

All this was going on as the band finished setting up. We couldn't believe our eyes. A polka band! A polka band during the height of the disco era?

Their name was the Henry Mack Orchestra featuring Two Kings and a Jack. Our advisor was Mr. Joblanski. With that last name, we should have known what kind of band he would pick for a prom!

In spite of how bad the band was, we still "boogied down" and danced. One of the funniest things that happened was Mike Renfro, who had obviously had too much of the "Ronnie Punch" asked the band if they did requests.

The bandleader, who looked like he had played at Herbert Hoover's inaugural polka in his East Side dialect, said yes. Mike asked them if they knew "Le Freak" by Chic. We laughed so hard that the bad sherbet punch was coming out of our noses.

I left the table to use the bathroom and assured everyone that it was okay to make more requests, but this time maybe a little Perry Como or Sinatra would be a better request for after-dinner.

As I walked from the bathroom, someone tapped me on the shoulder. It was Stephanie.

"Are you going to ignore me the whole night?" she asked.

She had a white high-heeled shoe in her hand as she asked me the question, her hair was up in a bun, and she was wearing a white dress that made her look like the queen of the prom.

"Are you going to hit me with that?" I asked.

"It's broken, stupid. The strap ripped. If I were going to hit you, I would use my fist," she said with a smile.

"Excuse me, I'm with a date, and it's rude to leave her sitting there too long. I want to get back to her as quickly as possible," I said, and I started to walk away.

She grabbed my arm. "Nick, you are supposed to be my friend, no phone calls, no visits to Burger Chef in the last month. How come? And answer this question truthfully, why aren't you talking to Jack?"

"He's no friend of mine, and I guess he never was" was all I said.

"Am I still your friend?" she asked.

There was another one of those patented "only Nick and Stephanie few seconds of silence" situations that seemed to last an hour before I answered.

I didn't know what to say. There she stood in front of me. The prettiest girl I had ever seen, asking me if I was her friend. Most people would have told her to get lost, drop dead, or leave them alone.

But I didn't.

I had never met someone that had put me on the spot as many times as she did. I thought back to my grandmother's wake and what we talked about. I thought about our walks and a crazy bus ride home from the Sabres game. And I thought about her smile that lit up every room she was ever in.

All this clouded what I should have told her to do and who to take with her.

"Stephanie, if after three years you don't know how I feel about you, I guess this conversation is over. Don't you think that you mean more to me than just a friend?"

I started to walk away, when she grabbed my arm and turned me back toward her.

"What is that supposed to mean?"

"Figure it out" was all I said.

171

"Would you please talk to Jack? He is afraid that you are going to hit him if he comes anywhere near you or your table. He likes me, and I think I like him. There isn't anything wrong with that, is there? And there isn't any reason why we all can't be friends."

I walked directly over to Jack who was sitting at the table. He looked up at me with a surprised look on his face. I think he thought I was going to jaw him.

"It's over," I said and walked away.

I looked over my shoulder and saw Stephanie smiling at me. For that split second, she was the prettiest girl at any prom, at any time.

When I went back to my table, I couldn't believe what had just happened. Stephanie had actually talked me into apologizing to Jack for what he had done to me!

I was in a daze when I heard, "Wake up" It was Ronnie in my ear.

"What now? Back to the punch bowl again?"

"A bunch of seniors need us in the parking lot."

I asked Carla if she wanted to go outside for some air. When we walked out, the senior class had moved Mr. Kelly's Volkswagen Bug to the other side of the parking lot. They had painted peace signs and smiley faces all over the car with watercolors. Everyone was getting out their Polaroid cameras and taking pictures of each other next to the car.

Tony walked over to me and told us that the seniors had also decided that there was going to be an after-prom picnic at Delaware Park the next day.

"Do you want to go to a picnic tomorrow?" I asked Carla.

She looked at the ground and stumbled for an answer.

"I have a family commitment," she finally said.

"Okay," I said, "no big deal."

I didn't think anything of it, and we went back into the restaurant. The prom ended with the band playing "My Way" by Frank Sinatra. Just before we left, our principal, Father Williams, grabbed the microphone and told us all to "go home, don't drink and drive, and we'll see you at the park in the morning."

Jaimie, Annie, Carla, and I got into the car for the ride home. When we got to Carla's house, I walked her up to the front door.

"I had a great time. I wish I could go with you tomorrow, but I have to go with my family somewhere," she said.

"It's okay. Maybe I'll see you at the dance on Sunday night."

I gave her a kiss, and she went into the house. When I returned to the car, Annie asked what was up with Carla and that she seemed nervous on the ride home.

"She was nervous because she figured she would have to kiss Nick at the end of the night. I'd be nervous too!" Jamie said, laughing.

"Jaimie, when you drop me off, I promise you won't have to kiss me," I said as we drove toward Annie's house.

After we dropped her off, we talked about being cheated out of our senior year. Every kid looked forward to senior year and all the excitement surrounding finally graduating. We weren't attending the same school next year. It was kind of sad knowing we were going our separate ways one year too early.

On the way home, we pulled up in front of The Elmwood Taco and Subs. It was on the corner of Delavan in a converted house. Walking in there, you never knew who or what would be in line in front of you. And that's what made it so much fun to get something to eat there late at night.

The whole neighborhood knew there was nothing like an Elmwood Taco to end a great evening. We bought a few them from my cousin Joe who was working there at the time. We definitely looked out of place in our loud tuxes ordering at one in the morning.

But then again, the hippies in front of us looked kind of funny too.

We ate our tacos on the bench out in front of the restaurant that every kid growing up on the West Side sat on at least once, and some people like me, every week. We talked about how cool it would have been to have our senior year at Brennan and how our high school experience had been great to this point. Jamie and I also lamented that our memories were all we were going to have about Brennan in a few weeks.

Sitting on that bench in our ruffled tuxedos eating tacos must have looked funny to everyone driving by. But we didn't care.

We drove to my house, and as I left the car, my prom chauffer named Jaimie looked in the back seat to see if anyone had left anything. He noticed that Carla had left her purse there. He handed it to me.

"I'll bring it to her in the morning," I said.

The next morning the phone rang bright and early. It was Stephanie calling.

"YOU'RE GOING TO THE PICNIC!" she told me.

"I have no date, and no ride, and why are *you* calling *me*?" I asked. "Shouldn't you be working?"

"I asked for the day off. You have a ride. Jack will pick you up, and it won't matter if you're alone. Half the people at the prom broke up with each other last night anyway. We'll pick you up at noon, and I won't take no for an answer."

The next thing I heard was a dial tone because she hung up and didn't even give me a chance to say no. What could I say? She was persistent. When they beeped in front of my house at noon, I walked out to see Jack driving his parents' Delta 88.

I had Carla's purse in my hand.

"That purse doesn't match your outfit," Stephanie said as I got in the car.

"Very funny, Phyllis Diller, can we drop this at Carla's house?" I asked sarcastically.

"We'll go right over now, and then go to the park," Jack said nervously, staring straight ahead.

As we drove over to Carla's, I couldn't help but think, *Here we go again, another crazy, awkward situation starring Nick and Stephanie, and anybody else that was around.*

All three of us sat in the front seat for the ride over to Carla's. *How bizarre is this?* I just kept asking myself. But maybe I had started something good with Carla the night before. Maybe she was going to be *my* girlfriend!

When we pulled up in front of her house, last night didn't matter anymore. She was walking down her front stairs, and in her driveway was a college-age guy driving a new white Corvette.

She hugged him, gave him a kiss, and got in the car.

Stephanie said, "That guy certainly isn't one of her cousins!"

I looked at Stephanie and said, "Give her the purse on Monday."

CHAPTER 24

The class of 1979 graduated from Cardinal Brennan High School on June 17. It was the last one to do so. All the underclassman had to find different schools to attend. I toured St. Michaels, Cardinal Rooney, and Washington High School. I would not go to St. Michaels after hating them for three years. The nun that was the principal at Rooney made it perfectly clear that she didn't want any Italians from the West Side at her school.

I was left with Washington High School, a public school.

I had never attended a public school before. Many of my friends from the neighborhood went there. It was a five-minute walk from my house, and there were about eight hundred girls enrolled there. For me it was an easy decision to make.

My mother was not happy with the idea that I was going to finish at a public school. She told me that I had to have a "Catholic diploma" or I would never get into a good college. After a series of rather loud family conversations, she eventually came to understanding that Washington would be the best choice for me.

A sad thing that happened at the end of June was our dog, Humphrey, became very sick. He wouldn't walk down the stairs to go out, so my dad started carrying him. It was not easy to carry a 120-pound dog up and down the stairs. When it got to the point that he wouldn't eat, my dad told me to go and get the car, even though I only had my permit.

My father had never driven with me before, but he still threw me the keys. When I pulled in the driveway, he came out the front door carrying Humphrey.

It was then that I saw him crying for the first time. He sat in back seat with the dog on his lap and told me to drive to the vet on Elmwood Avenue. I walked in and told the receptionist what the situation was. She opened the side door, and my dad carried him in.

It was so sad seeing my dog that had been with me for most of my life nearing the end of his. While we were waiting for the vet, Humphrey just lay there barely breathing. When the vet walked into the examining room, Humphrey stood up and walked toward him.

My father told Dr. Smith that he was going to bring the dog back home and that he was okay now. The vet told us that we would only be back tomorrow, that he was fourteen years old, had been a great dog for us, and that it was his time. He said that dogs know when it is their time to go and that he was being brave one last time for us.

My father hugged that dog for about five minutes until the vet came back in with the needle. In a few seconds, he was gone. We took his chain off and hugged him one last time.

My dad threw me the keys again and told me to drive home. We didn't say a word in the car. My father was crying too much.

Within a week, my parents had another puppy Airedale. We named him Rico after Enrico Caruso, the opera singer, and he gave us a run for the money chewing everything in sight and barking all night for months.

We still had the whole summer to look forward to before school started in the fall. We put our "Starz" baseball team back together. We added a few players, and Danny and Matt coached us again. Our practices were at Delaware Park, and as usual they were long and hard.

It paid off. We won our first ten games and were cruising along as the best team in the league. We were now called Brennan, mainly because our Brennan coach had given us all the jerseys at the end of the season, and we didn't have any sponsor to buy us new jerseys, so we used the old ones.

I took my road test on July 7, 1979, my seventeenth birthday. The mail brought my license two days later. What a feeling of freedom it was taking my first ride by myself in the Camaro. I went down Elmwood to downtown, back down Delaware Avenue to Hertel Avenue, and drove past all my friends' houses. I cruised the neighborhood in that muscle car like I was a big shot. Gas was up to sixty-two cents a gallon, and your parents didn't care how much you used as long as you never left the car on E.

The second day I had my license, I was driving down Delaware Avenue when I saw an unbelievable-looking 1964 black GTO convertible screaming toward me. As it got closer, the driver was pointing at me to pull over. It was my cousin Joel. He was a few years older than me and was really into muscle cars.

I pulled over as he made a very illegal U-turn right in front of me.

"Get in!" he yelled. "And hang on!"

My head slammed back as he burned out and down the street. It was a 389-tripower four-speed, one of the fastest cars produced in the sixties. The adrenaline rush of your hair blowing in a race car like that was amazing!

He told me that he found the car in a garage that he had painted a few weeks ago. The car belonged to a boy that was killed in the Vietnam War, and his mother left the car in the garage without touching it for almost ten years. Joel convinced her that selling it to him was a good idea. He repainted the car and had a neon dragon pinstriped on the hood. That car was absolutely the fastest car I was ever in. It was also the first convertible muscle car I ever was lucky enough ride in. Before that ride, I liked old cars, but now I *loved* them. I was instantly obsessed with finding another GTO convertible. It took me almost two years to find one, but I did.

At our last regular summer league baseball game before the playoffs, an incident happened that brought us all closer together. We were playing a team made up of players from Bishop Neumann High School. Their school had also closed in June like ours did.

The usual crowd was in the stands including Stephanie, Cindy, and a bunch of the girlfriends of the players on our team. I was up to bat and hit a double. When I was about to slide into second, the second baseman knocked me down and spiked me as I slid into the bag.

I stood up and was nose to nose with him. Without thinking, I punched him in the mouth. The benches emptied. While I was fighting him, Mike Muller grabbed the third baseman that was about to jump on me and threw him to the ground. Jack was the first one off the bench to defend me. He did his best to unscrew the shortstop's head as he was about to hit me from behind.

There were fights all over the infield. The other team was coached by one of the players' father. He hit Matt Pasquale as he ran onto the field. His brother Mitchell jumped on the coach's back.

Danny saw this and started fighting the dad. Needless to say, Danny wiped the field with him.

When all the fighting was done, the umps called the game. Our entire team sat on the bench while still screaming at the other team. I thought Danny was going to yell at me for starting the fight. I was sitting there looking down at the blood dripping from cuts in my newly spiked leg.

"What took you so long to hit him?" Danny asked me with a shit-eating grin and laughing.

"I thought you would get pissed at me if I did that," I told him.

"If anyone ever does something like that to you, or your teammate, in any game you ever play, you react exactly the way you did. You did what I would have done. You're the kind of player I would always want on my team."

I said, "Thanks, Coach," and I started to laugh along with the rest of the team.

By the way he said that to me, I knew I was not the kid anymore that he played football and hockey with and called "Freshman" because he couldn't remember my name. He was in college now and a great baseball player in his own right, and someone I looked up to, and he told me he would want me on his team.

That someone like him said that meant the world to me.

I also thought about what Jack did. He didn't hesitate to defend me and he had my back. It was at that point I forgave him for all our previous problems and I realized he was in fact, a good friend to have.

It's funny how a fight in a baseball game could teach me so many valuable lessons about friends and friendship. But it did.

"All right, pick all the equipment up! Let's get ready for the playoffs!" Danny told us.

We picked everything up and loaded Danny's 'Cuda with the equipment and started to walk home.

"What was that!" Stephanie said as we walked away from the diamond toward home.

She was smirking, so I think she knew exactly what it was.

"That was just a preppy jerk getting his ass kicked," I said with my own newfound confidence.

"You guys sure took care of them. You managed to turn a baseball game into a hockey brawl. Pretty cool, I guess," She said.

The North Buffalo kids turned right out of the park to go home, and the West Side kids took a left toward home.

"See ya later, guys!" I yelled as we crossed the Delaware Park bridge toward home.

After I got my license, my parents were really cool with the car when I asked for it. I drove to North Buffalo almost every night. I would pick up Jack and Andy and hang out with our Brennan friends. Most nights, we made at least one appearance at Stephanie's house.

At one of the Sunday night teen dances at the Elmwood Village, I met a girl that lived around the corner from me. Her name was Debbie. She was a sweet girl, tall with blond hair and pretty brown eyes. I would walk over to her house and sit on her porch or watch TV.

We went on a few summer dates to the movies and for ice cream. It only lasted a few weeks. And as usual, I ended up spending more time at Stephanie's house.

Jack and I hung around the entire summer. We put the prom situation behind us.

Andy spent a lot of his time helping his parents pack up his house because they were moving to the suburbs. He slowly started hanging out with a different group of kids that were going to Cardinal Rooney with him in September.

Our baseball season came to an end in the championship game. We won our first three-playoff games and made it to the city championship. We played a team from South Buffalo. It was a great game that went down to the bottom of the seventh inning. We had a chance to tie the game, but Bobby O. popped out to end our season.

They beat us 3–2, and our season was over.

With Andy not hanging around with us as much he used to, a new guy that was Dominic's next-door neighbor and his good friend joined our group. Bob was his name, and he went to South Tech School, and they had been friends since they were five years old.

Bob's father bought an old Mustang for his first car. We worked on it, got it roadworthy, and he had it painted. It looked brand-new. One night, Jack, Bob, Dominic, and I jumped in the car and went to the Broadway Drive-In.

When we pulled in, Bob kept his headlights on. Everyone started beeping their horns and flashing their lights at us. He got nervous and turned his lights off. Because it was dark, he started hitting the poles that held the speakers for the drive-in. He snapped a bunch of them before he stopped.

The front of the car looked like he had hit a brick wall. There was steam shooting everywhere, and radiator fluid was dripping on the ground.

"My father is going to kill me, then kill you, and then kill you," he said while we were staring at the damage to his freshly painted car.

"Your dad is going to just kill you. We weren't driving. That makes us kinda safe," I said.

"I have an idea," Dominic said. "Start picking up those broken pieces and put them in the trunk."

We listened to Dom and picked up the broken parts of the grill and fiberglass panel. We put them in the trunk and drove out without the lights on. We went to a corner store and bought some anti-freeze to put in the leaking radiator.

"Here's my idea, you know how cars on our block are always getting hit by drunks driving home? Well, we are going to put this beast on the curve of the street and make it look like someone hit it. We'll throw the broken pieces on the ground around the car, and then pour some fluid on the ground," Dominic said.

Bob drove home much more carefully than he did in the Broadway Drive-In. We had to stop multiple times to put in more radiator fluid.

"How are we supposed to do this when we get back without anyone noticing us? The whole neighborhood will be sitting on their porch watching everything that is going on." I asked.

"Bob, you're gonna park the car at around the block and go into the house like nothing happened, then you can get up and go downstairs for something to drink at 1:00 a.m., run outside, move the car, and spread out the pieces and spill antifreeze on the ground."

I had to admit it was a great plan if it worked. It did work, and his father never figured out what really had happened.

A few days after the drive-in fiasco, we decided that it was safer to go to the movies than the drive-in. I drove over to Stephanie's house and met up with her and a group of seven other kids. We were all arguing about the movie we should go see.

"I read *The Amityville Horror* book. It was great. Let's go see that," Stephanie said.

"Not me! I admit I'm scared. I hate those movies. I'll sleep with my covers over my head for a week if we see that."

I lost the vote, and we went to *The Amityville Horror* at the Colvin Theatre.

When we got to the movie, Stephanie had already bought my ticket.

"I bought your ticket. It's a late birthday present for you," she said as we walked toward the movie.

"Here's the money. You don't have to buy me anything."

She refused to take the money before and after the movie.

We stopped at Art's Hoagie Hut for some subs on the way home. My cousin Joel worked there and always had his GTO parked out in front. I knew with him working we would get an extra sub for free. We sat outside and ate our food with sand flies dive-bombing us from every direction.

It was one of those summer nights with lots of stars in the sky and bunches of kids cruising up and down Hertel Avenue. Every once in a while, two cars would drag race down the street right in front of us. Most of the time, it was the Battaglia twins in their '70 Superbird taking on all comers. The smoke from the burnouts and the sounds of the engine were music to my ears.

I started to get the feeling that fast cars were going to be part of my life. The faster and louder they were, the more I wanted one.

When we finished, I drove Cindy and Victor over to the Pacificos house and dropped them off. When Cindy was getting out of the car, I gave her $3 to give to her sister for my ticket. She took it and assured me Stephanie would have it that night.

A few days later, I walked into the house while my father was sitting at his desk doing paperwork.

He turned to me with his glasses on the end of his nose and said, "I guess I accidently opened a letter meant for you, sorry, I opened this. I thought it was a check from one of my customers. I know I'm stuck in the fifties, but it's another strange thing from that girl that's not your girlfriend, that you spend a lot of time with, talk to on the phone almost every night, and now I guess you are now going to marry."

That was the longest sentence my dad had ever said to me. I had to think quickly to try to cover my tracks.

"Dad, what the heck are you talking about?"

He handed the letter to me.

I opened the letter. It contained three dollars and a note.

I am retuning this three dollars to you. I have a job and could easily support us. And besides, it was for your seventeenth birthday!

Love,
Your future wife,
Stephanie

The Piña Colada Story

My cousin Ronnie's parents had their twenty-fifth wedding anniversary at the Granada Hotel's Ballroom. There were a couple hundred people invited, and it felt more like a wedding than an anniversary party.

One thing that they knew how to do was throw a party, and what a party it was!

The banquet room was huge, with high ceilings, with the plaster flowers painted gold. It seemed like our entire family, including all the kids, were there. When the orchestra took a break, there was a DJ playing music for the younger crowd. My cousin Harrison sang Sinatra with the orchestra, and my father sang a few big band era songs with my aunt Vera. My Uncle Paul did his Vaudevillian tap dance routine from the 1930s. I was proud to see my talented family performing all together for my aunt and uncle's party.

I hung out with all of my cousins by the staircase watching all the action. We were dressed in our disco best and watching all the activity in the busy hotel lobby.

"The bartender just quit," my cousin Jennifer told me while pulling me and her brother Ronnie back toward the banquet room.

"What can we do about that?" I asked.

"Get behind the bar and start pouring some drinks," she told us.

When my cousin Jennifer told you to do something, you did it without hesitation. And besides, what seventeen-year-old boy wouldn't jump at the chance to be a bartender?

"Ronnie, do you think we can use this opportunity to meet chicks?" I asked.

"Hey stupid, all the chicks here are related to us!" was all he said.

"Just our luck, the one time we're asked to bartend, there aren't any eligible girls around!"

My father then walked over and told me, "You two, stop talking and get behind there and start working," as he pointed toward the bar.

"Okay," I said. "We'll give it a try."

Before I knew what happened to me, I was behind the bar with Ronnie acting like I knew what I was doing. It was easy enough to open beers and serve them, and it was easy to pour the wine into glasses, but making piña coladas was another story.

The "Piña Colada" song was very popular at that time, and everyone was asking for one. "Piña colada," "Piña colada" we heard ten times in the first five minutes behind the bar. The supplies were there to make them, so was the oversized blender, but we had no idea what the recipe was. We kept throwing pineapples, rum, cream, and sugar into the blender until we finally hit it right. We made them as fast as we could, and put them onto the bar, and they were gone as fast as we made them.

Ronnie and I started to sample the leftover concoctions in the bottom of the blender. Neither one of us had ever drank liquor before. They were so sweet and tasted like a vanilla milkshake, but most milkshakes aren't loaded with shots of 90 proof rum made by kids that had no idea what they were doing.

Within a few minutes, we had a line of people asking us for one of our special piña coladas. We kept making them, pouring them, putting them on the bar, and drinking the leftovers.

Over the next hour, we both started to act and look like we were two drunken sailors on leave. Our version of the piña colada was filled with lots of sugar, tropical rum, and coconut juice. Ronnie and I didn't realize what was happening to us until it was too late.

When the party ended, both of us were still behind the bar trying our best to keep upright while still making the star drink of the night. Uncle Harrison came and got Ronnie and me when we started walking toward the car. We were doing our best to hold each other up when all of a sudden everything started spinning. I remember sitting up in the back of the station wagon surrounded by gifts wondering what was going on and seeing Ronnie passed out lying next to me. The next thing I knew, I was waking up in the attic at Ronnie's house, still in my silk shirt and polyester pants, wishing that I had never heard the lyric "If you like Pina Coladas, getting caught in the rain."

CHAPTER 25

As the steamy disco-fueled summer of 1979 continued to roll on, a major announcement allowed me to attend my first concert.

"Phone for you," my mother screamed up the stairs to me.

"Who is it?" I asked.

"It's Ronnie."

"Did you hear the announcement?" Ronnie yelled at me. "The Bee Gees are coming to Buffalo!"

Having the Bee Gees come to Buffalo was like the Beatles showing up in your town in the sixties. The effect they had on all of our lives could never be duplicated. They *were* the music we listened to. They *were* the clothes we wore. They *were* everything.

The flashing lights, the disco ball, the dancing—all came from them. They *were* the soundtrack of our lives. They *were* the entire disco era.

"When?" I asked.

"August 16, my brother can get us tickets, are you in?"

"How many can he get?"

"As many as you want, some girl that likes him and the band works in the Aud's ticket office."

I hung up and called Jack. Both he and Stephanie were in. Matt Pasquale was in. Cindy and Gina were in. Victor and Charlie were in. Andy wasn't in. He was too cheap to buy the tickets for both he and his girlfriend.

We needed eight tickets, and we got them. The tickets were nineteen dollars each with a one-dollar surcharge for a total of twenty dollars. I couldn't drive down to the Aud box office fast enough to buy them.

"Hey, Mom, I got them!" I said, walking into the house.

"Got what?"

"The tickets!"

"You got a ticket? Your dad knows a lot of cops. He probably can get you out of it."

"Mom, the Bee Gees! I got the concert tickets!"

My mom walked out of the kitchen. She was in a pantsuit and all dressed up. When she was dressed like that, I knew that something special was going on.

"I got you, ha. I think you might have to wear something special that night," she told me. "Tonight is coffee night. We will have to eat early and clean up the dishes and go somewhere special before everyone comes over."

On "coffee night," my parents' friends and our relatives would show up and eat doughnuts from Mr. Donut, drink way too much coffee, and smoke way too many cigarettes. The ladies would sit in the kitchen and gossip, and the men would sit in the living room watching television. They would laugh and argue until about ten o'clock, and then they would all leave at once.

My Uncle Paul and Aunt Lee would always come over first with a dozen doughnuts. Uncle Pat and Aunt June would bring pastries, and the Muffalettos would bring the almond rings. Aunt Pat and Uncle Joe would bring her famous brownies.

I knew what "wearing something special" meant. We would be going to Pantastik to get some new clothes for the concert. We went to the store, and I picked up my first pair of Jordace dress jeans and a new polyester print shirt. The usual salesgirls were there, and they approached us as we walked in. They steered me toward the newest jeans and the new shirts. I tried on a bunch of shirts in front of the floor-length mirrors and settled on a patterned peach-colored silk shirt.

I was ready for the concert.

My mother and I walked out of the store, and something made me stare up at the Pantastik neon sign. It was a hot summer night, and the sign's neon was so bright it made me look at it. It had two people shoulder to shoulder running wearing jeans in a Peter Max type of painting. It was such a great logo, and the colors were so seventies it made you want to run back in and buy another pair of jeans.

We got back in plenty of time for coffee night. I put my plastic Pantastik bag upstairs and greeted my relatives from the front porch. As the usual people arrived at our house, I was asked multiple times if I was ready for a new school and what it was like losing out on my senior year at Brennan.

I sat on the porch for the rest of the night and listened to the conversations of my parents and their friends. I remember thinking that when I get older I would be lucky to have the type of friends and relationships they had with the people closest to them.

Listening to the men argue about how bad President Carter was, how bad the Bills were going to be this year, and whether Fords were better than Chevys, always made me laugh. It seemed like every time they got together, the discussions were the same, but they still got together week after week, year after year, decade after decade, and spent time together like it was a new experience each time.

The ladies, on the other hand, only talked about what their kids were doing, who was getting divorced, and who was on a diet.

The day of the concert our entire group was at Bay Beach in Canada swimming and hanging out. You could feel the buzz about the concert all over the beach. Bee Gees songs were being played on every transistor radio that was stuck in the sand, getting us ready for the concert that night.

The topic of conversation all over the beach was the concert, and it seemed like everyone was going.

"Do you have tickets for tonight?" Augie asked me.

"I'm going with seven other people," I told him.

"Seven people, how did you get that many tickets?"

"Sometimes it ain't what you know, it's who you know," I said with a smile as I walked by him into the water.

Bay Beach was down the road from Crystal Beach. The beach was connected to an amusement park of the same name that we all loved to go to. It had a roller coaster called the Comet that was the greatest roller coaster I have ever been on. Crystal Beach was one of the most beloved places to go to in the Buffalo area for generations. Sadly it closed in 1989.

When I got home and showered up, I felt like Tony from *Saturday Night Fever* getting dressed. My tan looked good; my hair was blond, parted in the middle and shoulder length. I put on the peach-colored shirt, my gold chains, my Gruen LED watch, dress jeans, and platform shoes.

As I was getting dressed, I looked at myself in the mirror, and for that moment, I was Tony Manero, just like in *Saturday Night Fever*. And I was going to see the Bee Gees at the Aud with thousands of other people.

"Have fun at the concert, drive safe, and keep an eye on your friends while you're there" were my marching orders as I was walking out the door.

I said goodbye and ran out to the car. Matt was already waiting for me in the car.

"You ready?" I asked him.

"Ready as I'll ever be!" he yelled at me and high-fived me at the same time.

I drove over to Stephanie's to fill up the car with kids and get to the concert. Ronnie drove with his brother and sisters to the concert separately because they were sitting together.

KB 1520 was playing the Bee Gees nonstop the entire day, and that was what I had playing on my AM radio the whole way there. When we pulled up, everyone was waiting in the driveway.

Mr. and Mrs. Pacifico were sitting on the porch. All three of the sisters were dressed in their Funky brand polyester disco dresses, each one so pretty in their own way with their dark feathered hair and tans. I stared at them before I got out of the car.

"You guys all look so nice," Mrs. Pacifico said to me as I walked up. "I wish I were going with you!"

She laughed and went back to reading her magazine. Mr. Pacifico, as usual, didn't say anything. It was so hot that night it seemed like the entire neighborhood was on their porches cooling off and staring at us.

The girls all looked like they could have been dancing in the dance competition in *Saturday Night Fever*. The dresses were brightly colored polyester with high-heeled shoes. They had gold chains and bright lipstick on.

"Why didn't you ask Debbie to go?" Stephanie asked me as we waited for Jack to show up.

"She told me she didn't want to go."

"What girl wouldn't want to see the Bee Gees?" she asked me.

"And go with a guy as good lookin' as me!"

When Jack finally showed up, the girls got in with him. I looked at Stephanie as she got in the front seat with Jack, and I wished she were going with me instead. Victor and Charlie jumped in the Camaro with Matt and I, and we took off. They were as psyched as we were to be going to the concert. We had the windows rolled down and were blasting the *Saturday Night Fever* eight-track on the stereo. As we drove downtown, I started to think it was just my luck that three beautiful girls were going to be sitting with us, and my date was my next door neighbor.

When we arrived, there were people standing outside the Aud smoking and talking everywhere. It was such a hot, humid night you could cut it with a knife. Roaming through the crowds were people with large bags selling bootleg Bee Gees concert T-shirts for ten dollars. The popcorn and peanut salesman were there, and so was Mister Softee, all adding to the confusion and excitement.

When we walked through the front doors of the arena, it *was* the world's largest disco. The buzz in the atrium was deafening, people were walking in every direction, and they were dressed like they were going to meet the Bee Gees.

I saw Ronnie waiting for us in the corner and walked over to him.

"We're here, can you believe it?" he asked me.

"Thanks to Harrison, we are!"

Ronnie's eyes then went toward Stephanie and her sisters as they walked up behind me.

"They are so gorgeous, I don't know why you haven't dated Stephanie yet," he told me.

We walked to our seats past every kind of Bee Gees souvenir you could think of. There were T-shirts, sweatshirts, necklaces, and Bee Gees socks. There were posters, jackets, books, and even albums for sale.

Our seats were in the Oranges or the highest section of the arena. We were to the left of the stage. When I looked at the stage, roadies were all over it like worker ants, each one adjusting something and yelling at each other. They were testing the lights on the stage floor that were made to look like the dance floor from *Saturday Night Fever*. Laser lights were flying in every direction, and in white lights the name BEE GEES was flashing on and off. The speakers were stacked to the ceiling of the arena.

Stephanie and Jack sat on one side of me, and Matt on the other. The other four with us sat right behind us in the next row. The buzz from the atrium had now found its way into the arena. I had never felt such electricity in an audience before.

"I have never seen a laser," I told Stephanie as their green lights flew around us.

"Neither have I. Will you look at that stage, it's unbelievable!"

When all the sound checks were complete, the lasers adjusted and the lights working the arena went totally dark. There was no opening act, just the Bee Gees. Immediately people started lighting their lighters. It looked like thousands of little stars in the dark sky.

Girls were screaming, and everyone was yelling.

Then after a few minutes, as sudden as the lights went off, the spotlights went on, and there stood Robin, Maurice, and Barry Gibb all dressed in white pants with silver shirts. The first note of "Night Fever" was played, and the stage floor started to pulsate with the music. All sixteen thousand people stood up and stayed there for the rest of the concert. The band had an entire horn section, backup singers, and multiple guitar players. It looked like a full orchestra was behind them.

The green lasers started flying around the arena, the lights flashed, and we were all part of *Saturday Night Fever*. Barry did most of the talking. His long hair and beard made him look like some sort of a Greek god. He told us about how the brothers started out in

Australia and moved to England, how they developed their harmonies and wrote their music.

They played their new hits and their old ones for nearly two hours. The crowd roared for each song and went crazy for the disco songs. The floor of the stage pulsated with the music, and the Bee Gees sign flashed too. People were dancing in their seats, in the aisles, and with each other. The concert was done without missing a beat.

It was the best concert I have ever seen.

When we walked out to the now-cool summer night, our ears were ringing, and people were still dancing and singing the Bee Gees songs we had just heard. What a great time we all had.

Every time I hear a Bee Gees song, I think back to the night that a little bit of disco magic happened right before my eyes.

CHAPTER 26

As the summer came to an end, I tried out for the Washington High School football team. I thought it would be a long shot for me to make it. Washington always had a good team and had made it to the championship game two out of the last three years. The tryouts usually attracted over 150 players, and being an unknown senior, I didn't think they would take me.

I told my father how hard I thought it would be to make the team.

In his usual way, he told me, "Go out and play like it's your last game. You go out there tomorrow and find the biggest guy on the team and knock him into next week."

Well, at least he didn't tell me to "win one for the Gipper!"

The last week of summer was very busy with the football tryouts and a surprise party for my father's fiftieth birthday on August 29. Mom planned a dinner at Antonio's Italian Restaurant on Elmwood Avenue.

Antonio was a friend of my dad's since high school, and my parents ate there all the time. The restaurant was dark, had red fleck wallpaper, black vinyl chairs, and rounded booths for your 1970s ultimate dining pleasure. The bar had a piano in the far corner with a bartender that looked like Jimmy Durante.

It was my job to hide all the cars in the parking lot across the street so my father would be surprised when he walked in. The Thursday coffee group along with more of my aunts and uncles were there to greet him when he walked in. He was surprised when he made his entrance.

The smile on his face when everyone screamed "Happy birthday!" was great. We had the entire restaurant to ourselves. My father and Aunt Vera sang while Joe "Bags" played the piano.

Our Italian buffet was great, as was the cake from Bluebird Bakery.

At the end of the night, when my father told everyone goodbye, he had tears in his eyes. He had just sung "Mama" with Aunt Vera. It is an Italian folk song about a mother's love. I know he was thinking about my grandma as he sang that song.

When I was leaving, he called me over and told me how proud he was to have me as a son. He hugged me and gave me a kiss.

That was the last time he ever did that.

The next day was the first day of tryouts. I took my dad's advice, and I hit every big guy on the team. I didn't stop until the whistle blew. There were a bunch of Catholic school players that had transferred to Washington trying to make the team too. I had played against them before. They were good players, and we stuck together.

"Brennan, right?" John Hogan asked me during one of our wind sprints.

"Yep, Wedgewood?" I asked him.

"I hope we both make the team so we can show these public school kids how the Catholic school kids play."

There it was. I had made my first friend at my new school. John was a big, strong lineman that I knew would make the team. I remember lining up against him last year and having a tough time playing against him.

After the first five practices, the coaches were making their final cuts. A bunch of freshman had already been sent back to their West Side Little League Football teams. Another group of kids cut themselves by missing a practice.

As the coach called out the names of the players that should report back on Monday, I stood off to the side wondering if I had made it.

One of the neighborhood kids walked over to me and said, "If you made it, it's only because I put in a good word!"

I had to laugh because *he* got cut!

195

He hasn't said my name yet. If I don't make it, I'm going to Cardinal Rooney even if they don't want West Side kids there. I have to play football my senior year, I told myself.

The coach said my name. He terribly mispronounced it. His version sounded like "car navel," but it was close enough. He said my name. I made the team!

What a relief. I ran home from the Hidden Diamonds field and told my father.

"Made the team, made the team!" I yelled from our front hall.

Most of the other Catholic school kids made the team too. Coach Bumgarner said that the players that had transferred from Catholic schools to Washington in the past had been well trained and disciplined players, and the type of players he wanted on his team.

It was quite a rush making the team. The coach had over 150 players to choose from, and he picked me. I knew that I would be looked up to at the new school because I was on the team. I also hoped that there would be plenty of cheerleaders around to show me the ropes.

On Monday, defensive coach Mackiewicz asked me what position I played.

"You look like a good tackler, ever play any D?" he asked.

I told him I had played every position except quarterback and that I was willing to play anywhere as long as I was playing. I ended up running back kicks and punts and playing guard.

I walked to practice every day with Vinny Garino. He lived down the street from me, and we had played baseball together since we were kids. Vinny was definitely the "big man on campus" at Washington. Every single practice had groups of girls there watching him and waiting to talk to him after we finished. He introduced me to all of them. I have to admit it was going to be weird having girls in school with me after going to an all-boys school for the last three years.

The night before school started, I was very nervous. Ronnie wasn't going to be with me for senior year. Neither was Jamie, Johnnie Porkchop, Andy, or any other friends from Brennan. It sure was going to be different.

I tossed and turned all night and thought about how unfair it was that Brennan closed. I thought about how hard I worked to make all the teams I played on there. I thought about how important it was to me to have my graduation picture hanging in the hall outside the main office.

I thought about the friends I wouldn't be seeing again in homeroom the next day, especially my cousin Ronnie, who always looked out for me. I never was comfortable with change, and this was going to be a big one. I thought about all the fun times we had at the dances and how that school felt like home even when I walked in it the first time. The last thing I thought about before I fell asleep was would I still be as close with Stephanie and her family.

When the alarm went off, I jumped out of bed to take a shower, and of course my dad was in there using all the hot water.

"Hurry up!" I screamed. "I'm not going to be late on the first day of school!"

He walked out looking half asleep.

"Dad, I'm a senior in a school with eight hundred girls. I get first dibs on the shower in the morning, new rule!" I told him.

I ran downstairs and quickly ate a bowl of Quisp cereal. I grabbed a notebook and walked toward the door, and my first day of my last year of high school was about to begin.

"Do you want me to drive you to school this morning?" my mother asked me.

My mother knew that this day was going to be hard on me, and she was trying to help me out, as usual.

"No thanks, Mom, I am going to walk to school with Vinny."

The walk to school took about ten minutes. I approached the ancient school and looked at the huge purple doors. Washington's colors were purple and white, and when I walked into the hallway, almost everything was either purple or white.

I don't know what I expected when I walked into my homeroom. But what I found out was, kids are kids. It didn't matter if it was a public school or a Catholic school. Most of them sat there half asleep, still wishing it were summer vacation, or it was just a bad dream that they were back in school.

My homeroom teacher was a social studies teacher named Mr. Niro. I immediately liked him, especially when he pulled me aside and said that any way he could help me he would. He told me that it must be tough under the circumstances coming to a new school as a senior, and that he had looked at my folder, knew I was a good student, and had never been in trouble.

Wow, I thought, another teacher that cared about me.

He was right, and within a few days, I knew my way around and felt very comfortable in the huge school.

Jack also went to Washington. We had lunch together until we obtained early dismissal and were allowed to leave school at 11:30 a.m. He had many more neighborhood friends at the school than I did. He did his best to introduce me to as many of them as possible.

I kept in touch with Stephanie that first week, but I had to do my best to make friends at the new school. I hung around the football team in the halls and the cafeteria. On Friday nights, the team would get together and hang out, sometimes at a house or just walk around the neighborhood in our jerseys talking about the game the next day.

Some of the players were drinking, partying, and acting stupid. Once I figured out who the idiots were, I stayed clear of them. No drugs and no drinking for me.

As was true at Brennan, wherever there was a football team, the girls weren't far away. And if you were friends with Vinny G, there were usually ten girls around him.

He and I became good friends over the first few weeks of practice and school.

Most game nights after walking around the neighborhood, we ended up at Michelle's house. She lived in a large house in the well-to-do area of the Upper West Side. We usually ordered from Mr. Pizza and drank cherry Crush to celebrate.

At one of the parties, I noticed a girl that immediately caught my attention. I was never introduced to her, but she was so pretty that every boy there was looking her up and down. She looked familiar to me, but I just couldn't place her.

On Monday, I was at my locker getting ready go home when I noticed the girl from the party walking toward me. She had long black hair that I hadn't noticed on Saturday. She looked at me out of the corner of her brown eyes when she walked by.

This girl, I thought, could easily make me forget Stephanie.

I ran over to Vinny G's locker and asked him who she was.

"Her name is Renee, don't even bother," he told me.

"She has a rule to not date anyone from her school. It's written in stone, and she's out of your league."

Well, just my luck, another girl that was out of my league!

"We'll have to see about that," I told him.

He laughed at me and said, "Lots of luck with that one!"

So her name was Renee. I remembered seeing her at the Brennan dances, but she had gotten so much prettier since then.

The football season was going great. We were 5–0 and in first place. It seemed like Renee was everywhere I went. One day when I was getting books from my locker to go home, she walked by me again and smiled.

"Did you go to Brennan?" she asked me as she looked at my Brennan letterman jacket. "My cousin went there. He had the same jacket," she said and walked away.

As she walked away, she made the mistake of looking back at me. Right then, I knew I had a chance with her. My heart skipped a few beats; then I felt someone hit me.

"Wow, she actually talked to you! That's a lot further than most guys around here get," Vinny said.

"You haven't seen me work my magic. I'm going to get that girl to go out with me."

"I'll be by your house for practice at two thirty. Work some more of that magic and try to get the car so we don't have to walk to practice in the rain."

After going to a private school, the classes at Washington were very easy. For the first time in my high school career, I had over a 95 average. (It probably was a result of me not knowing anyone and actually paying attention in class.)

I asked Jack to come out with the team and go to the parties. He always said no. When I spoke to Stephanie, she told me that she wanted to start going out and having fun like I was instead of just watching TV at her house.

On one occasion, we did get the Brennan group together and went to our favorite place to eat, the Casa Di Pizza for subs and pizza like we had done so many times before.

The "Cas" hadn't changed at all. The food was still great, and our jukebox was still there with songs waiting for us to play, but what wasn't the same was all of us.

It was sad. We were at different schools, and we were now heading in different directions. Our friendships had sadly changed. Our lives, in a few short weeks at different schools, had changed too. Yes, our group would always be friends, but closeness we had felt was now gone.

Matilda was still our waitress and still didn't like to serve us. We made sure we asked her for separate checks for old times' sake. I wasn't sure, but I think she finally smiled at us a few times while we were there. So maybe she had changed too.

Stephanie was skating in the mornings and called me several times to take her to her practice. I had no problem going in the Camaro to pick her up and watch her skate.

I told her one morning that I had met a girl that I really liked.

"I met this girl in school, she was very pretty, and I think she likes me."

"What's her name?" she asked.

"Renee, she started talking to me after she saw the Brennan letterman jacket."

"I know who she is. She has friends that go to O'Malley with me. She's so cute!"

I have to admit, I didn't know if that was good or bad that she passed Stephanie's evaluation. But at least she didn't say she was "out of my league."

The football team continued rolling along. We were 6–0 before we lost our first game to South Tech. We ended our season with a win over Grover Cleveland, our rival, and made it to the playoffs with a seven wins, one loss, and one tie record. The team that we tied, Burgard, was the team we played in the first playoff game.

We easily beat them 18–6.

After that game, there was a party at Mike Scinta's house. When I got there, Renee was there too. When I looked at her, to be honest, she was the first girl that made me stop thinking about Stephanie. She was outgoing, well liked, and very pretty in a preppy kind of way. I wanted to believe that the fact that I had come from a Catholic school gave me a chance with her.

She congratulated me on the win, and we talked for a few minutes.

"I might have to eat my words, but I think she's interested in you," Vinny said to me while he stuffed a piece of cheese and pepperoni in his mouth.

"Can you stop talking with your mouth full? It's gross! She obviously has good taste and likes good-looking, well-bred Catholic school boys!" was my reply.

I couldn't help but think he was right because I caught her looking at me a few times during the night. Did I really have a chance with a girl as pretty as she was? I asked myself on the walk home that night.

The Buffalo Public Schools championship game was called the Harvard Cup. It was always played on Thanksgiving morning and televised on public television. My entire family was at the game—Dad, Mom, my Aunt Pat—and about three thousand fans were all screaming at the start of the game.

We played Jemison High School. They had won the championship the last two years. The weather was awful. It was pouring through the entire game.

I remember taking my helmet off during the National Anthem and getting soaked to the bone. Freezing water poured down my back all the way to my underwear. We were standing in about two inches of mud. I knew it was going to be a hard game to win against the defending champions.

Jemison had a great team and ended up beating us 20–6. Even though we lost, it was a great end to our season. We finished with seven wins, two losses, and one tie.

We had another party the next night to celebrate our season. The cheerleaders were in charge and had no problem filling a house on Parkdale Avenue with what seemed like the entire school. Again Renee was there, and I talked to her all night. At the end of the night, I asked her to go to the movies. She accepted.

Hey, Vinny, I guess there *is* an exception to every rule.

CHAPTER 27

Renee and I went to dances and hung out at teen night. I went to her house and watched TV. A couple of times we double-dated with Jack and Stephanie. Stephanie told me how pretty she was and that we made such "a cute couple."

We met each other at our lockers, and I walked her home nearly every day. Every night we talked on the phone and made plans for the weekend.

At one teen night dance, we held hands for most of the night. I gave her a kiss when I dropped her off. I really was starting to fall for her and forget about Stephanie.

In December, I tried out for the Washington hockey team. I made the team as the starting goalie. It was made up of a small group of players I knew from my Front Park days. The team was not very good. The year before they had won the championship, but nine seniors had graduated, and they had a bunch of lower classman that weren't ready to play varsity hockey.

One of the boys on the team was working at an Italian Restaurant called Upstairs Downstairs. He told me that they were looking to hire a busboy.

"I'll tell my boss, Mary, that you used to bus tables at Roseland's and you had to quit because of hockey," Joe told me.

"But I've never worked in a restaurant before," I told him.

"You should've seen some of the busboys they've hired since I've been there. Trust me, they'll hire you," he told me as we walked out of practice.

When I got home that night, I called and asked for an interview. My father told me to wear a suit because people that own restaurants like people working for them that dress well and present themselves neatly. I went into the interview not really knowing what to expect.

Upstairs Downstairs was named after a British television show on PBS. It was on Elmwood Avenue in an old house converted into a restaurant. Patrons were able to eat either "upstairs" or "downstairs" depending upon how busy it was.

I walked into the foyer, and I knew instantly that I was going to work there. I think it was because it reminded me of my grandmother's house with its ornate oak staircase and beautiful fireplace that greeted you as you entered. And one other thing, the smell of sauce cooking and garlic in the air was just like a trip back to her house too.

As I walked in and looked around the first floor, I was greeted by a man behind the bar with white hair and a warm smile. He introduced himself to me as Phil, one of the owners' father and the bartender.

I went into the office upstairs, and Mary, one of the owners, was sitting behind a desk with papers piled all over it.

She looked at me and asked, "What school do go to, honey?"

"Washington this year because I went to Brennan and it closed last year," I said.

"You went to Brennan?" she asked me.

"Yes, ma'am, I did," I answered.

"You have the job," she told me.

"Aren't you going to ask me anything else?" I asked.

"Nope, you Catholic school kids are always good people to hire. Be here Thursday, you start at five" was all she said.

So there it was. I was hired for my first real job just because I went to Brennan.

I later found out that one of her best friends, who eventually became mayor of Buffalo, was a Brennan graduate and always recommended the Brennan kids for jobs to Mary.

My first night working would have been a complete disaster except that Phil was behind the bar and more than willing to help me. His daughter, Carolyn, was the other owner, and he had come out of retirement to help them run the restaurant.

He took one look at me as I was running around having no clue what to do or how to bus tables and said, "Have you ever done this before, kid?"

"No, sir, I haven't," I said to him as sweat was pouring down my face while I juggled glasses trying to set a table.

"What's your name, son?" he asked.

"Nick Carnavale, sir."

"Who's Pat, Joe, Charlie, and Paul Carnavale to you?"

"They're my uncles, sir."

"They've been my friends for fifty years," he told me, patting me on the back.

"Is Nick your father?"

"Yes, he is," I told him.

"He has the best voice on the West Side!" he told me.

From that point forward, Phil was my best friend at the restaurant.

I worked on Thursday and Sunday nights from four until closing. It was a great place to work. The waitresses were college age and were wild, and I knew most of the cooks and dishwashers from the neighborhood.

Phil showed me how to quickly set tables and take care of the costumers. I poured water, served bread, answered the phone, took reservations, and ran up and down the stairs with dirty dishes all night. Time flew by, I made lots of tips, and I had money to spend on Renee.

My life suddenly was very busy with school, work, hockey, and a girlfriend.

I started to feel like I had a real girlfriend for the first time in my life, and a very pretty one at that. Walking around school, everyone asked me if we were going steady, and my response was "Not yet."

She came and watched every one of my hockey games. They were played at the Aud where the Buffalo Sabres played. It was a great feeling looking up in the stands having a special girl watching me.

When Valentine's Day came, I had to work that night. I made a lot of tips and worked until almost eleven. I went to Renee's house after I finished. I gave her a stuffed animal, a card, and some candy.

And since it was Valentine's Day, I thought that we had dated long enough and it was the right time to be going steady.

"Renee, will you be my steady girlfriend?" I asked her.

"No, we still have to get to know each other better, and we are too young to do that steady stuff," she said.

I didn't argue with her, but I thought that answer was kind of strange. We were meeting at our lockers three or four times a day, she was at every hockey game, we weren't dating anyone else, we were kind of going steady already, weren't we?

I should have recognized that something wasn't right when I opened my Valentine's gift. It consisted of a card and a coupon for a free Whopper at Burger King. *Maybe she's not very good at this dating thing*, I immediately thought. *I'll just have to give her some time.*

At the restaurant we were very busy, and I started to make really great tips. I was now working three nights a week until about ten.

Phil was the bartender, and I worked right along with him every night. I knew he liked me a lot, and he treated me like I was part of his family. As it turned out, he knew my entire family very well. He had stories about some of my uncle's exploits in the early 1930s that made me laugh. He always said that the only good about growing up during the Depression was baseball and that it was the most important thing in his life.

After a few months being a busboy, he started training me to be a bartender. I never told him about my previous bartending experience! My best friend during training was an old "Mr. Boston" drink-mixing book that my father gave me. When I didn't know how to make a drink, I just looked it up and made it. After a few weeks of training, Phil started letting me close the restaurant and take the night's receipts to his house down the street. I was only seventeen years old and responsible for closing a restaurant! I was very proud that Phil trusted me with such an important duty.

I would put the night's receipts in a paper bag, stuff it under my shirt, and deliver it down Elmwood Avenue to his house. He took me under his wing and taught me how to deal with crazy customers, deliveries, and how to handle the rush that restaurants get at certain times of the day.

He was truly a gentleman in everything he did. I enjoyed every second that I worked with Phil. He told about winning the MUNY baseball championship in 1932 like it happened yesterday. He just had a way with words that made you feel like you'd known him your entire life. He had great stories of playing baseball at the legendary Offermann Stadium in Buffalo too.

"They should have never torn that place down," he told me every time we talked about baseball. The twinkle in his eye every time he talked about baseball told me he must have been a great player.

He also reminded me daily how much he loved the Yankees. I never had the heart to tell him that I hated the Yankees as much as he loved them.

I never knew either of my grandfathers, but I would have wanted them to be like Phil. He was the first adult that treated me like I was an adult too. Whenever I think of Phil, I smile and get a warm feeling knowing that I was very lucky to have known someone as special as him.

Years after the restaurant closed, one of Phil's former customers became the producer of the Murphy Brown television show. She named the bartender Phil after my friend. What a perfect gesture for one of the nicest people I have ever met.

The Friday after Valentine's Day, I left work and went to Renee's house. I could tell something wasn't right. And it wasn't because I smelled like fish frys. We talked for a while, and I left her house at curfew time, 11:00 p.m. I went home very tired and went to sleep.

The next morning, my cousin Ronnie called me and said that he had seen Renee leaving a bar the night before with a bunch of her friends.

"Nick, I saw Renee leaving the Hotel California late last night. She was with a bunch of other girls."

"Are you sure it was her? At what time?" I asked.

"I'm positive, it was about twelve thirty."

I drove over to Renee's house. I asked her if she wanted to go to the Record Theatre to look at some new albums before I had to go to work. On the way there, I asked her if there was a problem with anything.

"No problems, why are you asking me something like that?"

"Renee, tell me the truth, did you go to Hotel California last night?"

She hesitated for a few seconds and said, "Yes I did, and I went with some of my older friends. We aren't going out steady, you know. I can do what I want."

The answer she gave sounded like one she had been practicing, waiting for the right time to use it on me for a month.

"So let me get this straight, I take you out, spend my money on you, and drop you off, then you get dressed up for a night of barhopping without me?" I asked her.

There was no response.

I felt like I had been stabbed in the heart. *Here we go again*, I thought. *I like this girl, and she is treating me like shit.*

"My friends told me I was too young to get tied down to one high school–aged boy. That I needed to start going out to the bars to start meeting some more interesting older men, and not spend all my time with you."

What a mean thing to say to someone that obviously liked you. If she didn't like me anymore, she should have just told me. And she shouldn't blame it on her friends. Just admit that your feelings have changed. That is, if she ever really did like me at all.

We never made it to the record store. I turned the car around and drove her back home without saying anything more. When we got to her house, I opened the door to the Camaro and told her, "I guess it's over."

She got out of the car without saying another word to me. I shut the door and drove over to Burger Chef to tell Stephanie what happened.

As I drove away, all I could think of was the Lee Michaels song "Do You Know What I Mean?" The lyrics never made sense to me before, but all of a sudden, they did.

"So I asked her if she still cared, she didn't hear me, she just stared, do you know what I mean?"

CHAPTER 28

I sat in the Burger Chef's parking lot thinking about how hard it was to find a nice girl. When Stephanie walked out after her shift, I called her over. At this point, I didn't care what people said or thought when they saw us together.

"It's over between Renee and me."

"What? What happened?"

"Well, I have been doing things with her, spending my money on her, and dropping her off at home, and then she was going out with her *older friends* looking for *older guys* and barhopping. I mean, I'm at home watching *The Late Show* on the couch, and she is going out behind my back looking for *older, more mature men*. How stupid is that!"

"Nick, slow down. What happened again?"

"I guess I got dumped by someone that wasn't even my girl-friend yet!"

"Nick, I'm so sorry."

"That's why she never wanted to be my girlfriend. I asked enough times to go steady. But the answer was always 'No, not yet, Nick.' It's going to be hard to see her in school every day, but I don't care. She made me feel like shit, and I'm going to make sure that that won't ever happen to me again."

"You didn't deserve that, and she made a big mistake listening to her friends. I have to ignore my sister a lot of the time when she is giving me advice. You seemed so happy with her. I know this is going to hurt."

"I guess I'll be hanging out a little more on Parkside Avenue, is that okay?" I asked.

She smiled and nodded.

"You're always welcome at my house," she said as she got out of the car.

That night at work I was not in a very good mood. The waitresses kept asking me what was wrong. I just ignored them and continued busing tables without talking to anyone.

When I got home late, my dad was waiting for me as he usually did. We talked and counted the dollar bills that filled my pockets. I made over one hundred dollars in tips that night.

"You made more than I did this week," Dad said with a wink.

"Dad, why are girls so stupid?"

"Where did that come from?" he asked me. "I thought we were just counting money."

I explained what had happened earlier that day.

In his "Dad knows best" voice, he told me, "Walk out that door. If you really want to look, there are plenty of other girls around. Did you really think you were going to marry that girl? Do you know how many girls I dated before I met your mom? Did you really think she was the last girl you'd ever date? Forget about her. Aren't there about five hundred other girls in your class you could date?"

When my dad talked to me like that, he made a lot of sense.

"But, Dad, I really liked her a lot."

"It's not easy to say this, but she didn't care about you at all, or else she wouldn't have done that to you. Forget about her. There are other fish in the sea."

I knew that I had to let it go. Even my father's corny "other fish in the sea" line didn't make me feel any better. And for the first time, it really got to me. I realized that all this girl stuff was really without rules, and sometimes it hurt, really hurts, like it did that night. I knew it wasn't the end of the world, but it felt pretty close.

I decided to look forward to the end of the hockey season and graduation in June. And I also started to think about the prom. My big plans for the prom and who I was going to take were ruined again. Who would I take this year? was what I thought about as I fell asleep.

I hung around with Jack and Stephanie for the next few weeks. The saying two's a couple and three's a crowd would have been appropriate to say the least.

Both Stephanie and I wanted to go and do things every time we got together. I was making money and had no problem spending it. Jack was happy staying at his house, or Stephanie's, instead of going out and doing things. Stephanie made a few comments to him that he should be more like me and want to go out and do things.

As winter ended and spring began, baseball tryouts were held. Washington had won the championship the last three years. I went to the tryout fully expecting to make the team. The coach didn't even look at me batting or fielding any balls. After the tryout, he said that he had enough seniors on the team and had to let the younger players stay.

It really didn't upset me that much. I had the feeling that high school was all but over. My high school sports career was over too.

I picked up more days of work at the restaurant and started saving my money for college. I had been accepted at Peter's College and would need all the money I could save.

A group of kids at Washington were talking about a party they were going to on Friday night. One of them asked me if I wanted to go. Being the recently dumped senior in high school that I was, and being asked by a girl in my class to go to a party, I accepted the invitation.

Friday I worked until after ten. I ran home as fast as I could, took a shower, and went to the address where the party was. As I walked up, Van Halen was shaking the house and the neighborhood. There were kids passed out on the front lawn and on the porch.

My intuition told me this wasn't a good situation to be in. When I walked into the front hall, what I saw was very disturbing to me. It immediately became very clear that I was somewhere I shouldn't have been.

The front porch smelled like pot, and when I walked into the apartment, there were people using drugs everywhere. Right in front of me there were two guys snorting cocaine through dollar bills on a glass table and another group with a water bong as big as mom's Hoover vacuum cleaner.

Before I was offered anything, I just walked back out and started walking home. I had become an expert at walking out of parties without being noticed the last few months.

I knew that drugs were all around me, but I had managed to avoid them up to this point in my life. I had to talk to someone about what had just happened. I couldn't talk with my father and mother, because in the seventies you didn't talk with your parents about such things.

I quietly walked back toward home. I went into Elmwood Taco and bought four tacos from Carl, the best basketball player on the West Side. We talked back and forth while he made my order. He asked me a couple of times if everything was okay. I told him it had been a long day as I walked out the door and continued home.

I really wasn't ready to go home yet. As I ate my first taco, I was passing my friend Don's house. I had met him when he owned a hot dog stand that my family went to when I was about ten years old. He had long black hair to his shoulders and ice blue eyes that stared right through you. The way he talked made you feel like you were back in the sixties talking to Jerry Garcia. And he was someone I knew I could talk to about anything that was bothering me.

Especially something like this.

I walked up to his door and saw the TV on and knew it was okay to knock. It was late at night, and he answered his door in his pajamas. His appearance made me laugh and lightened the moment.

"Don, I need to talk to someone about what just happened to me and about crazy girls that dump good guys."

"Come on in, you wan' a Coke?" he asked me.

"Funny you should say *that*," I told him as I walked by him and sat on his beanbag pillow on the floor.

I explained what happened at the party that night. I also told him what happened with Renee.

"You did the right thing just walking away tonight. Don't listen to anyone that tries to get you involved in that drug crap. You did the right thing. Stay away from that stuff and anyone that tries to get you involved in that scene. Nothing good ever comes from that shit."

He also told me that what happened with Renee "happened to me many times, and one day, when you least expect it, the right girl will bump right into you."

I listened to his advice and thanked him for being such a good friend. And I did share a bottle of Coke with him.

When I got up to leave, he told me, "What we just talked about is a secret between the two of us."

He swore that he would never tell anyone what we talked about. He has never mentioned our conversation to this day.

As April began, my thoughts turned toward the prom. Jack and Stephanie were going to both the Washington and O'Malley proms with each other. I began to think about whom I should ask to go with me. After the disaster that happened the year before, I wanted to make a better choice.

I decided to ask a girl named Sharon. She was a friend of Renee's that went to a Catholic school, and I knew she wanted to go to our prom. It was also a good way to get back at her, I thought. I asked her, and she accepted.

I have to say that some of the craziest situations happen as a result of proms. Many people ask their date weeks or months in advance. By the time the prom comes, they like someone else, aren't dating anymore, or are dating someone else. All this confusion leads to many uncomfortable moments.

But it's high school, and I guess it's supposed to be this way.

I knew that Sharon liked a boy that played on the football team with me. But that didn't matter. I wanted a date that would irritate Renee. That was all I cared about.

A few weeks before the prom, I was invited to a party on Baynes Avenue at Michelle's house. Most of the football team was there along with a bunch of the seniors from the neighborhood.

When I walked in, I saw Renee sitting in the kitchen. She immediately looked very nervous. I saw her in school all the time, and it didn't seem to bother her, but for some reason, me walking in bothered her.

Michelle made the mistake of telling me Renee was trying to ask a boy that was at the party to go to the prom with her.

Oh, so that's what is going on, I told myself.

I tried my best to make her as uncomfortable as possible. I wanted to hurt her feelings for what she had done to me. I wanted to hurt her for what Carla did to me. I wanted her to feel the way I did when she did what she did to me.

I definitely succeeded. I kept saying out loud, "Why would anyone want to go to the prom with a high school age boy? Don't older men like going to a prom with high school girls?"

Everywhere she went I stood close by just staring at her and the nerdy guy she was talking to.

I probably shouldn't have been doing what I was or saying what I did, but at this point I didn't care. She had treated me like shit, and this was my chance to get a little revenge.

I kept staying just close enough to her to make her uncomfortable. The guy she was trying to ask to the prom was from a prep school and looked very out of place with a bunch of disco-liking public school kids. He also was smart enough to realize what I was doing.

I'm sure he thought I was going try to pick a fight with him. I didn't. My problem wasn't with him. It was with Renee. He left the party without saying a word to me.

And Renee never got the opportunity to ask him to go to the prom. Mission accomplished!

For some very strange reason, the pizza from LaNova tasted extremely good that night.

CHAPTER 29

The prom was about two weeks away when Jack, Stephanie, and I went to pick out tuxes. The loud 1970s tuxes were giving way to the classic black tux look. In the car on the way to Tuxedo Junction, I sensed some tension between Jack and Stephanie. Both Jack and I were sized for a black tux.

In the car on the way home, the tension continued. Stephanie wanted to go out, and Jack wanted to go back to her house to hang out.

"Can I take you home first?" Jack asked me.

I knew what was coming and, quite frankly, didn't want to get in the middle of another argument.

"Okay," I responded.

The phone rang about an hour later. It was Jack.

"She dumped me, can you believe it? Two weeks before the prom, I have no girlfriend and no date, what am I supposed to do now?"

"I'll be right over," I told him.

I know I shouldn't have felt bad for him after what he did to me the year before, but I still did.

On the ride over to his house, I made another of my "Only with Stephanie" lists.

- The girl I dreamed about going to the prom with now has no date.
- I'm going to the prom with someone I didn't like in that way.

- And my date liked one of my friends from the football team.
- Jack had no date for his prom too.
- And I was right in the middle again.

Maybe I should have suggested that Jack should go with Sharon. She didn't care who took her, she just wanted to go to our prom, and I would go with Stephanie. Then maybe everyone would be happy.

When I got to Jack's, he was very upset.

"She said I needed to be more like you, go out and do things, and most of all, get a job so I can afford to do things like everyone else does."

Like I said, it just kept getting weirder. The girl I cared about the most used me as an example of what a good boyfriend was as she was breaking up with him.

When the prom finally came, I went with Sharon. We had fun. It was good because I had no romantic feelings for her, and she had none for me. Just friends. It was much easier that way.

Jack did not get a date for the prom and stayed home alone that night.

Sharon and I went with Joe from the restaurant and hockey team and his date Annette in his father's Cadillac. Annette was a year behind me at Coronation School. We had been friends for many years.

I also had a nice time making Renee as uncomfortable as possible by picking a table right next to hers. It was fun staring at the rich kid she went with. He already looked like a fifty-year-old accountant, and the look on his face told me he was definitely not having a good time.

The prom was at the Granada Hotel, the same place that my aunt and uncle had their twenty-fifth wedding anniversary. It was a beautiful old hotel built in the 1920s. But the week before, a local television station did an exposé on the terrible condition of the kitchens at the hotel.

Needless to say *no one* ate any food at the prom.

The DJ did his best and only played all 14 minutes of "Rappers Delight" three times.

We had a picnic the next day at Delaware Park. Sharon picked right up where my previous prom dates left off and went to the picnic with another boy from my class she met at the prom.

As I said before, anything goes at proms!

Because I had no romantic interest in her, I didn't care. Most of my friends were there, and we sat around talking by Delaware Lake. It was sad because the kids all sensed that it was the end of high school and we would all be going in different directions.

I knew that feeling all too well because of Brennan closing the year before. The only thing we had left to do was get through the final weeks of school and get through our graduation ceremony.

I did not talk to Stephanie at all for the next three weeks. I wanted to call her and level with her about my feelings, but I couldn't. I was still stuck on the idea that Jack was my friend, and friends don't do that to friends.

One day, Jack called and asked if Stephanie had asked me to go to her prom. I told him no. He hung up without saying anything else. I didn't think he believed me.

I later found out that Stephanie went by herself. I felt bad for her. But I was caught in the middle again. I knew I had to wait for all this craziness to calm down before I did anything with Stephanie.

Washington's graduation was at the end of June. I had my party the same night. It was great with my whole family coming to celebrate.

I did not invite Stephanie.

"Hey, where's Stephanie?" Ronnie asked me while we sat on the front steps of my house.

"Didn't invite her."

"Let me get this straight. She broke up with Jack, you have been chasing her for four years, and you don't invite her to your graduation? How stupid could you be? What are you waiting for? Now is the time to move in on her."

I didn't know what to say to him when he put it that way.

"Ronnie, I just don't know what I'm supposed to do when it concerns Stephanie. I've liked her since the first time I saw her. I've chased her for four years and never kissed her or even really held her hand. I have spent more time with her than any friend I've ever had, and I'm not any closer to going on a real date with her than I ever was."

"I've been telling you since seventh grade that you're too nice. Most of the time, girls don't like nice, they want the bad boys, the troublemakers. They want nice for a brother. You've had so many chances with that girl and you blew every one."

"Thanks, you have such a great way with words."

"Go over there tonight and talk to her. If I knew her, and I do, she is expecting you to go and see her. Don't blow it with her."

It just wasn't the right time. I didn't know when that time would come, but I knew it would be soon.

CHAPTER 30

Before I knew it, July 7, 1980, my eighteenth birthday, arrived. It was a Monday, and I went to work with my father cutting lawns. We worked until the late afternoon. My cousin Joe had called me the day before and told me he was going to bring sauce to my house for a special dinner. (Joe always told my mother that because she was Irish she didn't know how to cook sauce like a real Italian.) Mom told him that her contribution to the party would then center around the cake and other items for dessert.

Joe showed up with a pan filled with sauce, and the party was ready to start. My father, because it was such an important day, broke out the homemade wine a friend had given him. He also bought a box of smelly large cigars to celebrate.

Cousin Joe always enjoyed acting a lot older than he in fact was. When he asked for a glass of wine, my father reluctantly gave him some.

"You know how strong this stuff is?" my father asked him.

"Ya, I can handle it!" was the response.

"Can I interest you in a glass? After all it's your eighteenth birthday, and you're finally legal" my father asked me.

After my involvement in the piña colada bartending fiasco a few months earlier, I was in no hurry to try some of my dad's "Dago Red" wine.

"No thanks, no interest in that stuff!" I said.

My father had a huge smile on his face as he filled Joe's glass multiple times. I don't know what proof that gasoline in a bottle was, but it was definitely more than Joe could handle. Everyone ate spaghetti while Joe sat back and enjoyed the wine. He eventually started eating the pasta and homemade meatballs and topped it off with about five pieces of garlic bread. As my mother cleaned off the table and went to get my cake, my father brought out his cigars.

I sensed that the room was starting to spin by the look on my cousin's face across the table from me. His color was beginning to be a little off as we waited for the cake and other dessert my mother had prepared.

Joe asked for a cigar while he was sipping the wine. He took one puff from the stogie, his face started to turn red, and his eyes started popping out. He covered his mouth, ran through the kitchen and out the back door and into the driveway.

He started throwing up all over the side of our house.

My neighbors Matt and Donnie always came to my birthday parties and were sitting at the table. They jumped up and were staring out the dining room window at Joe as he was on his knees loathing the day he was born.

"Mr. C, he's yacking all over the driveway. Who's going to clean that up!" Matt asked.

"Nicky will, it's his fault, he invited him!"

As all this was going on, I sat quietly thinking about who I was about to go and visit.

When the sound effects and swearing finally finished in the driveway, we were laughing so hard we couldn't put the candles on the Jell-O poke cake my mother made for me.

Every year I looked forward to the Jell-O cake with the home-made whipped cream on top. We would finish it off with an Italian ice cream called spumoni.

When Mom lit the candles, my father was standing, cigar in his mouth, looking out the dining room window at Joe and shaking his head.

"Hey big shot, make sure you hose the driveway down before you come in and eat some of this cake with all that creamy whipped cream, Jell-O, and spumoni ice cream."

With the mention of food, Joe responded by throwing up some more!

"Very funny, Cousin Nick" was all I heard before he started throwing up again.

Once all the commotion stopped, everyone sang "Happy Birthday" to me. I thought about how high school was over and college was starting in eight weeks, and that it had been long enough. I had to go and see Stephanie.

I opened my presents and tried to sneak quietly out the door.

"Where you going?" my mother asked me.

"Mom, I don't have to answer that question anymore, today I am officially an adult!" I said as the screen door slammed behind me. "Don't wait up!" was all I said as I ran down the steps.

I drove to North Buffalo and walked up Stephanie's driveway. I rang the doorbell. She came walking out of her backyard and leaned on the gate. Her brown eyes were piercing me.

"What do *you* want?" she screamed at me.

"I'm here to talk to you."

"Get out!" she yelled at me, pointing at the street.

From inside the house, I heard Gina telling Stephanie, "Renee just called you. She wants to go to Hotel California with you tonight."

She was looking out the window and trying her best to pile on and hurt my feelings.

"You haven't called me for over a month. I had no date to my prom, went to my graduation by myself, and wasn't invited to your graduation. Now get out of my driveway. I never want to see you again. I hate you, I wasted four years of my life on you, I'm through, I'm going to college and don't need any *high school boys* like you in my life anymore, I guess we were never really friends."

At that point, I was going to say what I had to say.

"Are you kidding me? You wasted four years of your life! From what I've seen, you've done pretty much whatever you wanted to do since the first time I saw you. And I waited and waited for you! No one else, you! Stephanie, I've watched you date two of my best friends while I stood by from the back seat like a jerk. I've been there for you since I met you. I got up at four in the morning to drive you to skating. Do you know how hard it has been for me to be next to

221

you in every crazy situation you put me in? 'High school boy,' huh? I know where you got that one! Tell her I said hi too."

She just stared at me with a look of hate that I had never seen from her before. I kept talking without giving her a chance to say a thing.

"Go on tell me to leave! Throw me out! I don't care! Do you know I didn't date girls because I was always waiting, waiting for you! Oh, and one other thing, in case you don't remember, today is my eighteenth birthday and here I am again. I'm here, trying to talk to you! Not anywhere else. I wanted to spend it with you, and only you. Why? Because I care about you! Stephanie, since I met you, I have swallowed my pride so many times I can't count."

I stopped talking and for a few seconds, and we just stood there looking at each other from either side of the gate.

It seemed like we had become enemies, like we were breaking up with each other. But how could we? We weren't even dating. How confusing all this Nick and Stephanie stuff really is.

Then there was that strange silence that we had between us so many times before. *Say something*, I thought. *Don't just stand there staring at me!*

I turned and started to walk away, and then I had one more thing I had to tell her. I finally let her know my true feelings.

"One more thing, Stephanie, I've loved you since the first time I saw you. There I finally said it, after four years. Boy does that feel good that I finally said it! Shit ya, it sure does! Not that you ever cared about anyone except yourself! No one else, only yourself!"

I turned and walked down the driveway hoping she would say something, anything to me.

Call me back, I said to myself. *Say something!* I thought.

She didn't. It was two years before I saw her again.

CHAPTER 31

I couldn't go home the way I was feeling. It was my eighteenth birthday, and I was not going to spend it alone. This was a day to celebrate with friends and family. After all you're finally legal to drink and be held responsible for your actions.

And my plan to spend it with the girl that was most important to me had backfired. Everything was going wrong for me tonight. It's supposed to be a day to remember forever, for all the good things, not the bad ones. I jumped into what was my most reliable friend, my Camaro, and drove away from Stephanie's house.

And there I was driving around alone, through North Buffalo and back to the West Side with nothing but a broken heart and a feeling that I had never experienced before.

I had no girlfriend or anyone to celebrate my birthday with. The entire day had become a disaster. I couldn't go home and let the kids in the neighborhood see that I had no one hanging out with me on such an important day.

I drove down Elmwood past Upstairs Downstairs to see if anyone was still around. But it was already closed.

Continuing down Elmwood, I saw the taillights of Don's yellow Oldsmobile 98 pulling into his driveway. I pulled in behind him.

"What, you again?" he said to me as he got out of the car. "You here for more free advice?"

I didn't say anything and just sat in the car staring ahead.

"What's wrong?" he asked me.

"Everything's wrong," I told him. "It's my eighteenth birthday, another girl that isn't my girlfriend just dumped me. And I…"

He cut me off in midsentence.

"Take your car home and walk back over here. I need to take a shower, and it sounds like you need to take a walk in the fresh air and get your thoughts together. We will solve the world's problems when you get back over here."

I drove home and told my father that the car was back and that Don was going to take me for some tacos for my birthday.

As I walked down Bird Avenue back to his house, I was kind of numb. Everything familiar that I knew during my high school years was now gone forever. The routines, people, and the places were all changing faster than I wanted them to.

At that point, I don't think I really wanted to grow up. I wanted to hang on to everything that was familiar and safe. I knew that kids are supposed to want to grow up, and your eighteenth birthday is the time to leave the past behind and become an adult. But I didn't want to leave anything behind.

I was so confused.

When I got to Don's house, he was sitting on his porch wearing a Hawaiian shirt, jean shorts, flip-flops, and a Mexican sombrero waiting for me. His bushy black mustache along with the sombrero made him look like the Frito Bandito on his honeymoon in Hawaii.

"Can you explain how a girl you weren't dating just dumped you again? I have all night because I know how long your stories can be! I must be getting out of touch with all this relationship stuff as I near my thirtieth birthday!" he told me.

I walked up onto the porch and didn't say a word. He just stared at me as I walked across the porch and sat down on the swing.

I started to laugh. I laughed at the whole situation, especially his outfit. And I was happy he was my friend and that he cared enough about me to want to listen to whatever I had to say.

"You aren't out of touch. I just keep getting involved in all these situations that are so hard to explain. This growing-up stuff is so confusing to me."

I swung back and forth telling him the whole story of Stephanie and me. I told him the whole sad truth.

One thing you can say about Don is he is a good listener. He kept shaking his head every time I told him about another crazy situation I found myself in with Stephanie and all the goofy things that had happened since I met her. And I told him about how strange I was feeling about being officially an adult.

He finally interrupted me and said, "Enough of this crap. Tonight's your eighteenth birthday, right? I'm going to make sure you have some fun. For one night, I'm going to make you forget about this girl and your feelings for her and the other girl too and all the pressure of being a grown-up. Let's go, you're getting a shot at every bar on the strip! For free! My plan works every time! Let's go, and don't forget you're going to party hardy with the king of Elmwood Avenue!"

With that he got up, pulled me out of the swing, and headed me down the stairs. We walked down Elmwood toward Forest Avenue. Don moved like he, in fact, did own the street. Into Mr. Goodbar we went.

Everyone in there knew him. He announced that it was my eighteenth birthday. He told a couple of college-age girls sitting at the bar they had to kiss me for my birthday.

They did come over and kiss me, and the bartender gave me a free shot of Alabama slammer. These were college-age, nice-looking girls kissing me!

"One down!" he yelled as we left.

We walked to Coles next door. He repeated the same routine, and the results were the same. I got a free shot, and there were girls lining up to kiss me!

"Just stick with me, kid, and by the time the night's over, you'll have kissed fifty gorgeous girls, and you'll soon forget about what's her name"!

"It must be that goofy hat you're wearing," I said as we walked past Ozzy's Laundromat and the One Minute Stop.

With his moustache, skinny legs, and loud voice, as we walked down the busy street, it really felt like I was with the king of Elmwood Avenue!

"Two down! Hat or no hat, we're going to have some fun tonight! Let's keep rolling!" he said as he grabbed the handle of the door at the next bar.

When we walked into JP Bullfeathers, Don put his hat on the bartender's head, pulled her close, and whispered something in her ear. She smiled at me and gave me a kiss and a shot too! She had feathered hair and was pretty enough to stop traffic.

At that point I was starting to feel a bit tipsy, but we pressed on down the street with three bars left to hit.

"Three down!" Don screamed as we walked by the Parkview Pharmacy.

"You need to sit on this park bench for a second?" he asked me.

I agreed to sit on the bench and catch my senses. The bench was right in front of the Pantastik store. We talked with the green-and-white glow from the sign behind us.

"Nicky, my boy, you can't let the chicks know they're getting to you. No matter how hard it is, make your mind up that you won't show it. You got me?"

"I'll try, but what about this growing-up stuff?"

"Growing up just happens. When you try to make it happen, that's when the problems start."

We got off the bench and continued walking. We went into the No Name Bar. I got kissed again and drank another shot, a melon ball.

The patrons were all cheering "Nicky, Nicky" as I downed it.

"Four down!" he screamed while waving his sombrero at me as we walked past the Minuette Pizzeria.

So here I was, with a flip-flop–wearing, sombrero-wearing hippie having the time of my life on my eighteenth birthday. Don was making it easy for me to forget what had happened earlier that evening.

We hit Casey's Nickelodeon and Merlin's to round out my one shot at every bar on the strip birthday. At Casey's, another beautiful blond bartender gave me a shot and a kiss that made my head spin.

"Five down! And we'll be right back for something to eat, Pedro," Don yelled as we passed under the Elmwood Taco and Subs sign with the Mexican character on top.

At Merlin's, the owner let me sit on the bar to drink my shot. I knew him because I waited on him many times when he ate at Upstairs Downstairs. He also was a well-known graduate of Cardinal Brennan.

"Six down, Nicky, how you feeling?" the bandito asked me.

Surprisingly, I was okay. The melon balls and Alabama slammers apparently didn't affect me the way a piña colada did!

When we left Merlin's, it was way past midnight. There was only one place still open to get something to eat. We walked back to my favorite late-night place, Elmwood Taco.

Don was still wearing his sombrero when we walked in. He asked if they gave discounts to Mexicans. I thought I was going to die I was laughing so hard.

We bought six tacos, a sausage-all-the-way sub, and large loganberries from the fountain in the window. Outside we went and sat on the same bench I always did watching the world go by.

For a long time, neither of us said anything, just eating and watching the cars speeding back and forth in front of us. To me, at that moment, there was nothing better than sitting with someone that you knew always would look out for you, while eating a sub and tacos, on your eighteenth birthday.

We took turns shooting baskets into the garbage can with the wrappers and our cups. Neither of us had said anything up to this point. Then I looked up at the sign above us. It was a Dr. Pepper sign with "The Elmwood Taco and Subs" written on it. On the top was a caricature of a Mexican bandito. I looked up and started to laugh as hard as I ever had.

"Donnie, is that you?" I asked.

He looked up without missing a beat and said, "Do you know how hard it was for me to climb up there so they could take my picture?"

There is nothing better than a laugh with a good friend to make you feel like everything was ultimately going to be okay.

I thought about what a crazy day it had been. My birthday party, Joe yakking in the driveway, getting thrown out of Stephanie's house, hitting every bar on the Elmwood Strip, and finishing with a taco and sub underneath a sign that looked like the guy you were sitting with!

"Nicky, you know what? Life's too short, my man. You're going to be okay because you've always done everything the right way. It sounds like you really loved that girl you told me about. But it also sounded like you loved that Renee girl too. Promise me you won't get involved with any more of these girls because I don't know how many more nights like this I can take!"

Don walked me home to make sure I made it all the way without any problems.

When we got to my porch, he told me, "Remember what I said about the girls, as for the other stuff, just let it happen. You'll be able to handle whatever the big guy in the sky has planned for you. I know you will."

He gave me a hug, turned around, and started singing "All my friends know the low rider" as he walked back home.

I don't know how he did it, but a friend of mine dressed like the Frito Bandito did manage to make one of worst days of my life turn into a night I will never forget.

CHAPTER 32

In the two years that I didn't see Stephanie, I finished my freshman and sophomore years at Peter's College, continued to work at the restaurant, dated a few girls, restored a GTO convertible, made my college baseball team, started a house-painting business, and still thought about her nearly every day.

A few other things also happened. Disco was giving way to punk. Bands like The Cars, The Clash, The Police, The Go-Go's, and A Flock of Seagulls were replacing the Bee Gees and KC and the Sunshine Band on the radio.

We also started wearing our hair a little different. Now I had what would be described as a mullet. Hair cut straight above my ears and long in the back.

I don't know how our paths never crossed in the last few years. We still had a lot of friends in common, and I'm sure we went to the same places, but we never saw each other.

My group of friends had remained, for the most part, the same. Andy had slowly retreated out of our group. Jack, Big Bob, Dominic, and my cousin Ronnie were still my closest friends. I had also met Lenny Ricardo in college, and he and I formed the painting company.

My second college baseball season ended in May of 1982. Our team was terrible and didn't win a game. We were 0–19. We were so bad that it was the last year that Peter's College fielded a team.

I spent most of my summer days working and most of my nights barhopping on Elmwood and Hertel strips.

The most important thing to me during this time was my car. After taking that ride with my cousin Joel in his GTO, I spent all my time trying to find a GTO for myself.

I bought a 1968 GTO convertible after seeing a listing in the *Swap Sheet*, a local newspaper. It said the car had been off the road since an accident in 1971: $1,500. I took my father with me, and he did the negotiating. (No one, and I mean no one, was better at buying a car than he was.) The car was hit in the front, and it had a new fender and bumper in the box waiting to be installed. When the seller made a mistake and told my dad that his mother-in-law wanted the car out of her garage, immediately my father offered him $250.

I was embarrassed by his offer. He laughed and said he'll take it. No one wants their mother-in-law on their back.

Dad was right, he took it, and I was now the proud owner of a GTO convertible. We hooked the tow chain up to my father's Scout and towed the car home.

My cousin helped me with the car. We stripped all the paint, put the fender and bumper on, and tuned the car like an Indy Race car. He also had a friend of his paint it sky-blue lacquer for $200. With the new top, I was cruising in an unbelievable car for a little under $1,000.

When I wasn't working during the day, the beach was a great place to drive my GTO to hang out. We were still going to Bay Beach in Canada. It was a perfect place to try to meet girls and work on your tan.

If you wanted to stay late, the day would end with a trip to Crystal Beach Amusement Park. We would ride until it got dark, look at the amazing neon lights, and then the smells of cotton candy and cinnamon would take over the nighttime air. Our night would end with rides on the Wild Mouse, and our favorite, the Comet Rollercoaster.

When the last weekend in June came, I went to the beach with the Pasquales and Marones, my neighbors. Cruising to the beach in a convertible with the top down is the best feeling to have. We had all our supplies with us: blankets, Matt's portable radio, football, and a pitcher of vodka and orange juice all safely stored away in the trunk.

We didn't usually go to the beach to swim. It was more like a social gathering with everyone checking each other out. Boys were there to meet girls and girls there to meet boys. Since I had my "little sisters" with me, I felt it was my job to keep the boys away from them. Alisa and Paula were safe entering the beach with me. I might as well have put up a "Stay Away From Them" sign when they walked in with me. I treated them like they were the sisters I never had.

It was very hot that day, so we dropped our blankets in the sand and ran to the water as soon as we could. When I approached, the water my friend Dee was walking out. We talked, and Dee told me she was moving to California in a few weeks. We had been friends for a long time, and attended Peter's with me. It was quite a shock to say the least.

After a quick game of football in the water, I went back to set up our spot on the beach. I had just sat down on my Charlie the Tuna blanket to dry off when the guys I just finished playing football with started making comments and whistling at three girls walking by the edge of the water right in front of us.

They were all tanned, they were all very pretty, and they all had the same last name. The girls turned around and gave dirty looks and the finger to my friends. I started to laugh, and then I realized who the guys were gawking at.

I made eye contact with Stephanie and her two sisters. I hadn't seen her or Gina since my eighteenth birthday. Their younger sister, Cindy, was with them and had turned into a very pretty senior in high school.

Stephanie and I just stared at each other, and didn't say a word. I had the same reaction that I always did to her. My heart skipped a few beats, and I'm sure I started to blush. It was like I was a freshman in high school all over again.

I thought about that night, the last time I had seen her, and what had been said. Four years of high school and two years in college hadn't changed me at all. That girl still captivated me.

I watched as they walked to the far side of the beach and sat down. I wanted to go over and talk to them. After all it had been almost two years, and we had been such good friends. But the situation just wasn't right. My friends had just made fools of themselves, and I was sure the girls thought I had put them up to it.

So I just sat there, listening to the transistor radio. The Human League's "Don't You Want Me Baby?" came on. I couldn't catch a break. Even the songs on the radio seemed to be against me.

So I ate my cheeseburger, and as usual, anything bought at the old man Eli's Snack Shack came with free sand in it. I ate the gritty burger looking at the three of them wondering how things had gotten so messed up.

I thought about the Sabres game, the zoo trip, all the conversations on her front porch, and her mother's cookies. I thought about my grandmother's funeral and going to the movies. I thought about all the time we spent with each other and all our conversations about growing up.

It seemed like I had grown up the last two years alone. And most of all, I thought about two people that should still be friends, or maybe even more. Our friendship felt like it was a million years ago.

When we were loading the car up to leave, shaking the sand and water from the towels, I looked back at the beach and thought again about walking over and talking to Stephanie one more time.

For some reason, I didn't.

On the ride home, the top was down. It felt like I was alone with the sky and my thoughts. I wondered how long it would be before I saw Stephanie again.

And as happened so many times before, my life was about to be turned upside down by the same girl that had done that to me so many times before.

Chapter 33

During the summer, I worked nearly two full-time jobs, but I somehow found the time to go to the bars almost every night. In Buffalo, the schedule of what bar to go to was well-known. Monday, The Stuffed Mushroom and Cassidy's; Tuesday, Graffiti's; Wednesday, Uncle Sam's; Thursday, The 747; Friday and Saturday, Peppers, Mulligans, and the Hotel California. At the Hotel California, it was not uncommon to wait one hour to get in. At Mulligan's, the wait could be similar.

If you knew the bouncers, you could cut in line, or if you had a VIP pass, you didn't have to wait either. I was lucky. A friend of mine, Anthony Vincenzo, was the DJ at Mulligans. He gave me a VIP pass, and I never waited in line. At the Hotel California, my neighbor Stan was the head bouncer. He gave me a Hotel California "key." It was an oversized fob that was similar to the ones used in actual hotels. I never waited in line there either.

A trip to Mulligans would allow you to see the Buffalo's in crowd. Many times I saw Rick James, some of the Buffalo Bills and Sabres, and many of the local television personalities of the time.

The week after I had seen Stephanie and her sisters at the beach, I walked into the Hotel California to meet some friends for Dee's going-away party.

It was a steamy Friday night in July. I went to the bar and ordered a drink. I should have been home sleeping after working all day and night, but I went out anyway to say goodbye to Dee.

Sometimes it seems that things happen for a reason. I leaned against the bar and was surrounded by my friends, both male and female, from my Catholic high school days. It was like we were all in high school again.

The DJ was blasting "Rapture" by Blondie. The lights were blinking to the beat of the music. It was almost impossible to move because of how many people were packed in there. The entire bar was dancing and moving to the music.

Through the crowd I saw the girl that made my high school years interesting to say the least. That girl was staring out the front window of the bar all alone. I knew instantly that it was Stephanie. And I could tell she wasn't there for Dee's party. And she didn't care about dancing, and she wasn't having any fun.

I didn't hesitate this time. I squeezed my way through the crowd toward her. As I got closer, I could tell she was crying.

"What's wrong?" I asked.

"Nothing," she answered without looking at me.

"Why are you crying then?" I asked.

"I'm leaving, get the hell away from me."

She walked out of the bar without saying another word, and down Hertel Avenue she went.

I ran to my car, put the top down, and drove around the corner looking for her. She was slowly walking toward her house.

The street was filled with people walking back and forth between the many bars on the strip. The hot summer night had the sound of pounding beats coming from every open bar door from block to block. Groups of kids were walking, talking, and laughing from every direction on the street.

I caught up to her as she was walking past Gabel's Bar.

"Get in," I said as I pulled up in my GTO.

"No."

"Stephanie, get in this fucking car right now."

She stopped and asked me through her tears, "What makes you think you can talk to me like that?"

"Well, the last time I talked to you, who told you that you could talk to me like that? You remember, it was my eighteenth birthday? And I was dumb enough to want to spend it with you? Now get in the car before I get into an accident."

"Eat shit, Nicky."

"It's been two years, and that's the best you can come up with?" I asked her.

As she continued to walk toward home, her brown eyes were now glaring at me as she weaved through crowds of people on the street.

She continued walking, trying to ignore me. But I could tell my comments must have really offended her because she finally stopped crying and I now sensed her anger was redirecting toward me.

I continued driving alongside of her looking through parked cars, trying to keep pace. I was leaning to the passenger side trying to shift my car, talk, and avoid parked cars and all the jaywalkers at the same time.

"Get in the car, Stephanie Pacifico!" I kept saying.

"No, leave me alone."

"Get in the car before I run out of gas!"

"There's never a cop around when you need one!" she half-laughingly said to me.

Right then I knew the crazy roller coaster was about to have me as a passenger again.

"Get in this car right now before I hit someone crossing the street or sideswipe one of these cars!"

I thought again, *What exactly is it about this girl that makes me do these crazy things?*

"Where did you get that car?" she asked me when she finally stopped walking and turned to me in front of the Stop and Go.

The bright lights and neon from the gas station made her look like a ghostly silhouette talking to me from the sidewalk.

"I've been working on it for the last two years with my cousin Joel. I look pretty good in it, don't I?"

She smiled at me for just a second and kept walking, but a lot slower. That smile still lit up her face like she was in Ronnie's driveway six years earlier.

With a softer voice, I told her, "Come on now, get in the car, I'll drive you home."

She continued smiling at me through her dark hair that was framing her face. She was so pretty even as she was wiping the tears away.

"Just leave me alone, Nick, please."

"Stephanie, I left you alone the last two years, isn't that long enough?"

She smiled that smile at me again and asked, "You're not going to give up, are you?"

"Not this time, it's been too long."

She walked toward the car, looked directly at me, and got in. I drove off toward her house. And as I shifted into third gear, my tires chirped, and I thought, *Where is this going now?*

CHAPTER 34

I pulled onto her street, a few houses from hers, and turned off the engine. We sat for a few moments in silence, both of us staring straight ahead.

Again, here we were in yet another strange situation. How many of these moments had I shared with her?

"Start the car up!" She suddenly said ending the uncomfortable silence.

"I'm not leaving yet."

"I'm going with you."

"Where we going?"

"To confront a rat."

As we drove away, she started to tell me that she no longer worked at Burger Chef. She was working at a supermarket, was about to be a junior in college, and was still skating.

I barely got a word in.

She also told me that one of the customers at work had asked her out, and they had been dating for about a month. She was supposed to go out with him that night, and he stiffed her.

What a strange reaction to being stiffed, I thought.

"He stiffed me because he's on a date with another girl!"

I started to laugh.

"What? You date all the winners, don't you?" I asked.

"Yes, I mean no, he seemed nice enough, but I didn't know that he was, well a two-timing lowlife. He seemed like a nice guy when I first met him."

I just stared at her and said, "Your taste in men never ceases to amaze me."

That comment only got me a dirty look for the ages!

"Where are we going, and what are we doing?" I asked again.

She ignored my question and said, "I found out from one of his relatives that he is out with another girl tonight."

I couldn't believe what I was hearing and what I was doing. Here I was getting caught in another crazy situation with her involving some other guy. In two years, everything in my life had changed, and now in the last twenty minutes, everything was the same again.

"Drive to Mr. Goodbar on Elmwood."

"Stephanie, why Goodbar?"

"He's in there with the other girl."

"Who's in there, the Lance Romance you've been dating?"

"Ya. He's in there all right, and I'm going to take care of this situation right now."

"Stephanie, I'm not going to let you go into a bar by yourself and start an argument with some dirtbag that thinks so little of you that he would cheat on you."

"I don't need you to do anything except get me there" was all she said.

When we got to the bar, the music was flooding out into the warm night air. People were standing on the sidewalk in front trying to cool off and having a cigarette.

Before I could even stop the car, she was opening the door and getting out. I had to keep moving because of all the traffic on the street. I found a parking spot about a block away on Forest Avenue and ran back to the bar as fast as I could just in case she needed my help.

What I saw when I walked in was hilarious. She had the guy backed up to the bar, her finger pointed in his face, and she was letting him have it, like only Stephanie Pacifico could do.

Off to the side was a girl that was obviously there with him not saying a word. I have to admit, that girl couldn't hold a candle to Stephanie.

The crowd in the bar was parted like the Red Sea, giving me a full view of the situation. Everyone was staring openmouthed, watching all the action. Boyfriend-girlfriend arguments always draw a crowd, and this one was no exception. Everyone was waiting for the action to continue.

I stood back and sized everything up, and if the guy tried to do anything to her, I would have wiped the floor with him. But he didn't.

The look of "I guess you caught me" on his face was priceless.

Stephanie had the situation under control, so I just continued watching. She ended the shouting match with one drink, then a second poured over his head. She turned and then calmly walked out.

The entire bar was pointing at her and laughing at the guy as he tried to dry his hair and pink alligator shirt with cocktail napkins.

"He'll think twice before he ever pulls that shit with anyone else," she said as we walked back toward my car.

The look on her face was my cue not to make any more comments on what I had just witnessed or her choices in men. I didn't say much on the way back. I could tell she was about to cry at any second. She just stared ahead, and the silence was deafening.

I put on my radio, and the SOS Band's "Take Your Time Do It Right" was playing.

"I guess you did that right too!" I said.

We looked at each other and laughed. I knew that in my heart nothing had changed when it came to her.

Yes, this girl was as unpredictable a person as I had ever met. She also was as sweet a person as I had ever met. To top it off, she was the most confusing person I had ever met.

And one other thing, her smile still captivated me. It was then that I had to admit I still cared for her as much as I ever did. I purposely took the long way home.

We slowly started to talk about what happened between her and that jerk that was probably still trying to dry his shirt off.

"Did you see the look on that clown's face when you doused him with the drinks? And since when do you like preps in pink alligator shirts? He didn't even look Italian! And how about him using the napkins to dry his hair and shirt? Do you think he will ever have the guts to place an order with you again?"

"He's a jerk. I think it'll be awhile before he cheats on any girl he is dating again."

It felt so nice just to be talking to her. It felt like this was the way it was supposed to be. Stephanie and me, just the two of us, and the sound of the GTO's engine riding around the neighborhood with the top down.

The wind was blowing her hair as I looked at her and realized we weren't kids anymore. She was already twenty, and I would be in a few days too. I knew I was getting on that backward roller coaster again.

When I pulled into her driveway, I had no clue what to do or say.

Just that all too familiar Nick and Stephanie awkward silence.

"Can I call you tomorrow?" I finally asked.

"Nick, I've been waiting for you to call me since I broke up with Jack" was all she said as she looked back at me with that smile and ran into the house.

CHAPTER 35

When I woke up the next morning, I couldn't believe what happened the night before. It was almost like a dream.

Should I call her? I asked myself. *Do I really want to get involved with her again?*

My life had been okay the last two years without her. But there also was something missing in it. Was that something that was missing her?

I started work at the restaurant at four o'clock, and I never knew when I would finish. I had also promised Jack that I would go out with him after work.

"Hi, is Stephanie there?" I asked

"Nick, is that you?" her mother asked.

"Yes, Mrs. Pacifico, it's me."

"Where have you been?"

"On a long vacation, but I think I'm back now," I answered.

From the first time I met her, Mrs. Pacifico always made me feel like I was part of her family. What a special lady she was.

"I've got it, Mom!" Stephanie screamed as she picked up another line.

"I don't know what to say."

"We need to talk a whole lot more, Nick. We need to talk about us."

"I have to work today at four. I have some other commitments too. I'll try to call you from work."

As I was talking to her, I heard water splashing in the background.

"What was that sound?" I asked

"I knew that as soon as I got into the bathtub you were going to call, so I stretched the phone into the bathroom. I hope I don't electrocute myself."

"I'll call you later from work," I told her again.

That night the restaurant was dead. It was another hot and sticky summer evening. Not an Italian food kind of night. I managed to leave at nine. I called Stephanie and said I was coming over.

I drove home as fast as I could, showered, and was on my way. When I was leaving, Matt asked if he could borrow my convertible because he was going to the drive-in. I told him yes. He was driving a 1970 Catalina that his grandmother had given him, so that would be my car for the night.

I drove over to Stephanie's, and I was very nervous. After last night, who could tell what she had in store for me? I walked up the driveway and knocked on the door. She came to the door in a pair of jean shorts, topsiders, and a rugby shirt.

I didn't have much time because I had promised Jack I would be back at my house by eleven thirty to go out with him. Stephanie and I went right to her porch. On that porch, we had previously solved many of the world's teenage problems.

She sat down Indian style on the top stair. I looked at her, and I again couldn't help thinking how pretty she was without even trying.

"I'm sorry for what happened in my driveway on your birthday. I wanted to call and apologize a million times, but I'm stubborn, and then days turned into weeks, and weeks into years, and before you know it, here we are."

I don't know how she did it, but she made it sound like everything happened yesterday, not two years ago. Just then her brother came walking up the street. He was very surprised to see me.

"Nick, how you doin'?" he asked.

"Good. Nice to see you again."

He looked at me, shook his head, and smiled. His body language told me my visit was not unexpected.

"You have to understand that I was in a really weird situation with you and Jack, and you and Andy."

I was caught midsentence when Gina and her boyfriend pulled into the driveway. The thing I liked most about Stephanie's house, all the comings and goings, was now the thing I liked the least about her house.

"Nick Carnavale, are you still after my sister?" Gina asked when she got out of the car.

"Is your sister still after me? would be a better question," I responded.

"I always knew you two would end up together, one way or another. Nick, this is my boyfriend, Eric. Nick hung around our house for four years waiting for my sister to notice him."

I still couldn't read Gina. She shook her head just like Danny did and smiled at me. And for a split second, I actually thought she might like me. But I still couldn't get out of my head how mean she was to me the last time I was there.

"Let's go, we are going to the park to talk. There won't be twenty people talking to us when we get there," Stephanie said.

We got into the car and drove to Delaware Park. We talked about everything in our lives the last two years. College and time didn't change anything between us.

She told me how she had always liked me the most out of the group, that she would rather have dated me from the beginning, and she figured we would have started to date after she broke up with Jack.

"Why didn't you call me after Jack and I broke up?" she asked.

"Stephanie, you have to understand. There is an unwritten rule. You don't go after your friend's ex-girlfriend, and if you do, you better wait awhile. Jack was very broken up. He didn't go to the prom, he barely made it to our graduation. I wanted you at my graduation party. You have to know that. I was trying to get over Renee. Too many things were happening. I know it's a bad excuse, but it is the truth."

"If I would have asked you to my prom, would you have gone?" she asked.

I still didn't know the answer to that question.

"Do you know what people would have thought if I took my friend's place with you? Guys have rules they have to follow. Nobody really knows my feelings for you. Shit, I don't even know if you know my feelings for you. I don't even know if I know my feelings for you. About all I really do know is that I haven't been able to take my eyes off you since the first time I saw you."

Talk about an awkward moment, the two of us just sitting on a bench near Delaware Park Lake, looking at the water, and for the first time being totally honest with each other.

"Nick, can I ask another question? Why didn't you talk to me at the beach last week?"

"Stephanie, don't you get it? The normal rules of life don't apply when it comes to you and me. I don't know why. I have dated a bunch of girls since I met you. But there has always been something about you that made me feel different. Do you know how awful I have felt every time I saw you with someone else? I started the brother-sister club in high school for the sole purpose of getting to know you. Almost everything I did in high school was for you. I know I'm jumping around, but when I heard through the grapevine anything about you, I always cared. I drove up and down Hertel Avenue a hundred times in my convertible hoping to see you. I've driven by your street hoping to see you. I've never stopped thinking about you. Even when I was with other girls, I was thinking about you."

She moved closer to me on the bench. I had a feeling that everything between us was about to change.

I looked at my watch. "I have to go. I have to take care of that commitment I told you about."

I knew that Jack was probably at my house right now waiting for me. I told my mom to tell anyone that came over that I was still at work and that I was running late.

"Stephanie, we have to go, we have a lot more time to finish this conversation."

When we got into the Catalina, it was very quiet. I looked at her, and she shyly smiled back at me. When I pulled up in front of her house, she slid over next to me.

And then it happened. I started to kiss her.

CHAPTER 36

The next day I woke up and went to work with my father. Cutting lawns for hours gives you lots of time to think and figure things out. But as usual, I was in uncharted territory.

Should I call her? I asked myself over and over.

I had to. We talked for an hour on the phone and decided to go to the movies the next night. The movie was *E. T. the Extra-Terrestrial.* As I drove over, I realized that this was my second real date with her. The Sabres game and this, six years and two dates!

When I got to her house, she was waiting in the driveway. She had on a stripped Rugby shirt and jean miniskirt. I looked at her and couldn't believe someone that looked like her was going out with me. She ran to the convertible and jumped in.

"Hi," I said.

"What are we going to see?" she asked.

"*E. T.*"

We went to the Holiday Six movies in Cheektowaga, far enough away, or so I hoped, to not know anyone. My luck with the movies stayed consistent. Mr. Kelly, my teacher from Brennan, was sitting right in front of us. He asked how both of us were doing. He asked about Stephanie's brother and what he was up to.

And then he asked the question I knew he would, "Stephanie, I have to ask, what are *you* doing with *him?*"

Mr. Kelly never liked me in high school, and maybe he thought I moved his Volkswagen at the prom. And I was pretty sure he didn't like me now that I was in college.

We enjoyed the movie, went out for ice cream, and went back to Stephanie's house and sat on the porch. Again it seemed like the whole world was coming by to say hello. Victor and Charlie from down the street came over to check out the situation.

I knew this wasn't going to get any easier. If this was going to work, we would have to take it slow, and get as few of our friends involved in it as possible.

We did take it slow and didn't see each other every night. The summer was starting to slip away before I knew it. It just didn't feel the same as it did while we were in high school. Maybe the girls I had dated in college changed me. Maybe I changed me.

On Labor Day weekend, we went out on Friday and were going to go out again on Sunday. My parents were leaving Saturday morning to go and visit my aunt and uncle at the Jersey Shore. I had the house all to myself for the first time in my life.

On Sunday, Stephanie came over, and we watched the "Jerry Lewis Telethon" for a couple of hours. We were all alone for the first time. We talked, and one point we just stared at one another while sitting on the couch. My heart was beating faster than it ever had. We started to kiss, and our relationship was about to go to the next level.

I was still looking into her eyes, and all I heard was Meatloaf singing "Paradise by the Dashboard Light" and I was the one being asked, "What's it gonna be, boy?"

I just couldn't commit to her. And I cared too much about her for us to do anything that would jeopardize that. And yes, I still loved her. But maybe in a different way now.

I knew that my friends would have told me I was crazy for not taking advantage of the situation I found myself in. Again, here I was with the girl I'd wanted for so long, but it just wasn't right anymore.

And maybe it was never going to be right.

"We have to slow this down," I told her.

We stopped before anything went further.

While I was driving her home, I thought about college resuming for the two of us in a few days, and it felt very strange.

I started to feel trapped. My mother was constantly asking what was going on with Stephanie. Mrs. Pacifico even asked me when I was going to marry her daughter. I had school, a full-time job, and many doubts about what was going on.

I believe that Stephanie must have too. After school began, we went days without talking. I took her a few times to skating and watched her like I always had.

She still was beautiful, she still was sweet, but I had met a girl at the end of the spring semester that I was interested in. When school started again, I was continually bumping into that girl. The feeling that I used to have with Stephanie I now had for this girl.

Stephanie and I drifted apart. Our summer together was over. Perhaps it was just for old times' sake that we dated. Or maybe we owed it to each other to spend time with each other before our lives went totally in another direction. You know, for old times' sake.

And the other girl I mentioned, I did marry her. But that's entirely a different story.

CHAPTER 37

As the funeral service ended, the church emptied very slowly. Stephanie's family walked down the aisle and by me. We nodded in quiet acknowledgment of their mother.

Yes, each one of them was part of me, I'm sure of that, and I hoped I am still part of them. I walked down the church stairs and stood to the side waiting to talk to Stephanie.

Gina and Cindy walked over, and we hugged. Katie, now all grown up, hugged me too. I told them how much I loved their mother. Danny walked over. I told him he was still the coolest guy I ever met. After he was done laughing, I told him how I felt about his mother.

And when Stephanie was finally alone, with tears in my eyes I walked toward her. We hugged. I told her how special her mother was to me. She told me that her mother still spoke about me as the "one that got away." We talked as if we were still best friends and talked every day.

Funny how that happens when you see an old friend, you pick up right where you left off.

We continued to talk for several more minutes until her daughter walked up and said the limo was about to leave. We hugged once more. I watched her walk away. She looked back at me, nodded, and smiled before she got into the limo. I waved to her one last time.

It was then that I fully realized that first loves, as I mentioned before, never really go away. They are always with you to bring a smile to your face and remind you of another place and time, of a younger you when you were free of responsibilities and had your entire life before you.

And there is nothing wrong with that.

As I walked to my car, I had a smile on my face and tears in my eyes thinking about all the good times I had with Stephanie and her family.

I saw my life as a series of snapshots, each one of a place and time that perhaps is only important to me. The places and people contained in those snapshots were still, but the sounds and feelings are not. They are alive and move in my memory as if they happened yesterday.

What a great feeling it is to still see the past the way I do. And to be aware how it touches me to this day.

I realized that my teenage years were really special and worth remembering.

My neighborhood was great and filled with friends I will never forget. And what a loving family I had.

I also thought about my mother and father, now gone.

And I thought about my cousin Ronnie who was like a brother to me. He is now gone now too.

But they are never far away from me. Those memories are always with me, and they did shape me into the person I am. That's the great thing about those memories and the feelings they elicit. They never leave you. They stay with you forever.

And for me, that's all that really matters.

E P I L O G U E

I received a simple note in the mail a few weeks after the funeral that confirmed all my memories and feelings.

> Dear Nick,
>
> Thank you so much for honoring our mother by attending her funeral. She loved you very much, as we all do!
>
> Love,
> The Pacificos

About the Author

Frank J. Maraschiello is a middle school history teacher with a passion for the 1970s. His fond remembrances from his teenage years and the people that influenced him the most prompted him to write his first novel, *Dress Jeans, Disco, and Dating*. Frank is a familiar face at flea markets and estate sales searching for the past around his hometown Buffalo, New York. His other interests include playing and coaching hockey and restoring classic cars. He is married with two children and one grandchild.

CPSIA information can be obtained
at www.ICGtesting.com
Printed in the USA
BVHW082240210819
556464BV00001B/6/P